I0585625

The Ambivalent Detective in Victorian Sensation Novels

The Ambivalent Detective in Victorian Sensation Novels studies how the detective as a literary character evolved through the mid-nineteenth century in England, as seen in sensation novels. In contrast to most assumptions about the English detective, Yoon argues that the detective was more often tolerated than admired following the establishment of professional detectives in the London Metropolitan Police Force in 1842. Through studying the historical and literary contexts between the 1840s to the 1860s, Yoon argues that the detective was seen as a suspicious, even mistrusted and disdained, figure who was nonetheless viewed as necessary to combat rising levels of crime. The detective as a literary character responded to the often contradictory values and aspirations of the middle class, representing an independent masculinity and laying claim to scientific authority. This study surveys novels by Charles Dickens, Mary Elizabeth Braddon, and Wilkie Collins, alongside lesser-known writers like William Russell, James Redding Ware (pseudonym Andrew Forrester), and William Stephens Hayward. This book contributes to the study of mid-nineteenth-century Victorian culture and connects with broader studies of the detective fiction genre.

Sarah Yoon is Lecturer at Underwood International College, Yonsei University, in South Korea. She holds an MA in English literature from Yonsei University. Her research interests include Victorian literature and culture, the environmental humanities, and Korean-English translated novels. Her research has been published by international journals, such as *Brontë Studies* and *Critique*. *The Ambivalent Detective in Victorian Sensation Novels* is her first book.

Routledge Studies in Nineteenth Century Literature

For more information about this series, please visit: www.routledge.com/Routledge-Studies-in-Nineteenth-Century-Literature/book-series/RSNCL

The Ambivalent Detective in Victorian Sensation Novels

Dickens, Braddon, and Collins

Sarah Yoon

Routledge
Taylor & Francis Group

NEW YORK AND LONDON

First published 2024
by Routledge
605 Third Avenue, New York, NY 10158

and by Routledge
4 Park Square, Milton Park, Abingdon, Oxon, OX14 4RN

Routledge is an imprint of the Taylor & Francis Group, an informa business

© 2024 Sarah Yoon

ISBN: 978-1-032-43963-1 (hbk)
ISBN: 978-1-032-43965-5 (pbk)
ISBN: 978-1-003-36962-2 (ebk)

DOI: 10.4324/9781003369622

Typeset in Sabon
by Apex CoVantage, LLC

For my first daughter, Ha-yoon.

Contents

Figures

Acknowledgments

As a study that grew out of my PhD dissertation, I have many people to thank. Most significantly, I am grateful to my advisers Hyungji Park, Hye-Joon Yoon, and Kyung-sook Shin from Yonsei University, and Jina Moon and Donghee Om. I am thankful for their time in reading my drafts, insightful comments, and reading recommendations. Hye-Joon Yoon recommended early readings that helped set the parameters of this study, while Jina Moon highlighted key readings that brought my argument to fruition. Donghee Om suggested important changes to the manuscript, while Hyungji Park supported and encouraged my dissertation throughout. I also wish to thank Saverio Tomaiuolo, who kindly took the time to read an early version of the manuscript, offered invaluable suggestions, and pointed me to useful sources.

I am also grateful to the English Department at Yonsei University, particularly Suk Koo Rhee, who coordinates important funding and research opportunities for graduate students. Suk Koo Rhee tirelessly supports and encourages graduate students to publish their work, instilling a work ethic that allowed this book to germinate. I am also thankful for the thought-provoking conversations I have had with other faculty members, including Peter Paik and Kyung Won Lee.

I wish to thank my intelligent students at Underwood International College, Yonsei University, where I have been a lecturer since 2019. The students have encouraged me, through their hard work and questions, to interrogate and examine my own writing style and ultimately aim for clarity and detail rather than poetry or erudition. It has been a great pleasure to teach and learn from such gifted students at UIC.

On a more personal note, I wish to thank my parents for their unflagging support before and throughout graduate school. I have been blessed to have parents who respectfully listen to me and have helped me grow as a thinker and independent adult.

Finally, I am grateful to Keonhee for being my enduring support and stay. Ha-yoon, who does not yet know how to read, accompanied me *in utero* during the writing of this book and quickened its completion with her birth. This work is dedicated to her.

Introduction
The ambivalent detective in Victorian sensation novels

In Wilkie Collins's *The Moonstone* (1868), regarded since T. S. Eliot as an early progenitor of British detective fiction, the family steward, Gabriel Betteredge, views the detective Sergeant Cuff with simultaneous disdain and admiration. As Sergeant Cuff conducts his investigations into the disappearance of a diamond in the Verinder family home, Betteredge remarks, "I had got by this time . . . to hate the Sergeant. But truth compels me to acknowledge that, in respect of readiness of mind, he was a wonderful man" (W. Collins, *Moonstone* 135–36). Later, he adds, "I couldn't help liking the Sergeant – though I hated him all the time" (W. Collins, *Moonstone* 179). These seemingly contradictory reactions to the detective encapsulate the ambivalence felt towards the detective as a real figure and literary construct in mid-nineteenth-century England. These tensions and contradictions appear in Victorian sensation fiction, as sensation writers often depicted detectives in their mystery narratives. Detectives appear, for instance, in Charles Dickens's *Bleak House* (1853), and in Mary Elizabeth Braddon's earliest fiction, as well as *Lady Audley's Secret* (1862), and Collins's *Armadale* (1866). There are also other characters who may not be professional detectives but nonetheless resemble private investigators in other sensation novels by Dickens, Collins, Braddon, and Ellen Wood, often corresponding to a lawyer character. But in the mid-nineteenth century, critics like Anthea Trodd suggest that "the police detective [was] a character still in search of a genre" ("Policeman" 436). What is clear in these mid-nineteenth-century formulations and literary projections of the detective is that the figure was viewed neither as a heroic type, nor as an immediately identifiable type of ascendant masculinity. The detective was viewed with both suspicion and tolerance, with revulsion and admiration.

Detective fiction is often dismissed as popular fiction or as formulaic stories revealing little about their historical contexts. This assumption has been challenged in recent years by critics who have shed light on the detective's emergence from a set of historically contingent circumstances. This study contributes to that inquiry, disrupting the popular notion that

DOI: 10.4324/9781003369622-1

the detective was either a purely rational figure, embodying scientific rationality, or that he embodied quintessential English values. As this book shows, detectives were more often tolerated than admired in the mid-nineteenth century soon after their establishment within the London Metropolitan Police Force in 1842. The detective was both celebrated and reviled, both an embodiment of a new professional elite and a threat to middle-class values. The detective also reveals a complex negotiation of English masculinity, amid the changing social landscape of the mid-nineteenth century. The detective as a literary phenomenon in Victorian sensation fiction simultaneously defends a middle-class conception of social order, even as he resorts to underhand and covert tactics. The strategies employed by the detective sat uncomfortably with proclaimed ideas of English freedom, privacy, and gentlemanly conduct. Yet the detective could also wield a tantalizing power over deviants or threats to the social order, as projected by bigamous women or spying servants in popular literature.

Detectives have often been considered one-dimensional character types embodying a masculine rationality. As an example of this view, Fredric Jameson has suggested that the detective story may be "a form without ideological content" and a "purely intellectual mode of knowing events" (23). Likewise, Franco Moretti argues that the detective novel "furnishes only the sensation of scientific knowledge" that "perfectly satisfies the aspiration to certainty" (149). D. A. Miller likewise assumes in *The Novel and the Police* (1988) that the detective of the mid-Victorian period acted as an agent of social control, intruding into the private and domestic sphere to impose methods of surveillance and discipline (viii). By his own admission, Miller sets aside the historical circumstances that shaped "the modern institutional" establishment of the police, focusing instead on an assumed "culture of less visible, less visibly violent modes of 'social control'" (viii). Yet Miller, and other critics, too quickly assume that the detective enjoyed a privileged position of power and authority that is sharply contested – and even refuted – in the contemporary literature and journalism of this period.

In recent decades, critics have historicized the appearance of the detective in Victorian fiction, notably Samuel Saunders in *The Nineteenth Century Periodical Press and the Development of Detective Fiction* (2021). In his study, Saunders provides much overlooked detail and context about the establishment of the Metropolitan Police Force in the early nineteenth century, as well as the emergence of the police memoir as an early form of detective fiction. Sensation novels are also a revealing literary source about the appearance of the detective, but most critics have tended to focus on readings of criminality or deviance in such fiction. Hence, Andrew Maunder and Grace Moore argue that sensation novels reflect a "nineteenth-century reformulation of attitudes to crime" (1), while Mark Mossman hypothesizes that detective and sensation novels have served as "discursive tools that solidify a rigid dichotomy of the normal and abnormal in the nineteenth century" (483). Andrew Mangham has importantly drawn links between views of female degeneracy and psychological debates in sensation novels in his *Violent Women and Sensation Fiction* (2007).[1] But for the most part, theories about the detective have tended to be one-dimensional and somewhat flat. Even Ronald R. Thomas's seminal work *Detective Fiction and the Rise of Forensic Science* (1999) posits in a rather straightforward manner that the detective represented the rise of forensic rationality and scientific authority in the nineteenth century, without further exploring the character's moral complexity and ambivalence (see also Thomas, "Moonstone").

This study is intended to supplement a historical understanding of the detective's moral slipperiness and contingency through a reading of sensation novels. In brief, this book explores how the detective was more often viewed as a suspicious figure, particularly between the 1840s and the 1860s, a period that overlaps with the rise of sensation fiction.[2] The detective serves a functionally convenient roles in such novels, but is also viewed as a morally reprehensible figure. For the most part, sensation novels were met with scathing criticism from contemporary writers such as Margaret Oliphant, William Fraser Rae, and Henry Longueville Mansel. Notably, James Fitzjames Stephen wrote in *The Saturday Review* that, "of all forms of sensation novel-writing, none is so common as what may be called the romance of the detective" (712). In such novels, the detective emerges as a character with an obscure background who intrudes into the domestic space of middle-class families. The detective was seen, in the words of the novelist James Redding Ware (under the pseudonym Andrew Forrester), "as peculiarly necessary as he or she is peculiarly objectionable" (2). The detective embodied a masculinity detached from the domestic sphere, while conveying the aspirations of an emergent professional elite. Problematically, the detective frequently resorted to underhand means of extracting information, which were seen as at odds with the values of English freedom, autonomy, and gentlemanly conduct. Hence, as Haia Shpayer-Makov points out, the detective was frequently compared to the "spy" to convey a "derogatory attitude" and aversion to their covert tactics and surveillance activities (27–28).

To understand the ambivalent characterization of detectives in popular literature, it is important to note the shifting social circumstances of the mid-nineteenth century. The accelerated expansion of the middle class and their replacement of older forms of authority are crucial to understanding the detective's usefulness and the anxieties he provoked. As Mariaconcetta Costantini explains, the middle class superseded "old-fashioned ideas of rank and order," but remained a "multi-layered social entity" (100; see also Steinbach 124–28). The middle class was "a class of contending opinions and fluctuating markers of status," with "internal subdivisions, ranging from gentrified plutocracy to lower-class employees" (Costantini 100). Hence, the middle and the newly moneyed class were marked by "heterogeneity" and "multi-accentuality," arising from the "diversity of their social roles and views" (Costantini 100).[3] While sensation novelists exploited these tensions and disparities to sell their fiction, the detective as a literary construct flouted the boundaries between the working and middle classes. While the middle class stood to benefit the most from private investigators, the detective remained, as Trodd points out, little more than a "higher servant or lower tradesman," fluctuating between the "roles of private and public servant" ("Policeman" 436, 449). Hence, the detective as a "cultural construct" threatened the separation between public and private spheres, while aggravating anxieties within the middle class (Shpayer-Makov 6).

At the same time, the detective as a cultural construct or "fictional presentation" served the social order in upholding and restoring patriarchal authority (Trodd, *Domestic Crime* 7).[4] The detective exemplified the social mobility of the rising middle class, embodying the ideals of an emergent professional elite, while eluding clear moral or social categorization. Hence, the detective exposed, to borrow Brian W. McCuskey's words, "anxieties about the increasing authority and privilege of professionals in relation to the rest of the middle-class community" (374). McCuskey adds that mid-century Victorian novels demonstrate a "fundamental and shared concern . . . that the existence of a professional elite heightens competition and factionalism within the middle-class community, potentially undermining the solidarity and the authority of the middle class as a whole" (374; see also Kucich). Shpayer-Makov also points out that the detective's ability to escape detection further heightened these tensions, writing that "at a time when social differences between higher and lower origins were being re-encoded, the notion of concealed identity heightened anxiety about growing anonymity and alienation, particularly in the middle classes, whose status was often precarious" (29). The ambivalence of the detective as an imagined character folds into the uncertain boundaries and moral authority of the rising middle class. But even as the detective was portrayed as "an officious and misguided interloper" in many mid-nineteenth century literary texts (Trodd, "Policeman" 436), he also offered precarious enjoyment to the middle-class reader, divulging imagined private affairs and family secrets.

Despite the contrast between detectives and the police in late Victorian fiction, detectives were, through most of the nineteenth century, simultaneously seen as members of and yet also independent agents among the police. As Heather Worthington notes, there was a "conflation of policing with detection in the early years of the police" in the mid-nineteenth century

(143). Detectives from the Metropolitan Police Force could be suspicious because, as John Sutherland states, they could be "privately hired as 'confidential agents'" and seemed to hold no moral allegiances ("Explanatory" 484, 487). The famous Inspector Charles Frederick Field resigned from the Metropolitan Police Force and became a "private inquiry agent" by 1854 (see Chapter 7; T. Hughes 103). But in earlier sensation novels, the detective character is seldom cast as a professional agent. Instead, the detective-hero is cast as both a lawyer and a patriarch in Wood's *East Lynne* (1861), receiving rather than actively scouting for information. By *The Moonstone* (1868), seven years later, the detective develops as an independent male professional with his own idiosyncratic traits. The detective still intrudes into the domestic sphere, where crime occurs in sensation novels, but could be tolerated and even evolve into a heroic type. As a character, the detective exposes contradictions in an expanding middle-class society that prized domestic values and also celebrated independent rationality. Contradictory reactions to the detective could not be easily resolved because the detective did not fit neatly within a pre-existent idea of masculinity or a middle-class work ethic. Hence, the detective is usually depicted as an outsider who works alone for his own financial benefit. For him, information is means for a living, severed from their moral context. This book surveys a range of sensation novels from Dickens, Collins, Braddon, Wood, to the lesser-known Ware, William Russell, and William Stephens Hayward. In engaging with the development of the detective during this period, this book aims to flesh out contradictory perceptions of the ambivalent detective in the mid-nineteenth century.

Critics have long argued that Victorian masculinity remained in flux throughout the nineteenth century. Phillip Mallett has pointed out that "male identity is not an ahistorical given, but the outcome of shifting cultural contest and debate" (vi). Similarly, Richard Nemesvari argues that sensation novels reveal "the inability of Victorian versions of masculinity to cope with" conflicting sensations and excesses (89). Novels by Wood and Braddon portray, according to Nemesvari, "the fluctuating contingencies of masculinity" (113). James Eli Adams's *Dandies and Desert Saints* (1995) and Herbert Sussman's *Victorian Masculinities* (1995) have become established studies of Victorian masculinities, with both upholding the view that "masculinities identities are multiple, complex, and unstable constructions" (Adams, *Dandies* 3) with significant tensions over "normative bourgeois masculinity" (Sussman 4). John Tosh has argued, in contrast, that the domestic sphere was central to middle-class masculinity. Pushing back against an exclusive association between femininity and domesticity, Tosh observed that "to establish a home, to protect it, to provide for it, to control it, and to train its young aspirants to manhood, have usually been essential to a man's good standing with his peers" (4). In this context, the detective emerges as an ambivalent articulation of masculinity in resolving a domestic crisis arising from an unchecked female threat. In many sensation novels, a bigamous woman undermines and challenges middle-class masculinity, associated with the cult of domesticity. The detective serves as an ambivalent counterweight to this female threat, appearing to uphold domestic values even as he undercuts them.

Hence, while it is useful to view masculinities in flux throughout the nineteenth century, this study does not aim to separately chart an alternative vision of masculinity as represented by the detective. This is because the detective emerged as an independent masculine type in opposition to a seemingly depraved woman in sensation novels. It is not useful here to study masculinity in isolation from anxieties about women, since the detective was framed in a relationship of an alternative masculinity informed by errant femininity. The detective's independent masculinity also contrasts with the patriarchal authority that he helps to reinstate. The detective's role is simultaneously ambivalent and functional, in that he counterbalances and resolves an external threat to middle-class masculinity, as embodied by the deviant woman. In sensation novels, such deviance was increasingly reframed and transferred to representations of foreign others, whether colonized natives or Europeans. The detective acts as an independent masculine figure, contending with these threatening forces, even as he represents a less-than-ideal moral compromise in his own right. The detective admirably subdues malign threats to domestic masculinity, but refuses to be subsumed within the patriarchal order that he helps to reinstate.

Charting the long history of detective stories can be difficult because, as with all generic histories, there remains considerable debate about their origins. Edgar Allan Poe is often regarded as the first writer of short detective stories and he did indeed meet Dickens during the latter's visit to America in 1842. They had "two long interviews," according to Michael Slater, at a hotel in Philadelphia, and Dickens agreed to try to find Poe an English publisher (which he did but failed) (184). Poe had already read Dickens's *The Old Curiosity Shop* (serialized between 1840 and 1841), praising the novel in *Graham's Magazine* in May 1841. But further connections between Dickens and Poe seem more incidental, attributable to their shared preoccupations with urban life and criminality. In contrast, T. S. Eliot suggested that *The Moonstone* might be regarded as "the first and greatest of English detective novels" (377), but Collins and Dickens also influenced each other in their literary output through their careers. It makes sense, from a broad historical perspective, to view detective stories as following a distinct trajectory in England, rather than attempt to write a generic history of detective stories across centuries and continents. Another reason for focusing on a particular country and period is that detectives became a real presence in London from 1842. Following police reforms, the Detective Branch of the

Metropolitan Police Force was established as a small contingent of plain-clothed officers (see Chapter 1). Dickens met with and conversed with these detectives at his editorial office for *Household Words*, inspiring articles he wrote for the weekly journal and, later, novels like *Martin Chuzzlewit* (1844) and *Bleak House*.

Crime and injustice have always existed, long before the nineteenth century, and individual resistance can be read in novels like William Godwin's *Caleb Williams* (1794), which is sometimes described as an early detective novel (see Symons; Ousby; Cohen). While it foregrounds a central conflict between two morally opposed individuals, however, there is no major third-party detective in the novel. One could also include novels from the 1830s, preceding and contemporary with *Oliver Twist* (1838), such as Edward Bulwer-Lytton's *Paul Clifford* (1830) and William Harrison Ainsworth's *Jack Sheppard* (1839) in the crime fiction genre. Both these novels were certainly influential (see Chapter 5) and demonstrate the growth of sensation novels from crime fiction inspired by, for instance, the *Newgate Calendar*. For the sake of convenience and to more narrowly focus on the detective as a literary character, this study mainly restricts its scope to detective stories and sensation novels of the early 1840s through to the early 1860s. Defining a detective story may be challenging, but my aim is not to trace the long history or typology of detective fiction. Rather, this book aims to explore how the detective as a character emerged as a contradictory and, eventually, heroic masculine type. Sensation novels are distinguished from other novels of the Victorian mid-nineteenth century in that they were highly commercial, amplifying social anxieties in opportunistic ways (a trait repeatedly criticized by contemporary critics), and also in that they were intensely psychological. While these features are not exclusive to sensation novels, sensation novels often stage a psychological theater of opposing wills and intentions at the domestic hearth. Patrick Brantlinger has mentioned that the sensation novel is "a forebear of modern detective fiction . . . shar[ing] several of its psychological properties" in an influential essay ("What Is 'Sensational'" 2). On one level, this means that webs of deceit and fears of madness invite rational ordering. But the detective does not merely resolve such psychological disorder, he also exposes and sets them into motion, as seen, for instance, in Braddon's *Lady Audley's Secret* (see Chapter 6).

Sensation novels: an overview

Only a cursory overview of sensation novels is necessary here, but it is worth covering their major features and their critical response to avoid repetition in later chapters. The scope of sensation novels has been debated, but they are generally agreed to have peaked in popularity between the late 1850s and mid-1860s. Tracing the emergence of professional detectives, as reflected in British literature, necessitates a slightly earlier time frame to accommodate the cultural impact of the Detective Branch of the Metropolitan Police Force (of which more in Chapter 1). Dickens is generally believed to have included the first detective character in his novel *Martin Chuzzlewit* (see Haining 12; R. Thomas, "Detection" 178). Collins may be associated with the rise of detective fiction in Britain, but it is difficult to imagine his interest in detectives without the influence of his mentor and oft-times rival, Dickens, who published and edited the first of Collins's successful mystery novels. The literary rivalry between Collins and Dickens would extend to Dickens's unfinished mystery novel, *The Mystery of Edwin Drood* (1870), often read explicitly as a response to and stylization of Collins's highly successful *The Moonstone*. Dickens also featured a detective in *Bleak House* inspired by the real detective Inspector Field (see Chapter 2). Indeed, some have argued that *Bleak House* "launched sensation fiction," demonstrating that the development of detective fiction in Britain cannot fully be appreciated independently from sensation novels (Talairach-Vielmas 115). Besides Dickens, this book also studies three other sensation novelists, Collins, Braddon, and, to a lesser extent, Wood. I also survey lesser-known novels by Russell, Ware, and Hayward, who wrote commercial "railway" paperback novels, rather than serialized novels in the periodical press.

The prominent writers of the sensation fiction genre were Collins, Braddon, Wood and also Charles Reade and Sheridan LeFanu. These latter writers are not included in this study because their stories are rarely linked to detective fiction. Lucy Sussex makes this point about Reade, noting that he is "less ancestral to modern crime writing" than Collins, Braddon, or Wood, since he tended to write "episodic and action-packed" narratives rather than mysteries (82). In contrast, Sussex sees Collins, Braddon, and Wood as writing "novels that were crime both in subject and form, often structured around a detective search" (82–83). Thomas concurs that the three "big names" in sensation novels associated with detective fiction are Collins, Braddon, and Wood. Their novels, Thomas argues, reveal "modern characters . . . tangled up in very complex social plots of class and pretense – mysteries that required a specialized expertise to expose and clear up" (R. Thomas, "Detection" 179–80). Dickens is only occasionally included in the genre of sensation fiction, but most critics acknowledge his formative influence. Braddon consciously imitated Dickens in her first novel (see Chapter 5; Sussex 85; Pykett, "Mary Elizabeth Braddon" 125) while Collins continued to negotiate Dickens's far-reaching literary and cultural influence in his own writing (see Nayder, *Unequal*). Anne-Marie Beller argues that Dickens was "a key figure in the development of literary sensationalism," observable in his depictions of "everyday life and domestic relations" ("Sensation" 9; see also P. Collins 253, 308; Shpayer-Makov

225). Even Dickens's contemporary, Oliphant, described *Great Expectations* (not included in this study) as a "sensation novel," though she conceded that it lacked the startling realism and plausibility of Collins's *The Woman in White* (1859) ("Sensation" 570, 575; see also Mansel 488).

Among various definitions of sensation novels, Maunder provides a succinct outline of their emergence as a literary phenomenon from around the early 1860s. He states that sensation novels

> offered readers a cultural fusion of different kinds of popular forms, drawing not only on the techniques of popular melodrama, but on the earlier 'Newgate' tales of crime and villainy, broadsheet literature, newspaper reports of criminal trials and divorce cases, as well as the Gothic novel.
>
> ("General Introduction" x)

This description highlights the heterogeneous and hybrid influences that gave birth to the sensation novel. Costantini points out that the sensation novel, while often serialized in periodicals for middle-class readers, "retained distinct elements of working-class literature" (101). The hybridity of sensation novels has been noted by other critics, such as Jenny Bourne Taylor and Russell Crofts, who describe the sensation novel as "a hybrid, a combination of different genres, including Gothic fiction, the 'Newgate novel' (with its lurid portrayal of violence and crime), stage melodrama and domestic realism" (xii; see also Pykett, "Collins"). The influences on sensation novels were multiple, ranging from journalistic to melodramatic. But perhaps the most striking feature of sensation novels was their emphasis on sensationalism (hence the name) to opportunistic lengths. Hence, Brantlinger states the identifiable elements of the sensation novel includes the following: "violent and thrilling action, astonishing coincidences, stereotypic heroes, heroines, and villains, much sentimentality, and virtue rewarded and vice apparently punished at the end" ("What is 'Sensational'" 5).[5]

Nor was this blatant commerciality – or emphasis on heightening readerly sensations at the expense of plausibility – lost on contemporary critics. Victorian critics pointed to an ideal aim of literature as providing moral instruction and improvement, while seeing sensation novels as merely catering to the popular appetite for excitement and intrigue. *St James's Magazine* complained in 1862 about the complete "stagnation" in society, as evinced by the "feverish rushing after what are accepted as sensational gratifications" ("Philosophy of 'Sensation'" 16–17). The *London Quarterly Review* in 1863 deplored "the very marked degeneracy" of the sensation school of writing ("Thackeray" 77). The *Saturday Review* pointed to "a wave of materialism" that had contributed to the success of female sensation novelists ("Novels Past and Present" 152). Likewise, the *Broadway Review* opined that "novels of this sort must be mischievous, especially to the young and impressionable" ("Women's Novels" 221), while the *Westminster Review* compared "the Sensational Mania in Literature" to an epidemic (de Capel Wise 157).[6] "Bigamy is now its typical form," John Richard de Capel Wise wrote, "No novel can now possibly succeed without it" (157). Wood made a fortune from writing sensation novels, while Braddon was deemed "without a living rival" in her stylization of the genre (Rae 204).

Coupled with this criticism about the potentially degrading effects of sensation novels, and what they revealed about their readers' vulgar tastes, was ridicule leveled at the growing number of women writers associated with the genre. "No *man* would have dared to write and published such book as some of these are," Frederick Paget wrote,

> Women have done this, – have thus abused their power, and prostituted their gifts. . . . And O what a degradation it is . . . that the demand for works of such description should be so great, that the supply can hardly keep pace with it.
>
> (215, italics in original; see also "Mrs Wood" 58)

Such criticism against sensation novels reveals not only concern about the changing modes of literary production, increasingly driven by market forces and consumer demand, but also the democratization of literary contributors. These changes invited derision, with W. Fraser Rae memorably noting that Braddon had especially contributed to "making the literature of the Kitchen the favourite reading of the Drawing room" (204). The kitchen was commonly situated in the basement, out of sight to respectable guests. In contrast, the drawing room was a "feminized space" that displayed "the public positions and respectability of the entire family" in its design (Tange, *Architectural* 62, 66). As Tange writes, "The drawing room was not only a private space; it was also one that brought to the foreground women's actions in order to confirm the respectability and the status of the family" (*Architectural* 63). This distinction explains Rae's irritation that the literature of the vulgar kitchen, associated with working-class labor, had infiltrated into the more respectable quarters of the middle-class home. The popularity of sensation novels heralded a change in reading and writing, specifically, what was being read and consumed as literature, and who were producing such works. Hence, a study of sensation novels warrants attention to the shifting landscape of the publishing industry in the mid-nineteenth century, as traced in the next chapter.

Sensation novels were seen as aesthetically inferior and morally corrupting because of their frequent emphasis on mystery, crime, and personal secrets. A dominant theme of sensation novels was bigamy, as seen, for instance, in Collins's *The Woman in White* and Braddon's *Lady Audley's Secret* and *Aurora Floyd* (1863). This preoccupation with bigamy has been read in conjunction with the divorce court journalism after the 1857 Matrimonial Causes Act (see Chapter 1). Other themes in sensation novels are double identity, insanity, and adultery. Foreigners are often introduced as villains or suspicious characters in the narrative. Criminality is often framed as social deviance in these novels, whether through transgressive female behavior or treacherous servants. Sensation novels were highly attentive to crime, both moral and legal, while being informed and literally surrounded by criminal reports in the periodical press.

Sensation novels were seen as opportunistically blurring the boundaries between journalism and literature. Contemporary critics agreed that sensation novels were in part inspired by "the criminal reports of the daily newspapers" (Mansel 501). These reports, in turn, whetted the public's appetite for similarly intriguing and exciting serial stories. Mansel complained of "this ravenous appetite for carrion, this vulture-like instinct which smells out the newest mass of social corruption" (502). John Ruskin voiced a similar sentiment, lamenting the "partly satiric, partly consolatory" taste in stories, "concerned only with the regenerative vigour of manure" (157).[7] Braddon indeed confessed in a letter to her mentor Bulwer-Lytton that she had drawn ideas from her "lucky bag of the Newgate Calendar," a quasi-literary group of criminal biographies and legal accounts (qtd. in Mangham, *Violent Women* 87; see R. Thomas, "Detection" 173–74). Sensation novels were criticized for targeting and stimulating the public appetite for excitement. "Excitement, and excitement alone," Mansel wrote, "seems to be the great end at which [sensation novels] aim" (482). The sensation novel "aims at convulsing the soul of the reader," Mansel complained (483), while Oliphant decried the "feverish productions" in the commercial press ("Novels" 275). Such novels, Oliphant wrote, gesture to "nasty thoughts, ugly suggestions, an imagination which prefers the unclean, [which are] almost more appalling than the facts of actual depravity" ("Novels" 275). Similarly, in May 1863, *Punch* magazine carried a satirical advertisement for a journal to be entitled "The Sensation Times, and Chronicles of Excitement," aimed at "Harrowing the Mind, Making the Flesh Creep, Causing the Hair to Stand on End, Giving Shocks to the Nervous System, Destroying Conventional Moralities, and generally Unfitting the Public for the Prosaic Avocations of Life" ("Sensation Times" 193).

Partly as a result of their emphasis on heightened reactions, sensation novels are often seen as an extension or adaptation of the Gothic mode. While it is true that such novels emphasize feelings associated with the "negative aesthetics" of the Gothic tradition (the sublime or terror), they

MAY 9, 1863.]   PUNCH, OR THE LONDON CHARIVARI.   193

PROSPECTUS OF A NEW JOURNAL.

IT must be admitted by all, that a new Journal is one of the necessities of the age, that it is imperatively called for, and that there is plenty of room for it. Actuated by these considerations, the Proprietors of the Journal about to be introduced, beg to announce that on Thursday the 14th of May (anniversary of the execution of RAVAILLAC by torture), will appear the first number of

The Sensation Times,

AND CHRONICLE OF EXCITEMENT.

This Journal will be devoted chiefly to the following objects; namely, Harrowing the Mind, Making the Flesh Creep, Causing the Hair to Stand on End, Giving Shocks to the Nervous System, Destroying Conventional Moralities, and generally Unfitting the Public for the Prosaic Avocations of Life.

Its columns will be enriched with carefully selected Horrors of every kind, from the English and Foreign newspapers, and with the most remarkable narratives of what is (perhaps uncharitably) called Criminal Adventure.

The Editors flatter themselves that there is no mock delicacy about them, nor any real delicacy either, and therefore their Subscribers may be assured that no record of an interesting nature will suffer by any of the fastidious revision which weakens a narrative, or by any of the timid manipulation which substitutes the hiatus for the description.

Murder, of course, will have in these columns, the foremost place, and the aid of photography will be used in order to present with an accuracy hitherto unattempted, the most faithful portraits of the actors and victims, and the most vivid representations of the scenes where such tragedies may be enacted.

But no class of sensational record will be neglected, and readers may rely upon receiving the most graphic accounts of all Crimes with Violence, merciless Corporal Punishments (especially in the case of children), Revolting Cruelties to Animals, and other interesting matters. Accidents, if horrific, will also be duly registered.

Arsenical Literature will find in these columns its best exponent, and all Poison Cases will be watched by a staff of special reporters who have been medically educated. Cases of suspicion will also be treated, and the Editors are happy to say, that they are already in communication with the butlers in several aristocratic families in which it is suspected that persons are endeavouring to dissolve the nuptial contract without recourse to publicity. This department of the Paper will be under the direction of an eminent sensation novelist, who will shortly be at liberty under a ticket-of-leave.

A Sensation Novel itself, in which atrocities hitherto undreamed of, even by the most fashionable fictionists of Paris, will form a feature in the new journal, and a large sum, under the name of a subscription, has been handed to the Society for the Suppression of Vice, in order to ensure its non-interference with the forthcoming tale.

The Police Courts will be watched, but the columns of the *Sensation Times* will not be encumbered with the dry details of mercantile fraud, commonplace larceny, and similar uninteresting matter, and reports will be given of such painful cases only as Paterfamilias, having duly enjoyed them, tells his family "he thinks they had better not read."

It is needless to say that the proceedings in the Court over which SIR CRESSWELL CRESSWELL presides will be given in full, where they have interest, and a distinguished lady novelist has undertaken to do justice to the sentimental features in such cases, points usually neglected by the hard and cynical male reporter.

Some extraordinary revelations of the habits and actions of exceedingly Low Life will be offered, and a special detective has been retained in the exclusive interests of the journal.

An eminent Vivisectionist has undertaken to supply a series of papers, setting forth his own experiences in his art, which he will continue to practise upon various portions of the inferior creation, for the sake of supplying truthful details to the readers of the *Sensation Times*.

The Editors, fearlessly throwing themselves upon the Public, unhesitatingly embark in an attempt to supply the evident want of the Age, and pledge themselves to spare no efforts in promoting the cause which has hitherto been left to the vigorous but inadequate efforts of the sensation *littérateur*.

Confidential communications of a terrific, sanguinary, or vicious description, may be addressed to the Editors, care of MESSRS. NIGHTMARE AND SKELETONS, Publishers, Garbage Lane, near St. Luke's, E.C.

Figure 0.1 A satirical advertisement for a new journal, entitled "The Sensation Times," in *Punch* magazine, 9 May 1863 ("Sensation Times").

relocate such actions and sentiments to the domestic hearth and, in particular, to the marital relationship. The reactions of fear, suspicion, and dismay are linked with social anxieties, connecting with misgivings over gender, race, and colonial conquest. Despite the sensation novel's significant departure from the Gothic tradition, elements seen earlier in the Gothic mode frequently appear in sensation novels, such as the uncanny reemergence of superstitious beliefs or intuitive knowledge. Such access to knowledge, independent of a deliberative scientific process, is comparable to the effect of the supernatural in earlier Gothic stories. In Collins's *No Name* (1862),

Mrs Lecount becomes firmly convinced of Miss Bygrave's real identity through the "guess-work of a moment," despite the absence of "a single fragment of producible evidence to justify it to the minds of others" (377). This instinctive acquisition of knowledge can hardly be described as rational or scientific, but grants her a more immediate (and hence, more dramatic) access to knowledge that needs only be confirmed by material evidence. The fact that knowledge precedes evidence, in such novels, points to the residual appeal of the spiritual while also revealing the currency of immediate information in a rapidly transforming society. Sensation novels reveal the tensions and contradictions between earlier modes of thought and ascendant forms of authority, which would become an attractive formula for later mystery and detective stories. Likewise, the tendency of sensation novels to cast foreigners and racial others as potential suspects was also to become unfortunate staples of the crime fiction genre.

Sensation novels were also a product of the mid-nineteenth-century interest in scientific authority. Hence, the negative aesthetics of sensation novels frequently give way to a rational deductive process, which becomes an identifiable component in detective stories. The reliance on empirical reasoning in such novels highlights the increasing public faith and popular interest in scientific discourse, even as anxieties coalesced over areas seen as testing the limits of the scientifically knowable, such as in deviant psychology, concealed criminality, mental illness, and pharmaceutical influences on the brain. The resolution in sensation novels is often a reinstatement of patriarchal, bourgeois authority, rather than following a marriage plot. The threat in many sensation novels is posed by a deviant woman with a questionable sexual history. Altogether, sensation novels are as much about how deviance and criminality is understood, as the ratiocinative process through which such threats are defused.

Crime and detection in sensation novels

Crime should be conceived quite broadly to include wrongdoing and mischief-making in sensation novels. Sensation novels are more often preoccupied with moral vice, social pretense, and villainous psychology than with the actual enactment of a crime. The motivation for committing crimes, whether they be bigamy or murder, also leads the reader into a narrative of personal identity. Hence, James Eli Adams writes that the central question of many sensation novels is "who is she?" rather than "who did it?" (*History* 208). Adams observes, "As identity becomes something akin to a commodity, it enables new modes of self-invention, but it also creates new possibilities of self-estrangement" (*History* 208). Maunder and Moore concur, adding that "suspicion and speculation surrounded the origins of self-made individuals" in Victorian England (8). The detective as a plainclothes police officer aggravated these tensions, since he also assumed a false identity. As Shpayer-Makov notes, "the claim to be someone else was viewed as blurring [class] distinctions and threatening the sense of security and assurance of knowing who was who" (29).

Hence, criminality in sensation novels has only nominally to do with a forensic investigation into a missing body or unexplained occurrence and more to do with an exploration into an individual's concealed past. The revelation of mystery in sensation fiction exposes a hidden network of implication and culpability. Criminality may be interpreted as a culmination of such concealed connections that threaten to tear at the wider social fabric. In *Aurora Floyd*, Braddon writes that "the results of one man's evil-doing" can foment and fester like a parasitic weed in a society (256). Braddon continues,

> The seed of sin engenders no common root, shooting straight upwards through the earth, and bearing a given crop. It is the germ of a foul-running weed, whose straggling suckers travel underground beyond the ken of mortal eye, beyond the power of mortal calculation.
>
> (*Aurora Floyd* 256)

Criminality or deviance is seen less from a scientific perspective, as it would later be viewed in detective stories, and more from the perspective of social obligations. This is also why sensation novels often take place at the domestic hearth. Stephen Knight notes that, in early detective stories of the Victorian period, "crime is not seen as some foreign, exotic plague visited on the British public, but as a simple disease that can, by some aberration, grow from inside that society" (11). The prime example of a social unit, Knight observes, is the family: "The family mirrors . . . the social order: static, hierarchical and male-dominated" (11). Saverio Tomaiuolo concurs that sensation novels often depict the family as "infected and corrupted to its root by 'endemic' maladies such as economic eagerness, violence, (inherited) madness and repressed sexual drives" (*In Lady* 8). As a social unit, the moral collapse of the family and marital unit played into anxieties over social disintegration, amid enhanced social mobility and a burgeoning middle class.

More broadly, sensation novels also reveal a tension between the rising middle class and the traditional social hierarchy. Robin Gilmour has argued that the idea of the gentleman, between 1840 and 1880, reflected the ambiguities of the middle classes and their desires. The idea of the gentleman, according to Gilmour, "answered to the conflicting needs of the nascent middle classes . . . their desire to be accepted by the traditional hierarchy and at the same time to make their impact upon it" (9). Sensation novels have often been read along similar lines, revealing, to borrow

Gilmour's words, a preoccupation with "a new professional and adminis-trative elite" that retained a connection with "the values of the old society" (8). The detective resembles the Victorian gentleman in embodying these ambiguities and, at times, contradictions, revealing the conflicting desires of the Victorian middle-class readership. Importantly, one way in which the detective asserts his authority and attains the recognition of the older, traditional hierarchy is through his claim on knowledge. The detective often crosses social boundaries, but also achieves a unifying perspective and narrative about events that reinstate social harmony.

Chapter outlines

In Chapter 1, I begin by tracing broad historical contexts helpful to under-standing the ambivalent detective. The first chapter on historical contexts may be read piecemeal where necessary, but I have set this information as a separate chapter to avoid expounding at length on historical details in the literary analysis. In this chapter, I discuss the police reform of 1829, which influenced literary explorations of crime in Dickens's novels. I also survey the cultural impact of the Matrimonial Causes Act of 1857, which allowed women to divorce for the first time. I cover developments in the periodi-cal press that created an open market for sensation novels and detective stories. I discuss the Indian Mutiny of 1857 and perceptions of Europeans (mainly French and Italian) in the mid-nineteenth century. Such historical contexts allow modern readers to make sense of perceived social threats that the detective was intended to defuse.

In Chapter 2, I explore how Dickens's satirical portrayal of the police in *Oliver Twist* gave way to greater admiration for individual detectives around 1850. As the editor of *Household Words*, Dickens heard stories from detective officers, which he later documented as contributions to the magazine. The establishment of professional detectives from 1842 also influenced his novelistic writing in *Martin Chuzzlewit* and *Bleak House*. *Martin Chuzzlewit* is said to feature the first detective in an English novel, representing the anonymity of the London crowd. Mr Nadgett evades observation through his inconspicuous appearance, but reveals incriminat-ing information about Jonas Chuzzlewit at the moment when patriarchal authority is restored. The detective stands outside the social order, even as he contributes to reinstating patriarchal control.

In Chapter 3, I explore how the detective features both as a villain and as a hero in Dickens's *Bleak House*. Mr Tulkinghorn and Mr Bucket rep-resent the moral ambivalence of detective work. While Mr Bucket in *Bleak House* was influenced by the real-life detective Inspector Charles Field, he is preceded in the narrative by another detective character, the Dedlock family lawyer, Mr Tulkinghorn. The detective's ambivalence partly stems from his unlikability, as Mr Tulkinghorn pries into and observes secrets, with damaging implications for other characters. Together, the detective characters of Mr Tulkinghorn and Mr Bucket reveal a negotiation of the detective's moral slipperiness, as a private investigation comes to resemble targeted persecution.

Chapter 4 explores detective characters of the late 1850s to the early 1860s in stories by William Russell, Collins, and Wood. This chapter begins with the real-life detective, Inspector Field, who was involved in the 1854 *Evans v. Robinson* trial. The trial ignited a debate about the "abuse" conducted by detectives and spies, underscoring a perceived distinction between a free England and oppressive European countries (*Daily News*, 24 Aug. 1854). The trial was mentioned by Russell in his *Revelations of a Detective Police-Officer* (1856), which recounts the memoirs of a fictional detective. This chapter also explores two sensation novels, *The Woman in White* by Collins and *East Lynne* by Wood. Neither novel features an identifiable detective in the strict sense, but nonetheless feature elements of detection and investigation that influenced other sensation novels. Detection in these novels is allied with constructions of masculinity, that, ironically in *The Woman in White*, relate to a female character. Masculinity in this landmark sensation novel is de-biologized, as Miss Marian Halcombe emerges as a masculine-looking, sexually unattractive, and yet highly observant investigator who drives the narrative. Mr Carlyle in *East Lynne* acts as a "passive detective" who enjoys the credit of a resolved mystery, even though he stands aloof from its more ambiguous investigative process (Kucich 186).

In a 2017 overview of recent critical work on Victorian sensation fiction, Beller stated that "it is undoubtedly Braddon who has received the preponderance of attention" since the late twentieth century ("Fashions" 467). Much of the scholarly attention, however, has focused on her best-selling novel *Lady Audley's Secret*, with scant critical interest in her earlier novels. Braddon's first novels feature detectives, but have been "relatively unexplored" and generally dismissed as her immature work and commercial literature (Cox, "Introduction" 2). Yet *The Trail of the Serpent* (1860), Braddon's first novel, exemplifies the moral ambivalence and slipperiness between the criminal and the detective. The novel also reveals a masculine claim to modern science, based on a method of reasoning that excludes and undermines more emotional women. Braddon's third novel, *The Black Band* (published anonymously in 1861), features detectives who practice "that wonderful science which tracks the dark pathway of crime with such marvelous success" (117). "Nothing is hopeless to the detective police of London," declares one of the characters – nothing except the international network of crime and blackmail known as the Black Band (Braddon, *Black Band* 105). Even "two of the cleverest detectives in London" are confounded by the extensive deception and intrigue practiced by this pan-European secret society of spies and criminals (Braddon, *Black Band* 105). *The Trail of the Serpent* and *The Black Band* reveal negotiations between crime and detection, as well as the ambivalence between the activities of criminal spies and detectives in Braddon's early work.

In Chapter 6, I explore how detective work places contradictory pressures on Robert Audley's character in *Lady Audley's Secret*, even as Braddon attempts to cast him as a gentleman. Through tracing the socially ambiguous position of the gentleman, I argue that this middle-class ideal of the gentleman conflicted with, rather than corresponded to, popular associations with detective work. In *Lady Audley's Secret*, Robert participates in an empirical and methodical process of reasoning, probing into a deceptive woman's past. This process of deduction and inference becomes a discursive strategy that claims to authoritatively interpret Lady Audley for the reader. Robert presents Lady Audley as "the most detestable and despicable of her sex," even though reflection on her life and background would suggest a more sympathetic reading of her character (Braddon, *Lady* 228–29). As other critics have already pointed out, the detective restores existent power structures and social distinctions (see Reitz; R. Thomas, *Detective*; Mossman).

The threat to the social order is framed, for the first time in this study, as bearing an overtly Eastern or Oriental mystique in Braddon's subsequent novel, *Aurora Floyd*. Chapter 7 explores how Oriental mystique dramatizes female disobedience, over which patriarchal authority must be reinstated. But the principal threat in the novel stems from spying servants, or household members who surveille and collect clues about their mistress. This sort of treacherous behavior recalls the recent memory of the Sepoy Rebellion (as briefly outlined in Chapter 1), with Braddon exploring the imperial trauma within a domestic context. The connection between empire and detection would become even more pronounced in subsequent sensation novels and in Arthur Conan Doyle's *The Sign of the Four* (1890) (see Chapter 10). But the criminal threat, while imbued with imperial memory, emanates from defiance against the domestic ideology, initially by Aurora and subsequently by the household servants. The professional detective (Mr Joseph Grimstone) helps restore the social order, even though he does not emerge as a hero in the novel.

Female detectives were not professionally employed by the Metropolitan Police until 1883, but they became the subject for imaginative exploration in two "yellow-back" books in 1864, as explored in Chapter 8. Hayward's *Revelations of a Lady Detective* and Ware's *The Female Detective* (written under the pseudonym Andrew Forrester) were published not in the periodical press, but as cheap railway books. Such books often wore glazed coverings with eye-catching illustrations, earning the name "yellow-backs" from the mid-1850s. Both *The Female Detective* (1864) and *Revelations of Lady Detective* (1864) play on the moral ambivalence, even popular "aversion" towards detectives (Forrester 3). The female detectives amplify the detective's moral ambiguity by masquerading as innocuous, middle-aged women. As Hayward's detective states, "Men are less apt to suspect a woman if she play [*sic*] her cards cleverly, and knows thoroughly well how to conduct" her investigations (43). Chapter 8 concludes with a discussion of Collins's *The Law and the Lady* (1875), which presents a wife as a female detective delving into her husband's affairs (albeit not a professional detective, in the sense of either Ware or Hayward's novel).

Collins's *The Moonstone* has been deemed the first English detective novel by T. S. Eliot, a view echoed by more recent critics (377). Chapter 9 focuses on the character of Sergeant Cuff, the first detective to take an active and prominent role in Collins's novels. Sergeant Cuff's investigations take place in the context of a missing diamond, which threatens to unleash mystical, unknown forces in the novel. Against this exotic and implicitly colonial threat, the detective's investigations restore faith and confidence in reason, filling missing gaps in the narrative to achieve a sense of rational comprehension. This chapter also explores elements of detection in Collins's earlier novels *No Name* and *Armadale*, though these may more properly be regarded as domestic melodramas, rather than detective narratives. Detectives and spies do feature, however, in *Armadale*, revealing the moral complexity and ambiguity associated with covert surveillance.

Detectives continued to feature in stories and develop after the peak of sensation novels. Dickens's *The Mystery of Edwin Drood* is widely seen as his own attempt at mystery writing, informed and inspired by the success of Collins's *The Moonstone*. Chapter 10 discusses the characterization of racial outsiders in this unfinished novel, while exploring the context in which detection is likely to have occurred. In this context, a sense of mystery and intrigue is amplified by the presence of foreign others, such as Neville Landless, who is cast as constitutionally violent and "tigerish" (Dickens, *Mystery* 47). This chapter briefly delves into Doyle's stories, *A Study in Scarlet* (1887) and *The Sign of the Four*, charting the trajectory from the mid-nineteenth century to the *fin-de-siècle*, as imperial adventure gave way to disenchantment. The early Sherlock Holmes is a product of this imperial fatigue, as his detective work is presented as a rarified intellectual activity, distanced from the moral complications of covert surveillance and spying.

Notes

1 For more recent criticism of sensation novels, see (Harrison and Fantina x–xi).
2 For a study of earlier detective narratives in the nineteenth century, see (Worthington).

3 Costantini continues that sensation novelists, in particular, "wove criminal plots that exposed the performative nature of respectability, [while] reveal[ing] ideals of worthiness and trust pertaining to middle-class mobility" (100). Such models of middle-class conduct were, in Costantini's words, "seldom . . . unambiguous" (100).

4 See also (Cox, *Neo-Victorianism* 73–84).

5 Brantlinger also writes that sensation novels were a "unique mixture of contemporary domestic realism with elements of the Gothic romance, the Newgate novel of criminal 'low life,' and the 'silver fork' novel of scandalous and sometimes criminal 'high life' " ("What is 'Sensational' " 1). For more on crime stories in the *Newgate Calendar*, see (Knight 8–38).

6 As Lucy Brown notes in *Victorian News and Newspapers*, "journalism was nearly always anonymous, though authorship can sometimes be found out from memoirs" (3). James A. Secord concurs that, in the nineteenth century, "almost all periodical journalism was anonymous," with anonymity sometimes seen as "guaranteeing independence and freedom from personal bias" (18–19).

7 While Ruskin did not restrict his criticism to sensation novels, he would surely have had these in mind in 1866. Ruskin also deplored the mood of "indignation, without any curative self-reproach," which he saw as "dull[ing] the intelligence, and degrad[ing] the conscience, into sullen incredulity of all sunshine outside the dunghill" (157).

1 Historical contexts
Police reform, marriage, empire, and the periodical press

Since the ambivalent detective as a literary figure emerged from a set of historical circumstances, it is worth surveying the major relevant contexts in the early to mid-nineteenth century that informed this development. Central among these was the formation of a professional group of detectives within the London Metropolitan Police Force in 1842. A broad overview of the police reform is included in this chapter, as well as the specific debate that surrounded the formation of the Detective Branch. Also important to understanding the detective as a literary construct, pitted against particular social threats in sensation novels, are the broader contexts of the Victorian gender ideology, divorce reform, imperial expansion, and colonial resistance. Since the sensation novel was shaped by particular market forces, it is also wroth covering the newspaper tax repeals that allowed the periodical press to flourish and court a wider audience. This chapter aims to flesh out the historical contexts that shaped the literary phenomenon and cultural construct that became the ambivalent detective.

In *Oliver Twist* (1838), Dickens ridicules the London Bow Street Runners, an older police force later subsumed by the Metropolitan London Police. In the novel, Inspectors Blathers and Duff attempt to trace a burglar, but are led down a false end. The police magistrate, Mr Fang, is also memorable as a cold-hearted and unjustly draconian character, who seems more interested in intimidating and threatening others than in meting out justice. From the 1840s, however, Dickens's literary depictions of the police would become more positive, particularly following his acquaintance with detectives from the London Metropolitan Police. While it would be hyperbole to argue that the establishment of the Detective Branch was a defining moment for sensation fiction, it did make possible literary explorations of individual agents of the law. The profession of detectives opened up a new vista of imagining law enforcement and individual ingenuity. Professional detectives were simultaneously part of and also distinct from the police force, occupying an ambiguous position between apparent members of the public and covert enforcers of the law.

DOI: 10.4324/9781003369622-2

The Victorian gender ideology has been widely studied and only a brief summary is provided here. Importantly, while women were deprived of many legal rights upon marriage, the patriarchal institutions and primogeniture ironically made it plausible for certain women to climb the social ladder. A woman could still theoretically (and imaginatively) come from a poor and obscure background, and marry into wealth or even aristocracy. The concealment of a woman's true identity is one of the recurring themes of sensation novels, and the detective often becomes embroiled in an investigation into an enigmatic person's past. Significantly, critics like Lisa Surridge and Marlene Tromp have argued that divorce reform in the mid-nineteenth century influenced the literary concerns of sensation fiction (Tromp, *Private Rod*). The 1857 Matrimonial Causes Act allowed married Englishwomen, for the first time, to separate from their husbands on the grounds of desertion or cruelty.[1] The divorce court journalism of this period, according to Surridge and Tromp, likely informed the acute attention to domestic trouble in sensation novels like Collins's *The Woman in White*.

Reforms in the London police force and the first police detectives

The London police force prior to 1829 was known as the Bow Street Runners, established in 1749 by the author and magistrate Henry Fielding. This police force was seen as woefully inadequate and ill-matched for the increasingly complicated task of combatting crime in early nineteenth-century London.[2] The Bow Street Runners were mocked in *Oliver Twist* through police characters depicted as drinking on their job. Philip Collins writes in *Dickens and Crime* that England was "the worst-policed nation of the civilized world" during Dickens's boyhood with the public frequently mocking police incompetence (8, 197). In 1829, the Home Secretary Sir Robert Peel founded a new police force in London that remains to the present day. The London Metropolitan Police Force differed from the Bow Street Runners in their emphasis on discipline. As an anonymous writer in the *Quarterly Review* recalled in June 1856, there was "some well-founded alarm" in the early days of the new police force, which resembled "a standing army of nearly six thousand men, drilled like soldiers, [and] taught to act in masses" like a "veritable gendarmerie" ("The Police and the Thieves" 438). Rather than await reports of crime at their office, officers of the Metropolitan Police Force were employed in patrolling designated areas of London, a practice that became known as the "beat" system. Their increased visibility on the streets as uniformed police officers was intended as a deterrent to crime, as a method of surveillance, and as a swift remedy to criminal acts. While the Metropolitan Police Force recruited officers from across social ranks, including the working class, officers were prohibited from drinking on duty and could be dismissed or punished for drunken behavior. Indeed, drunkenness was the main reason for dismissal and penalties among the Metropolitan Police Force, while another vice was relations with prostitutes.[3]

Even after the Metropolitan Police Force was founded, the Bow Street Runners continued to operate until 1839, when they were formally disbanded and merged with the Metropolitan Police Force. The Metropolitan Police were not immediately well-accepted, remaining, in P. Collins's words, "a mocked and hated body of men" before they won gradual acceptance and recognition (8). P. Collins writes that they "became quite soon an accepted and then a respected part of the London scene," with "general agreement that the New Police were more efficient and diligent, and less corrupt, than their predecessors" (8). Indeed, Dickens continued to lampoon police officers as ill-matched to criminal activities in London. In 1838, while Dickens was also writing *Oliver Twist*, he contributed sketches to *Bentley's Miscellany* (in which Ainsworth would also serialize his novel *Jack Sheppard*). In a sketch about the fictional town of Mudfog, modelled on Dickens's naval hometown of Chatham, he mocked the establishment of an automaton police force. In "Displays of Models and Mechanical Science," Mr Coppernose guides the members of the Mudfog Association towards prototypes of an automaton police force aimed at the "harmless and wholesome relaxation for the young noblemen of England" (Dickens, "Full Report of the Second Meeting" 221). The prototypes are to be stationed throughout London, with heads made of wood and bodies "made of the toughest and thickest materials that can possibly be obtained" (Dickens, "Full Report of the Second Meeting" 223). Mr Coppernose touches a small spring that enables the automatons to speak. Dickens writes, "One of the figures immediately began to exclaim with great volubility that he was sorry to see gentlemen in such a situation, and the other to express a fear that the policeman was intoxicated" (Dickens, "Full Report of the Second Meeting" 223). The members of the Mudfog Association applaud the ingenious invention and the President retires with Mr Coppernose to lay the idea before the council.

Dickens's view of the police force as largely ineffectual and incompetent would change in the 1850s, partly due to his acquaintance with detectives from the Metropolitan Police Force as editor of his own journal, *Household Words*. Even before this time, however, Dickens began shifting focus away from depicting criminal life in London (partly due to public disapproval), and instead explored the literary potential of apprehending criminals. In the process, he incorporated perhaps the first detective character in an English novel in *Martin Chuzzlewit* (of which more in Chapter 3). For the most part, the Metropolitan Police Force began to win public acceptance and approval due to discipline among their ranks. Through the County Police Act of 1839, they were expanded to absorb older police forces, including the Bow Street Runners and the Marine Police Force. But the establishment of the Detective Branch of the Metropolitan Police Force in 1842 indicates that apprehending crime was seen not only as an issue of institutional discipline, but also as requiring further stealth and covert surveillance. Peel had emphasized in the 1829 parliamentary debates that he would not countenance a system based on spying, but, as Gregory J. Durston writes in *Burglars and Bobbies* (2012), "the value of covert detection was never entirely rejected, even in the new force" (185).

The Detective Branch of the Metropolitan Police was founded to comprise a special and selective group of officers, who wore plain clothes in contrast to ordinary policemen. Instead of being a visible presence on the streets, these detective officers were able to imperceptibly blend into their surroundings as apparent members of the public. Their inconspicuous presence on the streets was intended to support police activity, even as their deployment hints at the limits of the preventative patrol system. Detectives were better able to surveille their targets and elude suspicion, since they were not uniformed. They were also more highly paid than their uniformed counterparts and were expected to have certain skills, such as knowledge of street slang and foreign languages. As Shpayer-Makov notes, the detectives "constituted the more esteemed branch" and were entitled to a "special set of compensations" denied to uniformed policemen (5). According to John Wilkes in *The London Police in the Nineteenth Century* (1977), detectives were expected to have "patience, persistence, courage, and cunning," especially as they often worked alone (29). According to Shpayer-Makov, later in the nineteenth century, the requirements for a detective officer were, according to one account, "considerable knowledge of the world, good education, good address, tact, and temper" (Vincent qtd. in Durston 213). The Detective Branch remained a highly selective group, beginning with less than ten members and comprising of only about fifteen members by 1867 (Wilkes 29–30; Durston 192; Shpayer-Makov 34; see also White 404; "The Police and the Thieves" 174). Additionally, John Sutherland writes that "detectives from the Metropolitan Police Force . . . could be privately hired as 'confidential agents,' " or as private investigators ("Explanatory" 484, 487). Shpayer-Makov concurs, noting that the state did not have a monopoly on crime control and that "private persons and agencies continued to provide detective services to the population" (3).

The reality in 1840s London was that immigration and population were surging, leading to higher crime rates. Throughout the nineteenth century, Britain maintained an "open-door policy towards immigration" and immigration to London was associated with the most destitute people, particularly from Ireland (Lloyd). Irish immigrants, such as those fleeing the Great Famine of 1846–49, were among the poorest of Ireland's rural population and often settled in London areas with poor living conditions, such as in the East End (White 133). Even before the wave of immigration, however, Irish Londoners had been associated with poverty and crime, living in areas such as St Giles, dubbed "Little Dublin" or "Little London" (White 11). Immigration continued to increase from further overseas. While the largest group of immigrants were Irish, there was also another "major source of immigrants" from continental Europe, including those fleeing political repression (Lloyd). Immigrants inspired suspicion and even hostility, as seen, for instance, in Braddon's portrayal of an Italian foreigner in *The Black Band*. This foreigner appears like "one of those shabby, penniless adventurers, who, rejected from their own country by reason of some evil deed, are thrown upon the wide sea of London for a refuge" (Braddon, *Black Band* 91). Braddon continues that such "disreputable adventurers . . . every day figure in the English newspapers, linked to some act of audacious swindling" (*Black Band* 104).[4]

Even though there were reservations about deploying non-uniformed police officers on the streets and concerns about their constitutionality, they were seen as a necessary part of law enforcement operations. The resemblance between detectives and spies inspired some unease, even though they had fewer powers of search, arrest, questioning, and detention than their uniformed counterparts (Durston 190). Even as late as the 1860s, there remained public concern that detective work was underhand. Durston writes that there was "acute concern about where these tactics might lead" and "the general public felt 'repugnance' for the use of many detective ruses" (188). The frequent association between the detective and the spy appeared, in Shpayer-Makov's words, "to personify the deepest threat to freeborn Englishmen" with implications of espionage (27–28).

Of particular concern was the resemblance between detective officers and the criminals they were pursuing. As Durston writes, it seemed that "the police [were] exercising the same degree of ingenuity that criminals employed against society" (188–89). The *Quarterly Review* argued in 1856 that both the detective and the thief were "using their wits to get their living . . . [with] a sort of tacit understanding between them that each is entitled to play his game as well as he can" ("The Police and the Thieves" 176). Again, the newspaper noted, "If . . . the swell mobsman's eye is for ever wandering in search of his prey, so also is that of the detective, and instances may occur where the one may be mistaken for the other" ("The Police and the Thieves" 182). Heather Worthington and Shpayer-Makov point out that, since most police officers were drawn from the working class, detectives could be imagined as former petty criminals (Worthington 159; Shpayer-Makov 257–59; see also Saunders 119).[5] The moral ambivalence here means that detectives, as members of the police force, were generally regarded as necessary but also as a less-than-ideal solution. As Ware writes in his 1864 novel *The Female Detective*, the profession of detectives might be "despised," but "the spy is as peculiarly necessary as he or she is peculiarly objectionable" (Forrester 2).

In the sensation literature of the 1850s and 1860s, detectives appear less frequently as police officers and more often as private spies and enforcers of the law. Their presence often inspires rage and disgust, mixed with some respect for their inconspicuous behavior. In Collins's *Armadale*, the townspeople react with disdain and indignation when they learn that Allan Armadale has enlisted the services of a private eye to tail Miss Lydia Gwilt. Ozias Midwinter describes "the means of a paid spy" as "the vilest of all means," while Major Milroy denounces such behavior as ill-fitting a gentleman (480). Major Milroy states to Armadale,

> if a man made private inquires into a lady's affairs, without being either her husband, her father, or her brother, he subjected himself to the responsibility of justifying his conduct in the estimation of others; and if he evaded that responsibility he abdicated the position of a gentleman.
>
> (W. Collins, *Armadale* 423)

The connotations of a sexual gaze and voyeuristic intentions were also not lost upon Victorian readers, potentially conflating the detective with a male predator. In the same novel, the spy James Bashwood embodies the perceived moral deficiency and questionable tactics of detectives, particularly as he is willing to make money from his father's sexual obsession with Miss Gwilt. The detective was seen as an investigator of information, but one employing means that resembled criminal activity rather than sound legal procedure. The association between detectives and ungentlemanly, even un-Christian, behavior meant that their deployment and presence often inspired ambivalence and mistrust. Petty criminals among the "swell mob" in urban areas had often dressed as respectable tradesmen to evade suspicion, as depicted in *Oliver Twist*.[6] Detectives would also conceal their identities by disguising themselves as members of the crowd, attempting to blend in while hiding their motives.

Both uniformed and non-uniformed police officers were trained to take handwritten notes on duty. Not all officers in the Metropolitan Police Force were well-educated and some detectives even struggled to make daily comprehensive reports due to their lack of education (Wilkes 32). However, they were expected to record and write down important names, places, and instructions while on duty, even if they were not able to compile extensive notes or diaries (see Wilkes 21). The police force was also unusually late in adopting new technologies, such as the camera or the telegram. Even though the telegraph had been available from 1846, the police force only set up telegraph wires to most of their stations after 1868. The police force also began to use photographs and identify fingerprints from the 1880s, even though the camera had been widely used before then.[7] Hence, in the mid-nineteenth century, detective and police work was associated with patrolling or surveilling the streets and taking written notes. In connection to this, the incriminating evidence of one's handwriting could serve as important proof of identification. In mid-nineteenth-century England, one's handwriting was seen as a distinctive (though, by no means, foolproof) marker of identity. Several sensation novels take the potential of identification through handwriting to imaginative lengths. In Braddon's early novel *The Black Band*, a forger is capable of "deceiv[ing even] the most experienced banker's clerk in the City of London or Paris" by imitating a person's handwriting (90). In Braddon's later *Aurora Floyd*, an unsigned letter is identified by their "peculiar hand; a hand about which there could be no mistake" (184). Collins's *Armadale* similarly relates a crime enabled through the forgery of another person's handwriting. His later work, *The Law and the Lady*, relies on the recovery of a torn handwritten letter as legal evidence to vindicate a man's innocence. Hence, detective investigations in mid-nineteenth-century literature relied on the circumstances of time and place, as well as the evidence of written notes, rather than technological or forensic analysis to investigate crime.

The Victorian gender ideology and the Matrimonial Causes Act of 1857

The Victorian period was a time of contradictions, evinced in the increased visibility of men on the streets but simultaneous suspicion towards unaccompanied women. The history of sensation fiction and the rise of detectives are intimately intertwined with urban developments in London. In the mid-nineteenth century, it remained unusual and even taboo for young women to walk the streets alone. Victorian society imposed limitations on female movement outside the domestic sphere, but unchaperoned young women on the London streets gradually became an increasingly common sight and, by the end of the nineteenth century, an acceptable phenomenon (see Altick, *Presence* 421). As Nina Auerbach and Judith R. Walkowitz have stated, the appearance of women on the London streets threw into relief contradictions between the popular fascination with feminine innocence and the imagined possibilities of female depravity. Added to this was the reality that, in nineteenth-century London, one could reinvent one's identity amid the London crowd. The possibilities of social mobility and self-fashioning meant that London was often associated with criminal intrigue, while the labyrinthine streets made it virtually impossible to locate specific individuals without a lead. Throughout the nineteenth century, London was contrasted with rural England in its association with "squalor, vice, misery, and crime" – but also as "the fountain of opportunity" (Altick,

Presence 384–85). It was in this city that individuals could reinvent their identities at will and merge indistinguishably into the crowd. The presence of young women on the streets of London raised questions, therefore, about their identity, their history, and their associates. In sensation novels, the possibility of reinvented identity reach new imaginative heights, with seemingly endless possibilities for character development.

As scholars have already highlighted, the Victorian gender ideology was closely intertwined with an idealized view of the marital union. Ben Griffin highlights in *The Politics of Gender in Victorian Britain* (2012), "the [Victorian] idea of [marital] unity referred not to a partnership of equals but to a couple united under one will – that of the husband" (46). In the mid-nineteenth century, anxiety over the erosion of traditional values and domestic harmony through the assault of modernity was expressed in popular fiction. Anxiety over manipulative or self-promoting women reached the fore not only in sensation novels, but other literary works of the period, such as William Makepeace Thackeray's *Vanity Fair* (1848). The gender ideology, intertwined as it was with the domestic ideology, was seen as a moral frontier to the encroaching influence of modernity. The perceived importance of a woman's role in the home was also linked with a perceived weakening of morality and religious values in society. As Griffin writes, many Victorians believed that

> the home needed to be peaceful to allow a man to contemplate God and to provide him with the peace and love he required to develop his character, so that he could protect himself against the sinfulness of the public sphere.
>
> (B. Griffin 41)

Hence, the visible presence of young women in the streets highlighted a discrepancy for Victorians, as women were seen venturing out into the "sinful public sphere" and possibly being corrupted by its influence. The moral need to protect the gender ideology and the domestic sphere meant that mystery, intrigue, and drama in sensation novels often coalesce at the domestic hearth. It was the domestic sphere that required protection and that was under assault, as female characters simultaneously seek new opportunities afforded them by opportunities in London. While these were hypothetical possibilities, exaggerated by far-fetched imaginations, they did touch upon a social anxiety over the perceived erosion not only to the gender ideology and the image of innocent femininity, but also to the weakening of the domestic sphere as a moral refuge from the public sphere.

Another contradiction of the Victorian period was that the domestic ideology was not seen as inclusive of the working class, as it was of the middle class. The widespread belief that working-classes families were abusive inspired the parliamentary debates that led to the Matrimonial Causes Act of 1857 (see B. Griffin 70–71). There was intense public and parliamentary discussion in the 1850s about working-class married women trapped in abusive and violent marriages. The belief that working-class women were subject to domestic violence motivated an eventual change in the law that enabled judicial separation on the grounds of physical cruelty or of desertion without cause for two years. A judicial separation restored some rights to married women, but did not allow them to remarry (B. Griffin 10). Access to divorce remained restrictive and also prohibitively expensive for working-class women. Ironically, the divorce court established as a result of the Act overseeing petitions for separation exposed instances of abuse and violence among the middle and upper classes. In 1862, the journalist Frances Power Cobbe decried in *Fraser's Magazine* the "many hundreds of such tragedies [that] underline the outwardly decorous lives . . . of the middle ranks in England" ("Celibacy" 57).[8] In her article "Celibacy vs. Marriage," Cobbe discussed how these private details had come to light as a result of the Divorce Court.

> Who imagined that the wives of English *gentlemen* might be called on to endure from their husbands the violence and cruelty we are accustomed to picture exercised only in the lowest lanes and courts of our cities, where drunkard ruffians, stumbling home from the gin-palace, assail the miserable partners of their vices with curses, kicks, and blows? Who could have it imagined it possible, that well-born and well-educated men, in honourable professions, should be guilty of the same brutality? . . . Now these things *are* so. The Divorce Court has brought dozens of them to light; and we all know well that for one wife who will seek public redress for her wrongs, there are always ten, who, for their children's' sakes, will bear their martyrdoms in silence.
>
> (Cobbe, "Celibacy" 57, italics in original)

As Cobbe notes, the divorce court journalism contributed to the sense that marital violence was not solely a working-class phenomenon – "in the lowest lanes and courts of our cities" – but also existed in middle- and upper-class households. Marital "brutality," in Cobbe's words, could also exist in families held by "well-born and well-educated men, in honourable professions." The divorce court journalism shook public confidence that the middle class was intrinsically morally distinct from and insulated from the domestic troubles plaguing the working class. As Griffin writes,

> For most of the century domestic abuse had been seen as largely a working-class problem but, once in operation, the Divorce Court

shattered this complacency by exposing to public view the behavior of middle- and upper-class men whose wives demanded relief.

(B. Griffin 71)

A. James Hammerton in *Cruelty and Companionship* (1992) concurs that, by the late nineteenth century, failed marriages were generally seen as the result of "men's unreasonable and selfish behavior," rather than female wrongdoing (166).

The Matrimonial Causes Act and the establishment of the Divorce Court in 1857 coincided with developments in the periodical press, outlined later in this chapter, that resulted in a wider readership and greater consumption of newspapers. The newspapers covered hearings in the Divorce Court and opened, in Hammerton's words, a "vivid window" into the marital relationship (102). Readers were invited to read and discuss private details of unhappy marriages, to an extent that would earlier have been inconceivable. In Hammerton's words, the privacy of marriage became "compromised by intrusive scrutiny and surveillance," as a result of the divorce court journalism, "facilitated by the ... shared newspaper culture among the middle class" (102). Indeed, Surridge and Tromp have argued that the "shared newspaper culture" of reading about other people's marriages directly inspired sensation novelists, who also wrote for the periodical press (see also Hammerton 102). Surridge argues that while domestic violence and marital abuse had featured in novels prior to 1857, such as in Anne Brontë's *The Tenant of Wildfell Hall* (1848) and Dickens's *Dombey and Son* (1848), novels after 1859 reveal "a wider phenomenon of ideological upheaval caused by the divorce court and the newspaper" (141). According to Surridge, the public debate over married women's rights opened an imaginative window into Victorian domestic life (137). Tromp also argues in *The Private Rod* (2000) that sensation novels achieved a popular readership "in the midst of growing concern about codes of behavior in marriage" (3).

The divorce court journalism laid open to public view the vulnerability faced by married women, who, regardless of their social rank, had few legal rights or privileges. Under Victorian law, married women were legal non-entities, whose property and rights were subsumed under those of her husband. Hence, Françoise Basch writes in *Relatives Creatures* (1974) that women, upon marriage,

lost at one stroke all her rights as a "femme sole", that is to say a free and independent individual. ... she entirely lost her own legal existence, and with it, any legal recourse against her husband or anybody else.

(16–17)

The coverture laws meant that married women could not make contracts, could not hold personal property, and had no rights to custody over her children (see B. Griffin 9–10; Basch 22). Cobbe scathingly wrote in *Fraser's Magazine* in 1868 that a "woman who commits Matrimony" receives the same sentence as "the woman who commits Murder," with the entire forfeiture of her property ("Criminals" 91). Through marriage, the wife and the husband achieved an absolute union that Cobbe compared to the tarantula spider, whereby one spider "gobbles" up the other ("Criminals" 103). Cobbe vividly wrote, "The victorious spider visibly acquires double bulk, and thenceforth may be understood to 'represent the family' in the most perfect manner conceivable" ("Criminals" 103). The complete dependence of married women on their husbands reflected the value of domestic harmony based on patriarchal authority in Victorian England. But married women were left, as the divorce court journalism showed, defenseless in cases of abuse or mistreatment.

Prior to the Matrimonial Causes Act of 1857, married women were unable to divorce their husbands, unless they could provide evidence of aggravated adultery. Evidence of adultery alone was insufficient as a basis for divorce, but aggravations of adultery, such as bestiality, incest, sodomy, or bigamy, were accepted conditions for divorce on the provision of evidence (see Wolfram 157; Chase and Levenson 186; Basch 24).[9] The double standard that allowed men to divorce their wives on the basis of adultery alone, while married women had to prove an additional offense, was unchanged in the Matrimonial Causes Act. Hence, though the 1857 Act was seen as a "watershed" moment in legal history (Wolfram 158), ushering in one of the most "agitating" anxieties of the period (Chase and Levenson 186), it was in reality an extension rather than a remedy of embedded inequalities between women and men. Modern historians see the 1857 Act as "quite conservative" and not touching "the double standard of traditional patriarchal structures" (Humphreys 43), with provisions that were "merely palliatives and . . . no substitute for legal equality" (B. Griffin 11). It would only be until the Married Women's Property Acts of 1870 and 1882 that married women would be able to exercise independent property rights.

Even though the Matrimonial Causes Act of 1857 threw open the theoretical possibility of divorce and separation, in reality, such petitions were infrequent as married women preferred to apply for "protection orders" that restored to them the property rights of unmarried women (see B. Griffin 10). Divorce remained difficult to obtain and was not widely accepted as an option by Victorians. As Anne Humphreys writes, divorce may have seemed "tantalizingly available as a resolution to an unsatisfactory marriage," but it remained hedged with "deep shame and severe social ostracism" (45). Despite this, critics have argued that divorce remained "intractably within the repertoire of possibilities" following the 1857 Act, operating as an "overdetermined set of anxieties" even where marriages remained intact (Chase and Levenson 187). In any case, sensation novels explore not so much divorce as bigamy, seen as its imaginative twin. The possibility of divorce conjured up ideas of remarriage and bigamy, since Victorians were used to viewing marriage as an inseparable and lifelong union. Remarriage could consequently be seen as illegitimate and even bigamous. According to Karen Chase and Michael Levenson, the bigamy novels of the 1860s may be seen as "divorce novels" to the extent that they are "novels about the failure of divorce to achieve a true separation" (203). In their view, Victorian culture was "still struggling to represent the change" heralded by the 1857 Act (Chase and Levenson 203).

Foreigners and colonial threats in sensation novels

The most notable event of the mid-nineteenth century crystallizing fears of instability in Britain's colonies was the Indian Mutiny of 1857. Much has been written about the Indian Mutiny, also known as the Sepoy Rebellion, and a mere outline of events is necessary here. The causes are disputed, but the rebellion escalated when the Hindu and Muslim sepoys ("soldiers") stationed at Meerut in the Punjab murdered their British officers and many of their wives and children on May 10, 1857. They subsequently seized nearby Delhi and killed more Europeans the following day. Over the following weeks and months, bloody uprisings occurred across military stations and towns in Bengal. General Sir Hugh Wheeler resisted a siege at Cawnpore for twenty-two days, before surrendering to rebel forces and their commander, Nana Sahib, on the promise that they would be allowed to leave unharmed. But on June 27, the British forces were massacred in the Ganges at Cawnpore, while many of their women and children were captured and imprisoned. Nana Sahib recruited butchers from a bazaar to hack these survivors (over two hundred women and children) to pieces with swords and axes. Supporting British troops, led by Henry Havelock, arrived at Cawnpore the next day, suppressing suspected rebels and rebel sympathizers on the way. They discovered the remains of the massacre, prompting public outrage across England. Historian Christopher Herbert deems the Indian Rebellion to be "the supreme trauma of the age," despite its contained geopolitical repercussions (2). The uprising marked, in Herbert's words, "a traumatic expulsion from a known world into a frightening new historical era" for the Victorians (2–3).

The impact of the Indian Rebellion was felt in Victorian society, even though the events unfolded thousands of miles away in Britain's colony (see Tange, "Picturing"). Memorably, Dickens wrote to Angela Burdett-Coutts in October 1857 that, if he were "Commander in Chief in India," he would "strike that Oriental race with amazement" and "do [his] utmost to exterminate the Race upon whom the stain of the late cruelties rested" (*Letters* VIII, 459). By the time of the letter, British and loyal Indian troops had already recovered control over Delhi after a prolonged siege. Rebels continued to lay siege at Lucknow, but this was lifted under British pressure in March 1858. Nana Sahib escaped into the mountains of Nepal, but other high-profile rebels (such as Rani of Jhansi and Tantia Tope) were killed in battle. Despite the containment of this uprising, it continued to be replayed and revisited in the Victorian imagination for at least a decade to come. Culturally, to borrow Brantlinger's words, "no [other] episode in British imperial history raised public excitement to a higher pitch" (*Rule* 199). The drama of the uprising and conservative sympathies meant that popular writers could imbue their narratives with a sense of conflict and tension through allusions to the Indian Mutiny. These allusions are seen in the sensation novels of the early 1860s, such as in Braddon's *Lady Audley's Secret* and *Aurora Floyd* (see Herbert 239–72; Nayder, "Rebellious" 31–42).

Since sensation novels were primarily focused on the domestic hearth, such imperial anxieties and concerns could be referenced through alluding to a domestic uprising and social collapse. The patriarchal authority that held sway over the domestic sphere could be seen, through imaginative extension, as a microcosmic version of British imperial power. Lillian Nayder concurs that "the oppression of Englishwomen and that of native figures are closely tied" in sensation novels, "as gender relations and imperial relations prove analogous" ("Empire" 445). This is not to suggest that domestic relations are necessarily as politically fraught as imperial relations, nor that events portrayed at the domestic hearth necessarily reflected concerns about British imperial power. But sensation novelists could, through a sleight of writerly hand, link these two tensions through allusion. This occurs most memorably in Collins's *The Moonstone*, but also, as I argue in Chapter 7, in Braddon's *Aurora Floyd*, which opportunistically plays on suppressed memories of the traumatic Indian Mutiny to raise the stakes for a domestic rebellion in a middle-class family. The intractable silence of Aurora Floyd and, later, the treachery of two servants at Mellish Park are dramatically stylized through allusion to the Indian Mutiny. As Nayder has argued, domestic betrayal could be represented as colonial resistance and the bigamous wife could be portrayed as a colonial rebel ("Empire" 452). Challenges against patriarchal authority could imaginatively figure as colonial disobedience, reenacted in the domestic sphere.

Since sensation novels freely appropriated events, concerns, and anxieties likely to inspire a strong reaction, the representation of a foreign threat was not limited to colonized people. The imaginations of foreign intrigue did not necessarily have to involve colonized or even racial others. In fact, Europeans feature more often as potential suspects than Indians or colonized people in sensation novels. This includes exaggerated depictions of the French as morally corrupt and easily swayed by their emotions, as seen in Braddon's *The Trail of the Serpent*. The French were seen as politically oppressive, with a police and intelligence network seen as invasive and abusive of civil liberties (see Shpayer-Makov 30). Italians were also associated with cunning, stealth, and conspiracy, fueled by the news of secret societies in Italy following the Napoleonic Wars. The Congress of Vienna in 1815 had restored control over Italy from France to the Austrian Empire and the Habsburgs, but a number of secret societies plotted a *Risorgimento* ("rising again") movement that would unify Italy as an independent nation. During the 1850s and early 1860s, when sensation novels were at their peak, Italy remained divided and, to the British observer, hopelessly plagued by political unrest and economic decline.[10] As Michael Cotsell indicates, Italy even featured as an "election issue between Conservatives and Liberals" in British politics (840). The inclusion of Italians as potential suspects in sensation novels underscores the theme where Britain defined herself in opposition to her neighbors or other countries. Britain was not, as was Italy, unstable or fragmented, but a prosperous empire built on rational principles and modern ideas. Nonetheless, Italian nationalist fervor, internal conspiracies, and secret societies animated the British imagination and served as inspiration for sensation novelists. Collins possibly drew the name of his Italian character, Count Fosco in *The Woman in White*, from the nationalist writer Ugo Foscolo, who had criticized French control over Italy in the early years of the nineteenth century. Sensation novelists deflected attention to less politically or economically stable countries, thereby gratifying the Victorian audience and allowing them to temporarily forget or minimize their own social problems.

Tax repeals in the periodical press and sensational cases

From early in the nineteenth century, the newspaper had circulated dominant ideas and influential theories that could potentially become radical. Henry Stebbing memorably wrote in 1828 for the *Athenaeum* that the British periodical press was "the most powerful literary engine in Europe" (qtd. in Sanders 327). The newspaper had been instrumental, according to John Stuart Mill in an 1836 essay, in enabling the whole country "to combine in that simultaneous, energetic demonstration of determined will which carried the Reform Act" ("Civilization" 4). Mill also wrote that the

> the newspaper carries the voice of the many home to every individual among them; by the newspaper, each learns that all others are feeling as he feels, and that if he is ready, he will find them also prepared to act upon what they feel.
>
> ("Civilization" 4)

For this reason, Parliament continued to impose duties and taxes on the periodical press, concerned that they could channel radical ideas and sentiments among the wider public. The taxes imposed on the newspapers included a fourpenny newspaper tax (from the Stamp Act of 1819), a tax of advertisements (3s.6d. each), and a paper tax.[11] Collectively, these taxes created friction on the periodical press, making them an unprofitable venture. As Richard D. Altick writes in *The English Common Reader*, "cheap journalism [was] a decidedly unattractive field for the profit-seeking enterpriser" in the early nineteenth century (331). Lawmakers and critics continued to debate these taxes from the 1830s, with *The Times* deeming them "taxes on knowledge."

Decisively, the newspaper tax was repealed in 1855, followed by the paper tax in 1861. Subsequently, the periodical press dramatically expanded and played an even greater role in Victorian public life. Described as one of "a few landmarks and turning points" in British newspaper history, the repeal of taxes meant that newspapers could circulate more widely, not only among the upper middle-class or urban commercial readership, but among rising members of the middle class (Brown 4). The repeal of taxes set the stage, in John Drew's words, "for a dramatic expansion of what can now genuinely be considered a mass media market" (110), leading to "a diverse, richly populated, and prolific cheap press" (Saunders 15). Newspaper circulation rates among some weekly newspapers and cheap miscellanies reached over 200,000, a record number never achieved before 1855. Eventually, some newspapers achieved circulation rates of 500,000 in the 1880s (see Altick, *English* 395–96). Together with improvements in printing technology from the 1860s, the periodical press was able to provide a wider platform for writers to produce – and readers to consume – sensational and exciting stories. The history of sensation novels is intimately tied with these changes in the periodical publishing industry. Sensation novelists experimented with formulas intended to secure strong readership, reflecting commercial tastes and public anxieties in their serialized stories. Newspaper publishers preferred writers who avoided weighty or introspective subject matter, encouraging thrilling stories. In Altick's words, the business formula for a successful newspaper after the 1870s was clear – "a price of 6d. [pence] or lower; plenty of light fiction and amusing non-fiction; and as many illustrations as possible" (*English* 363).

During the mid-nineteenth century, the middle-class continued to expand as the price barrier to novels continued to decline. Before 1852, books had been prohibitively expensive for all but the middle-class. Charles Edward Mudie's circulating library, established in 1852, granted readers greater access to books at an annual subscription of only one guinea a year, which was less than the sale price of some popular novels (see Altick, *English* 295; S. Eliot 39–41).[12] Even before the repeal of newspaper taxes, however, many novels were serialized in newspapers before their book-form publication. This allowed novelists to test their readers' reactions and to generate publicity for the novel. Most novelists would arrange for a volume publication to coincide with the final serial installment, banking on the interest that their stories had garnered in the newspaper. Some critics blamed this serial format for the sensationalism of these stories. Oliphant wrote that "the violent stimulant of serial publication – of *weekly* publication, with its necessity for frequent and rapid recurrence of piquant situation and startling incident – is the thing of all others most likely to develop the germ, and bring it to fuller and darker bearing" ("Sensation" 568, italics in original). Braddon also wrote in a letter to Bulwer-Lytton that serials "force one into overstrained action in the desire to sustain the interest" ("Devoted" 13). The blatant commerciality of sensation novels was a by-product of these market constraints. The emphasis on "the most original and startling impressions," in Oliphant's words," came at the expense of character or moral complexity ("Sensation" 580). The emphasis on plot suspense coincided with the serialized format, leading Mansel to write in 1863 that "a commercial atmosphere floats around works of this class, redolent of the manufactory and the shop" (483). Mansel denigrated the public taste for such cheap fiction, bemoaning that "unhappily there is too much evidence that the public appetite can occasionally descend from trash to garbage" (486). But as, Janice M. Allan notes, these criticisms of sensation novels reflected their origins through "the changing material conditions of literary production and consumption" (88).

Sensation novels were serialized in the periodical press, but they also resembled journalism in their narrative and dramatic style. They drew inspiration from reports of murder, bigamy, and fraud, blurring with non-fiction paratextual reports in the periodical pages. Sensation novelists alluded to highly publicized cases, such as the Mannings' case of 1849, to lend credibility to their sensational narratives. In this case, Frederick and Maria Manning were convicted and hanged for murdering Maria Manning's lover, a case directly referenced by Robert Audley in Braddon's *Lady Audley's Secret*. Robert Audley tells Lady Audley that "fouls deeds have been done under the most hospitable roofs, terrible crimes have been committed amid the fairest scenes, and have left no trace upon the spot where they were done," such as in "that common-place, plebeian, eight-roomed house in which Maria Manning and her husband murdered their guest" (Braddon, *Lady* 124). The Mannings' case is also referenced in Collin's *The Woman in White*, where Marian Halcombe reflects on whether "Mr. Murderer and Mrs. Murderess Manning were not both unusually stout people" (218). Another murder case alluded to in sensation novels was Dr. William Palmer's notorious poisoning of at least six people in 1856. In 1860, Dr. Thomas Smethurst was also convicted for poisoning of his wife and for bigamy. Braddon would write in *Aurora Floyd* that "if Mr. William Palmer had known that detection was to dog the footsteps of crime, and the gallows to follow at the heels of detection, he would likely have hesitated long before he mixed the strychnine-pills" (241). In *The Moonstone*, Collins borrows details from the Road mystery of 1860, when a teenage girl was accused of killing her four-year-old stepbrother based on the incriminating evidence of a stained nightgown (see Altick, *Presence* 526; Heller 249; Trodd, "Policeman"). Collins alludes to the case of Madeleine Smith, who was held on trial in 1857 for poisoning her lover, but acquitted amid widespread public sympathy. Speaking through the lawyer Mr Pedgift, Collins writes in *Armadale* that "if [Miss Gwilt] had attempted to murder . . . the first object of modern society would be to prevent her going into it" (W. Collins, *Armadale* 444).[13] The case was also the inspiration for his plot in *The Law and the Lady* (1875) (see Chapter 8). While nineteenth-century novels in general tended towards contemporary concerns, sensation novels were perhaps the most prominent genre that closely resembled and freely borrowed from journalism.

Notes

1 Divorce was not only morally unthinkable for many in Victorian England, it was also legally and financially impossible for most women and men. Hence, in *Oliver Twist*, the titular character is born in wedlock despite his father's wish to divorce his wife and marry Oliver Twist's mother. Similar fates would await real-life persons, such as George Henry Lewes (with whom George Eliot co-habited) and the publisher John Maxwell (with whom Braddon co-habited and bore six children).

2 For more historical context on the Bow Street Runners, see (Shpayer-Makov 23–26).

3 As John Wilkes notes, many officers in the Metropolitan Police Force came from families where beer-drinking, at least, was considered normal (19). For more on drunkenness among the Metropolitan Police see (White 403; Wilkes 19; Durston 69–70). For a more detailed comparison between the Metropolitan Police and the Bow Street Runners, see (White 383–404). See (Emsley) for a historical overview of police reforms and (Altick, *Presence* 529–31) for the literary impact of the Metropolitan Police. For more references to the establishment of the Metropolitan Police Force, see (Pool 135; Slater 313; Haining 13; Wilkes 24; P. Collins 197; Shpayer-Makov).

4 Amy J. Lloyd points out that, in spite of the hostility or suspicion towards immigrants, emigration from Britain "vastly exceeded immigration" in every decade after the 1830s (Lloyd).

5 There is some historical ambiguity here, since the *Quarterly Review* in 1856 observed that, "as every policeman must be able to read and write, have a good character, and be of sound body and mind, the mere over-flowings of the labour-market are excluded from the force" ("The Police and the Thieves" 170).

6 Later, Dickens would argue that "for the detection and punishment of such imposters [as the 'swell mob'] a superior order of police is requisite" ("Modern" 368; see Haining 61).

7 For more on the history of photographs in the early nineteenth century, see (Briggs 123–41).

8 Cobbe would further discuss domestic violence and marital brutality in her essay "Wife-Torture in England" (1878).

9 Such legal procedures remained notoriously expensive and beyond the reach of most married couples. Between the late seventeenth century to 1857, there were over 200 divorces granted by Act of Parliament, only six of which had been requested by women (see K. Thomas 201).

10 Emma Griffin points out that one reason for Italy's uneven economic development in the nineteenth century, in contrast to Britain, was the paucity of coal deposits in Italy. Industrialization in Italy, Griffin notes, "was largely delayed until the early twentieth century" until the use of electricity (E. Griffin, "Patterns" 100). Historians have also noted that the secret societies were comprised of alienated members of the educated classes, university students, and retired army officers (see Hearder 162; D. Smith 13; see also Duggan). Italian nationalist sentiment continued until 1870 when Italians captured Rome, following the withdrawal of French troops. Harry Hearder writes that the "epic phase" of the *Risorgimento* ended around 1861 (198).

11 For more on these taxes, see (Altick, *English* 331; S. Eliot 46–48; Hewitt). The newspaper tax was reduced in 1839 to a penny a sheet, but this was seen as only a slight improvement (Altick, *English* 341).

12 For comparison, both Jane Austen's *Emma* and Walter Scott's *Waverley* cost a guinea (21 shillings) on first publication. Scott's novels could cost upwards of 25 shillings, well over a guinea (see Altick, *English* 262–63). While circulating libraries existed before the nineteenth century, the quality and range of their fiction were usually quite low.

13 Further details on the Madeleine Smith trial are discussed in chapter six. See, for instance (Hartman 57–94; Mangham, *Violent Women* 21–23). For more details on the other cases, see (Altick, *Presence* 522–25).

2 Early detectives in Dickens's *Household Words* stories and *Martin Chuzzlewit*

Dickens's evolving attitudes toward detectives

Dickens was critical of the police force in earlier novels such as in *Oliver Twist*, serialized between 1837 and 1839. In this novel, Dickens presents two police Bow Street Runners (not to be confused with the Metropolitan Police Force), Mr Blathers and Mr Duff, who display general ineptitude and drink during their investigation into a burglary. They accept "a little drop of spirits" when called to investigate an attempted burglary and are depicted as an extension of the corrupt social system in *Oliver Twist* (Dickens, *Oliver* 240). The police magistrate Mr Fang is the epitome not only of an ineffective system, but also the hypocrisy of utilitarian values. Dickens's dismissive portrayal of the police in *Oliver Twist* was shaped, in part, by his own experiences in his childhood. As P. Collins states, England was "the worst-policed nation of the civilized world" during Dickens's boyhood and there were continued jokes about the police's incompetence (8, 137). In Ainsworth's *Jack Sheppard*, a contemporary novel with *Oliver Twist*, the police are also corrupt and in the pay of criminals (see 120, 152–53). The negative perception of the police would change through Dickens's conversations with detectives from the Metropolitan Police Force, which had been established in 1829 but took time to gain public recognition.

Around the same time that Dickens serialized *Oliver Twist*, he also contributed satirical sketches to the same journal. Between September 1837 and July 1838, Dickens portrayed the proceedings from the "Mudfog Association for the Advancement of Everything" in *Bentley's Miscellany*. Mudfog was the initial name of Oliver Twist's hometown, demonstrating Dickens's ability to expand his novelistic world through a series of extratextual insertions. In the second report of the Mudfog Association, which parodies British scientific societies, Dickens depicts an association member revealing a display of automaton policemen. Mr Coppernose gestures to "a position of great magnitude and interest, illustrated by a vast number of models" aimed at the "harmless and wholesale relaxation for the young noblemen of England" (Dickens, "Full Report of the Second Meeting"

DOI: 10.4324/9781003369622-3

221). These automaton policemen would be stationed throughout London, with heads made of wood and bodies of "the toughest and thickest materials that can possibly be obtained" (Dickens, "Full Report of the Second Meeting" 223). Professor Muff declares himself "quite satisfied" with the invention, though Professor Nogo raises an objection that the policemen should be able to speak. Mr Coppernose deftly touches a small spring in the models and one of them begins to "exclaim with great volubility that he was sorry to see gentlemen in such a situation," while another expresses "a fear that the policeman was intoxicated" (Dickens, "Full Report of the Second Meeting" 223). The members of the Mudfog Association applaud the invention and the President retires with Mr Coppernose to propose the idea to the council.

The negative perception of intoxicated policemen was earlier reflected in the 1829 police reform (as outlined in Chapter 1), as officers of the Metropolitan Police Force would be prohibited from drinking on duty. Despite this, Dickens's novel and sketches indicate that even some ten years after their establishment, general views of police incompetence amid crime in London remained firmly in place. Dickens's view of the police

Figure 2.1 Illustration by George Cruikshank for Dickens's satirical sketch "Full Report of the Second Meeting of the Mudfog Association for the Advancement of Everything" in *Bentley's Miscellany* in 1838. Public domain/scanned by Periodicals Archive Online (Boz).

would change after 1842, as he met and conversed with officers of the newly formed Detective Branch of the Metropolitan Police Force. From the 1850s, Dickens heard stories from detectives at his editorial office for *Household Words*.[1] Articles inspired by such meetings include "The Modern Science of Thief-Taking" (13 July 1850), "A Detective Police Party" (27 July 1850), "The Metropolitan Protectives" (26 April 1851), "On Duty with Inspector Field" (14 July 1851), and "Down with the Tide" (5 February 1853).[2] Such sketches focus attention on the detective as a new cultural figure, contrasting with the ineffectual police force. In "The Modern Science of Thief-Taking," Dickens compares detective work to scientific inquiry (369). In contrast to the incompetent policeman, the detective identifies and apprehends a thief through his visual senses, his "eye" serving as "the great detector" (Dickens, "Modern Science" 371). This contrasts with the "wandering" gaze of the thief or swell-mobsman, according to the *Quarterly Review* in 1856: "The principal sign by which a thief may be distinguished in any assembly is the wandering of his eye. Whilst those about him are either listening to a speaker or witnessing a spectacle, his orbits are peering restlessly, not to say anxiously around. When the thief-taker [detective] sees this he knows his man" ("The Police and the Thieves" 181). It is worth noting that this emphasis on visuality supported ill-founded notions of physiognomy. Even though the detective appears "a plain, honest-looking fellow, with nothing formidable in his appearance, or dreadful in his countenance," he is highly observant and has a commanding presence (Dickens, "Modern Science" 370). His key strength is his power of observation even amid a crowd. Such observational astuteness is akin to a "modern science," with Dickens writing that "it is . . . impossible to give even an imperfect notion of the high amount of skill, intelligence, and knowledge, concentrated in the character of a clever Detective Policeman" ("Modern Science" 372).

This characterization of the detective from the early 1850s projects a new kind of individual hero undeterred by and able to filter through the excessive visual stimuli of the city. The defining characteristics of the detective in these early sketches are his powers of "keen observation, and quick perception," his ability to navigate London, and his individuality, as contrasted with older establishment forces (Dickens, "Detective Police Party" 410). The detectives are stylized in these sketches almost as urban guardians, with Dickens writing in "A Detective Police Party" that detectives proceed "in such a workman-like manner, and [are] always so calmly and steadily engaged in the service of the public, that the public really do not know enough of it, to make a tithe of its usefulness" (18). But through his powers of observation and detection, he also resembles the criminal or pickpocket in the crowd. The detective engages in the same tactics of blending unnoticeably into the crowd as employed by criminals, thieves, and burglars. The detective represents the popular fantasy of piercing through the heterogeneous mass of information, but also problematically mirror the stratagems of the London "swell mob." This swell mob, Dickens writes, requires "the greatest amount of vigilance to detect," thereby necessitating a novel approach (370). But the slippage between the detective and the criminal in these stories foreshadows the general suspicion of detectives even after the 1850s. While the resemblance between the detective and the crowd demonstrates a kind of wish-fulfilment to cognitively master the stimuli of the city, the detective's tactics parallel those of the criminal, staging an uncomfortable and mutually reinforcing dualism.

In "A Detective Police Party," published two weeks after "The Modern Science of Thief-Taking," Dickens narrates stories told by detectives at his editorial office. The humor and camaraderie expressed in this story convey the same "workman-like" ethic and the individual ingenuity he had earlier portrayed. The detectives are described as "so well chosen and trained, proceed[ing] so systematically and quietly," yet also capable of an "amicable brotherhood" among themselves (Dickens, "Detective" 409–10). About a year later, in "The Metropolitan Protectives," Dickens would further elaborate that detective work requires a cool-headed and implicitly masculine stoicism. He writes, "Emotion is no part of a policeman's duty. If felt, it must be suppressed" (Dickens, "Metropolitan" 98). The rational, analytical, and methodical skills involved in detective work contrast with the working-class squalor in the poor neighborhoods that the policeman investigates.

Individual intelligence, resourcefulness, and judgment were crucial to the professional detective's work. Hence, the detectives embodied a fantasy among members of "the lower but still respectable classes of society," to borrow Ian Ousby's words, who were promoted in a "democratic system" (89). The fantasy here is that through his powers of perception and observation, a hard-working individual could theoretically emerge as a new authority figure and cultural hero. But these qualities, while appealing to certain members of the public, could also seem threatening to members of the middle class. The idea that a lower-class individual could observe and identify wrongdoing within a middle-class household was an extension of the fantasies – and anxieties – surrounding the newly formed detective force. Detective work as a private undertaking exemplified freedom from the "jobbery that riddled the older bureaucracies," to cite Ousby (89), but could also be seen as a threat, since ordinary members of the crowd could turn into imagined spies. The detective as a cultural figure evolved not just from the establishment of the Detective Branch in 1842, but also the subsequent suspicion that the crowd could surveille individuals. Any member of the crowd could be secretly watching others, whether to conduct criminal activity, or to surveille and inspect wrongdoing.

These were, of course, fantasies, anxieties, and mere possibilities, but Dickens leverages their literary potential both in *Martin Chuzzlewit* and *Bleak House*. The detective stories and sketches in *Household Words* were published between these two novels, but *Martin Chuzzlewit* and *Bleak House* reveal the trajectory of Dickens's ideas about detectives between the early 1840s into the 1850s. The full trajectory of these ideas culminates in Dickens's unfinished *The Mystery of Edwin Drood* (of which more in Chapter 10). In brief, the detective in *Martin Chuzzlewit* represents the seemingly inconspicuous individual in the crowd, who observes and attains incriminating information. The detective is further developed in *Bleak House*, as Mr Bucket was directly inspired by the real-life detective Inspector Charles Field. Inspector Field had guided Dickens in 1850 around the London "rookeries" (slum areas and criminal neighborhoods) (see Slater 314). As Trodd notes, "Field is for Dickens a model of courage, mental sharpness, and knowledge of the urban labyrinth" ("Policeman" 439). Mr Bucket is not merely a watchful and secretive individual in the crowd, like Mr Nadgett in *Martin Chuzzlewit*, but also has a family and a developed personality. Mr Bucket restores public order and aids the virtuous protagonist, Esther Summerson, in an almost chivalrous capacity. But the first detective character, though not a professional detective, appears as a lawyer in *Bleak House*. Mr Tulkinghorn and Mr Bucket should both be seen as detective characters, I argue, since they both pursue Lady Dedlock (though for different reasons) and are described as watchful observers. Mr Tulkinghorn pursues Lady Dedlock "doggedly and steadily, with no touch of compunction, remorse, or pity" (Dickens, *Bleak* 423). He is an "obdurate and unpitying watcher" of her suffering, and is "mechanically faithful without attachment" (Dickens, *Bleak* 537–38). He guards the power he acquires from family secrets, and is described as "very jealous of the profit, privilege, and reputation of being master of the mysteries of great houses" (Dickens, *Bleak* 537; see Chapter 3). As Dickens would discover, exploring the detective as a heroic type could present difficulties, chief among which was their potential unlikability. Detectives could represent individual heroism, but not necessarily for the middle-class readers who read his novels.

The epitome of secrecy: Mr Nadgett in *Martin Chuzzlewit*

It is fitting that Dickens should be the first novelist studied here, as his novels tend to be ambitious, far-reaching, and expansive in their scope. *Martin Chuzzlewit*, published in monthly parts between January 1843 and July 1844, presents a heterogeneous and bustling world that replicates the unordered chaos of the London crowd. The numerous opportunities and complex human ties in the novel mimics the city's infinite potential and labyrinthine streets. The novel sketches a maze of possibilities and interactions, ranging from the younger Martin Chuzzlewit's quest for success in America, to Tim Pinch's moral dilemmas as Mr Pecksniff's charge, to the whims of the elder Martin Chuzzlewit. When the younger Martin Chuzzlewit learns of Jonas Chuzzlewit's suspected murder of his grandfather, he and his friends are thrown into a "maze of difficulty" from which every escape seems to "lie through some perplexed and entangled thicket" (Dickens, *Martin* 634). It is in this context that the detective serves an organizing function, restoring clarity, closure, and order. The detective's revelations play an important role in the climax, when Jonas is freed from suspicion of one death and apprehended on charges of another. The detective resolves the dramatic tension in the novel, allowing for a restoration of patriarchal authority and the completion of two marriages (between Martin Chuzzlewit and Mary Graham, and between Ruth Pinch and John Westlock). The detective aids in the narrative closure and social reproduction of middle-class values.

Mr Nadgett has occasionally been described as the first detective in an English novel (Haining 12; R. Thomas, "Detection" 178), but he is a private spy rather than a public official. He is comparable to Poe's man of the crowd, who merges imperceptibly with the London crowd and also seems to embody its anonymity. On his first introduction, halfway throughout the novel, he is described as a profound mystery, "born to be a secret" (Dickens, *Martin* 385). Dickens writes, "How he lived was a secret; where he lived was a secret; and even what he was, was a secret" (*Martin* 385). It is not just that Mr Nadgett's identity and personal history are shrouded in mystery, but that he seems to manifest the secrecy and anonymity of the London crowd as a whole. Mr Nadgett is a product of the city and also a representation of London. Dickens continues that Mr Nadgett "belonged to a class; a race peculiar to the city; who are secrets as profound to one another, as they are to the rest of mankind" (*Martin* 386). The unknowability of individuals in the London streets, their ability to refashion their identities (as seen in Mr Tigg) means that tracing their histories becomes a convoluted and monumental task. Mr Nadgett is a direct representation of this unknowability about London life, whom viewers (and the reader) are encouraged to disregard amid the multitudinous crowd that may harbor unspoken mysteries.

Mr Nadgett is, as earlier argued, a representation of London's opportunity for self-fashioning. In his pocket-book, he carries multiple and "contradictory cards," which identify him alternately as a coal-merchant, a wine-merchant, a commission-agent, a collector, and an accountant, "as if he really didn't know the secret himself" (Dickens, *Martin* 386). Mr Nadgett loiters around the London Exchange, "looking at everybody who walked in and out," as if waiting for a person who never seems to arrive (Dickens, *Martin* 386). Even his financial status seems unclear from his appearance. Dickens writes, "He was that sort of man that if he had died worth a million of money, or had died worth twopence-halfpenny, everybody would have been perfectly satisfied, and would have said it was just as they expected" (*Martin* 386). His principal trait seems to be carrying a pocket-book "full of documents," and, as the reader later learns, he tends to write important observations rather than speak them (Dickens, *Martin* 386).

But if Mr Nadgett represents the London crowd, as a watchful observer who himself eludes observation, this speaks to a desire to make sense of the external stimuli in the city. Mr Nadgett, as an early detective in an English novel, represents the fantasized possibilities of making sense of and not being drowned out by the excess of information both in Dickens's novel and in nineteenth-century London. Mr Nadgett represents the ability to see through people's false appearances and guises to attain concrete knowledge. This link between knowledge and power would later be transformed in late-twentieth-century detective stories, but the potential was there from their early inception.[3] The heterogeneity of urban life, the mingling of unknown people, and the infinite possibilities for observation means that an individual with the power to pierce through and observe revealing information becomes more compelling. Mr Nadgett represents inconspicuous secrecy, but also a privileged vantage-point from which to observe others.

Mr Nadgett serves an important role in restoring narrative order and clarity, but he makes few appearances and remains distant even from the reader. The reader is never made privy to his private thoughts or impressions, hearing only his spoken words. Nor is the reader granted access to the written report he submits to Mr Tigg, which details his observations and suspicions of Jonas. Mr Nadgett is often absent from the action, seeming to merge into the bustle of the urban background. Indeed, he disappears from the book for about ten chapters before remerging with information about Jonas. Mr Tigg even refers to Mr Nadgett as inconspicuous as "a mere piece of furniture" in one scene (Dickens, *Martin* 510). Mr Nadgett's success as a private detective depends on his apparent inconspicuousness and unreadability. Like the old man in Poe's "The Man of the Crowd" (1840), Mr Nadgett seems to meander through the streets without a clear intention or knowable history. His lack of distinctive individuality and his ability to merge into the crowd means that he can somehow seem to be everywhere and nowhere at the same time. This reticence about Mr Nadgett's private world contrasts with Dickens's exploration of Jonas's interiority. Dickens dwells on Jonas's frustrations and his desire to "[set] himself free" from the hated Mr Tigg (*Martin* 619). The free indirect discourse exploring Jonas's guilt and frustration presents a tension between his inner life and outward interactions, rendering the novel a kind of moral maze through which Jonas has to negotiate his options. In contrast to this intimacy of inner experience, Mr Nadgett is all observation and outward interaction. As would also be seen in subsequent Victorian detective stories, the detective remains unknown and shrouded in mystery, even as he uncovers and adds to the knowledge the reader gains of other characters.

Mr Nadgett is distinctive for his near-supernatural powers of observation and detection. Somehow, his eyes "were seldom fixed on any other objects than the ground, the clock, or the fire; but every button on his coat might have been an eye: he saw so much" (Dickens, *Martin* 505). Jonas is unaware that Mr Nadgett is watching him, since the private detective seems "so wrapped up in himself, that the whole object of his life appeared to be, to avoid notice, and preserve his own mystery" (Dickens, *Martin* 505). This focus on inconspicuous observation adds to the already rich discussion on the visual imagination in Victorian culture (see Flint; J. Smith). It further lends credibility to the detective's methods, based on the now-discredited "science" of physiognomy. Braddon reiterates this connection between detectives and physiognomy in her early novels, *The Trail of the Serpent* and *The Black Band*. For instance, in *The Black Band*, Braddon writes that professional detectives have a "peculiarly searching glance known only to themselves – a glance in which the clever detective can read the inmost secrets of a man's soul" (110). Mr Nadgett exerts control over the stimuli of urban life by recording memoranda and notes in his pocket-book. The act of writing and collecting information becomes a way to salvage order from the city's fragmenting tendency. Writing also allows Mr Nadgett to avoid the brief lapses of memory that affect, for instance, Mr Chuffey, meaning that he can be ever watchful and attentive without being overwhelmed. Mr Nadgett presents these written findings to Mr Tigg and declines to read aloud from them, stating that "we never know who's listening" (Dickens, *Martin* 508). The written word conveys a secrecy that oral communication does not, underscoring Mr Nadgett's preference for silent observation. Collectively, his written observations seem to incriminate Jonas, likely pertaining to the attempted poisoning of his grandfather, but the reader is never made privy to their contents. A "terrific Truth" is unveiled as Mr Nadgett states that he had been "watching [Jonas] so long" and that he had "never watched a man so close" (Dickens, *Martin* 672). Before the reader's gaze, Mr Nadgett seems to "[cast] off his shrinking, purblind, unobservant character, and [spring] up into a watchful enemy" (Dickens, *Martin* 672).

Mr Nadgett's revelations reinstates patriarchal authority, as manifest in the elder Martin Chuzzlewit literally striking down the false Mr Pecksniff. But it should be pointed out that Mr Nadgett's detective work remains morally ambiguous in the novel. Mr Nadgett's ability to shift character in the moment, as in the earlier quotation, reveals a suspicion about detectives that would continue to dog their literary reincarnations. Mr Nadgett is hired by Mr Tigg to uncover compromising information about Jonas so that he can blackmail him into joining his fraudulent insurance company. Such information would enable Mr Tigg to pursue his own likely criminal aims. As Mr Tigg plainly states to Jonas, "I am not the least in the world affected by anything you may have done; by any little indiscretion you may have committed; but I wish to profit by it, if I can" (Dickens, *Martin* 544). (It is even possible that Jonas would never have murdered Mr Tigg had he not felt cornered by Mr Nadgett's initial disclosure of compromising information about him.) To the extent that Mr Nadgett represents a man of the London crowd, he is as morally ambiguous as many other characters in the novels, including Mr Pecksniff and Miss Gamp. Unlike Mark Tapley and Tom Pinch, Mr Nadgett does not seem to altruistically serve an established form of authority or abstract ideal (such as justice), but uncovers secrets about individuals for morally vague ends. As a character without a personal history, Mr Nadgett is a fluid and mysterious character who seems to elude attempts at moral categorization. Even as he serves as a catalyst for moral resolution, his own motivations seem unclear, as the rest of his character remains shrouded in secrecy.

Ironically, even though Mr Nadgett embodies secrecy in the city, he also uncovers the histories and motivations of other characters. He gratifyingly reveals the actions and intentions of characters among the anonymous crowd, even as he remains unreadable. He unmasks Jonas, who attempts to hide from the unflinching light of truth. Dickens writes that this "truth, which nothing would keep down; which blood would not smother, and earth would not hide . . . came swooping down upon him" (*Martin* 668). Rather than having a religious quality, this truth corresponds to empirical facticity that deals with his private history. In exposing Jonas, Mr Nadgett engages in an investigative work that alleviates Victorian anxieties over self-fashioning and social mobility in nineteenth-century London. As identity becomes open to self-construction, such investigative work into real identities becomes more appealing. The effect of the exposed truth is to dispel irrational fears and anxieties. Before Mr Tigg's death, for instance, he is haunted by vivid dreams and an evil conscience. He has an ominous "presentiment, or superstition" about his journey with Jonas to Mr Pecksniff (Dickens, *Martin* 558). Jonas is similarly haunted by fears of being discovered, as he "fearfully [surveys] the multitude" of the crowd in his dreams (Dickens, *Martin* 615). Such fears are dispelled by Mr Nadgett's calm revelations of observed facts, restoring a sense of cold reality to the novel and casting off supernatural fears. The detective character would perform a similar role in sensation novels of the 1850s and 1860s, restoring a sense of factual clarity that alleviates a hyperactive imagination. The detective pivots the narrative mood from one of mystical uncertainty to an empirically ordered world. Even as the detective's revelation gains momentum from these irrational fears, the detective fulfils the reader's desire for factual clarity and coherence.

What is the kind of order that such detective work reinforces? The detective story is often characterized as a conservative genre and such a view may apply to this novel, as the detective's revelations dispel fears about social contamination and moral outsiders. As R. Thomas writes, "what begins as an investigation and critique of the prevailing regime ends as a consolidation of it" in detective stories (*Detective* 164). The detective's climactic revelation sets into motion a series of events that reinstates the elder Martin Chuzzlewit's patriarchal authority. Martin Chuzzlewit chastises and strikes Mr Pecksniff, who represents the vice of "selfishness" and "the love of self" (Dickens, *Martin* 679, 688).[4] Martin Chuzzlewit's moral reinstatement follows Mr Nadgett's discovery about Jonas's treacherous attempt to poison his grandfather. While such a criminal act of poisoning is explained away by Mr Chuffey, Jonas is simultaneously found guilty of another crime – that of murdering an imposter and fraud in the woods. Jonas's murder eliminates the social and moral threat of Mr Montague's fraudulent insurance company, while also catalyzing a series of events that instates the younger Martin Chuzzlewit as his grandfather's legitimate heir. In effect, the detective aids in restoring patrilineal inheritance, while restoring the Chuzzlewit patriarch to health. When the younger Martin Chuzzlewit emerges from the "maze of difficulty" through an entangled thicket, he finds that social relations have been reconstituted through this patriarchal structure. If "self" is the vice that Dickens chastises in this novel, the idea of social integration and order, as held together by the male head of the family, seems to supersede these individual desires and self-aggrandizing tendencies.

The restoration of legitimate patriarchal authority in this novel contrasts with Mr Pecksniff's disregard for his two daughters and personal failings as a father to care for them. Mr Pecksniff represents a false patriarchal figure who must be punished, since he used his daughters to secure desirable connections to wealth. The spectacle that ensues when the elder Martin Chuzzlewit strikes down Mr Pecksniff before numerous characters gathered at his home illuminates the kind of social function the detective serves (Dickens, *Martin* 687–88). The detective acts within a narrative that punishes moral vice, self-promoting individuals, and false patriarchal characters, ultimately helping to reinstate a social order based on male authority and moral father figures. The elder Martin Chuzzlewit embraces his role as a patriarchal figure, stating that he "must play the part of father" in marrying off the two "daughters" on the same day (Dickens, *Martin* 703). By stating that the curse of his family had been the love of self, he also implicitly calls female characters (like Mary Graham and Ruth Pinch) and loyal servants (like Tom Pinch and Mark Tapley) to their rightful places within the social order. Hence, the novel ends with two marriages, while leaving unresolved Tom Pinch's romantic misfortunes and Mark Tapley's plans to marry Mrs. Lupin.

Notes

1 *Household Words* was rare among newspapers at the time in that it offered high-quality literary content at a modest price of 2*d*. While this was still above the reach of most working-class readers, the newspaper helped, in Altick's words, "to break down further the still powerful upper- and middle-class prejudice against cheap papers" during a period when cheap periodicals were still suspected of harboring radical views (*English* 247).
2 These stories are also compiled in Peter Haining's *Hunted Down*.
3 Much has been written about postmodern detective fiction, such as those written by Jorges Luis Borges, Paul Auster, Vladimir Nabokov, and John Barth, among others (see Yoon).
4 Critics generally believe that Dickens modelled Mr Pecksniff on Samuel Carter Hall, a public figure and journal editor, who came to be associated with snobbery, self-righteousness, and moral puritanism (see Slater 208).

3 The detective as villain and hero in Dickens's *Bleak House*

If Mr Nadgett epitomized the secrecy and anonymity of nineteenth-century London, remaining unreadable and unknowable to others even as he pierced through their pretenses, the detective in *Bleak House* is a more fully formed character with a private life to which the reader is briefly made privy. Published in monthly parts between March 1852 and September 1853, Dickens had been working on *Bleak House* for over a year before publication. His writing process coincided with his rising interest in detectives, as manifest in the sketches and articles he contributed to *Household Words* during this time. As I argue, there are two detective characters in *Bleak House*, the lawyer Mr Tulkinghorn and the detective Mr Bucket. Mr Bucket's work picks up from where Mr Tulkinghorn's inquiries cease, allowing the reader to see their work as a continuum of investigations into Lady Dedlock's past.

Bleak House is often read as a legal drama, revealing institutional corruption and anxieties over the Victorian gender ideology. But it is also a story that, like *Martin Chuzzlewit*, culminates in the reinstatement of proper father figures. Like the elder Martin Chuzzlewit, Mr John Jarndyce in *Bleak House* is a helpless father figure, who is dramatically reinstated as a patriarchal authority by the novel's resolution. Like *Martin Chuzzlewit*, Dickens's *Bleak House* resolves a sprawling and heterogeneous narrative through the restoration of patriarchal authority over the younger characters. Mr John Jarndyce's weakness and passivity through much of *Bleak House* is also caused by the vices of self-interest and hypocrisy, which are more deeply institutionalized and legally embedded than in *Martin Chuzzlewit*. Mr Pecksniff's singular love of self gives way in *Bleak House* to simultaneously a more ambiguous and more widespread form of corruption, as dense and impenetrable as the London smog into which the reader is immersed from the novel's opening pages. As in *Martin Chuzzlewit*, the question of inheritance hangs in the balance. Unlike *Martin Chuzzlewit*, however, the main culprit in *Bleak House* is a woman with a secret past. These themes (inheritance, female deviance, and patriarchal

DOI: 10.4324/9781003369622-4

authority) have collectively led some critics to suggest that *Bleak House* may be read as an early sensation novel.

Male detectives and female deviance in *Bleak House*

As with *Martin Chuzzlewit*, *Bleak House* is a rich novel with multiple layers and narratives that deserve close critical scrutiny. For the purposes of this study, however, I have limited my attention to the role and characterization of detective characters and their relations to the primary female figures, Lady Dedlock and Esther Summerson. One reason for this is that detective work in *Bleak House* shifts from secret observations of criminal behavior into more normative investigations into women. Male investigators (Mr Bucket, Mr Tulkinghorn, and Mr Guppy) pursue and expose a female subject, Lady Dedlock. The consequent process of detection reveals female wrongdoing and a woman's moral shortcomings. This micro-narrative contrasts with the overarching macro-narrative of institutionalized incompetence and corruption. While the former is associated with a specific female individual, the latter corresponds to a more ambiguous, but distinctly male presence. *Bleak House* follows an investigation into a female character's background and birth, specifically, the virtuous protagonist Miss Summerson. The work of detection becomes a process of divulging how Lady Dedlock had earlier been engaged to Captain Hawdon, "a young rake . . . nothing connected with whom came any good," before her marriage to Sir Leicester Dedlock (Dickens, *Bleak* 601). Both Sir Dedlock's lawyer Mr Tulkinghorn and the detective Mr Bucket find evidence that Lady Dedlock bore a child from her romance with Captain Hawdon, who grew to become Miss Summerson. Mr Tulkinghorn threatens to reveal this incriminating information to Sir Leicester, which prompts Lady Dedlock to murder him in a rage. Towards the end of the novel, Mr Bucket together with Miss Summerson pursue Lady Dedlock, knowing that she has escaped, and eventually discover her disguised body.

Ruskin complained about the number of deaths in *Bleak House*, mostly of "inoffensive, or at least in the world's estimate respectable persons" (159). He also stated that Lady Dedlock was "less reprehensible in her conduct than many women of fashion have been and will be," adding that it was not "poetically just" that her daughter should discover her dead body (Ruskin 160). But the perceptive shift in criminal wronging from a legal to moral crime reflects the direction of sensation novels and the development of the detective in English literature. Ruskin complained that novels such as *Bleak House* evinced a general degeneration in the reading public's sentiments, due to the "peculiar forces of devastation induced by modern city life" (154). Whether or not their tastes had been corrupted, it is true that sensation novels catered to what were seen as dominant fears, anxieties, and concerns that coalesce over female deviant behavior and secret sexual experience. In Ruskin's view, sensation novels belonged to the group of novels revealing a new set of values, "partly satiric, partly consolatory, concerned only with the regenerative vigour of manure" (157).

Throughout *Bleak House*, detection involves men seeking out female wrongdoing, but there are more comical attempts at detection by women. The focused investigations led by Mr Bucket, Mr Tulkinghorn, and Mr Guppy, sharp and bracing in their search, contrast with the laughable and misguided detections by Mrs Snagsby, who believes her husband is the secret father of an orphan boy. Detective work is not only associated with men, but also demonstrates an assertion of masculine authority over women. Detective work can only reasonably be conducted by men, and is used to expose and thwart female misbehavior. As in *Martin Chuzzlewit*, the male detective in *Bleak House* investigates female secrets and makes use of their shame in the service of patriarchal authority. As Mr Tulkinghorn informs Lady Dedlock, "the sole consideration in this unhappy case is Sir Leicester," a foreshadowing of Robert Audley's remarks in Braddon's *Lady Audley's Secret* (Dickens, *Bleak* 608; see Chapter 6). Mr Tulkinghorn continues, "He [Sir Leicester] and the family credit are one. Sir Leicester and the baronetcy, Sir Leicester and Chesney Wold, Sir Leicester and his ancestors and his patrimony . . . are, I need not say to you, Lady Dedlock, inseparable" (Dickens, *Bleak* 608). Nor does Lady Dedlock qualify as a "prominent consideration" in Mr Tulkinghorn's calculations (Dickens, *Bleak* 610).

Bleak House reveals a pattern of uneven gender representations that would become a hallmark of sensation novels. There is much irony in the castigation of female wrongdoing and the perceived failure of mothers in the novel, when read alongside the weakness of fathers and juvenile men. Mrs Jellyby is described, for instance, as a short-sighted philanthropist who neglects her home and children in her charitable concern for Africa. But there are also remarkably child-like men in the novel, such as Mr Skimpole and Mr Turveydrop. Even Richard Carstone is humored, in spite of his shortcomings, having secretly married Ada against Mr Jarndyce's orders, and is allowed to survive and redeem himself in the novel, unlike Lady Dedlock. Lady Dedlock is far from negligent as a mother, even though social norms prevent her from raising Miss Summerson herself. Sensation novels and detective work aim to expose and eliminate female vice and sexual wrongdoing to preserve the social order. Miss Summerson comes to embody the female counterpoint to her mother, adhering to duty over affection and deferring to patriarchal authority. Detective work culminates in the eradication of female transgression and the elevation of a redeeming female counterpart. Miss Summerson's growth as character counterbalances her mother's wrongdoing, as Lady Dedlock is not allowed to survive and enjoy her privileged position once her secret is revealed.

Hence, in addition to being male, the detective also represents a specific kind of masculinity. The detective is not just a male investigator into a female subject, but also allied with a rising professional class associated most closely with London. To understand the difference here, and before discussing specific detectives in the novel, it is worth turning to Mr Skimpole as a male antithesis to the detective. Mr Skimpole was originally modeled on the aging Romantic poet and critic Leigh Hunt, who was later hurt by the characterization (see Slater 343; Altick, *Presence* 617). Mr Skimpole is introduced as a "grown up" child, with a child's "simplicity, and freshness, and enthusiasm, and . . . fine guileless inaptitude for all worldly affairs" (Dickens, *Bleak* 80). Miss Summerson observes that Mr Skimpole's words seem "so free from effort and spontaneous, and was said with such a captivating gaiety, that it was fascinating to hear him talk" (Dickens, *Bleak* 81). Mr Skimpole may be the same age as Mr Jarndyce and have children of his own, but he is incurably carefree, irresponsible, and even indifferent to those closest to him. But while his child-like nature may seem charming on first appearance, it eventually degenerates into a child's inability to adjust to an urbanizing world. He protests his constitutional inaptitude for worldly affairs, but these protestations also belie an unwillingness and stubborn refusal to adapt. He has no ability to keep track of time ("I have no idea of time") and completely disregards money ("I don't care about it [money]") (Dickens, *Bleak* 262, 863). These child-like traits contrast with the detective's empiricism, worldliness, and departure from romantic ideals.

Mr Skimpole represents the antithesis to a more morally ambiguous type of male professional. While Dickens may have incorporated him to counterbalance the heavy weight of the Chancery case overshadowing Bleak House, unaffected as he is by self-interest and greed, Mr Skimpole eventually becomes isolated from the other characters. An extreme manifestation of the male professional, in contrast, is Richard's lawyer Mr Vholes. Mr Vholes assiduously takes care of his family and daughters by performing his professional duties. He is introduced as "diligent, persevering, steady, acute in business," who eschews emotional expression while rigorously carrying out his responsibilities (Dickens, *Bleak* 574). The detective is more aligned with this type of self-made and urban individual, reflecting in part the recruitment of detective officers from "the lower but still respectable classes of society" (Ousby 88). To some extent, the detective embodies the potential for self-improvement and social mobility through hard work that Dickens often depicts in his novels. But Mr Vholes as a male professional is cold, calculating, and unswayed by emotional attachments. He is eminently unlikeable, even though he may warrant some respect, due to his inability to feel any compassion for his clients. Miss Summerson remarks that there seems "something of the Vampire" in Mr Vholes's prioritization of his respectability and professional reputation, particularly as Richard begins to mentally break down under his diminishing hopes of legal success (Dickens, *Bleak* 854).

It is another lawyer, no less cold or calculating, who acts as the first detective character in the novel. Indeed, detectives are often associated with, work closely with, or feature as lawyers in the sensation novels of the 1850s and 1860s. In *Bleak House*, Mr Tulkinghorn hires Mr Bucket, a private detective, but also becomes an incarnation of the detective character himself. He pursues a private investigation into Lady Dedlock's past, with the fallout resolved by Mr Bucket. Mr Tulkinghorn seems to merge with Mr Bucket in their narrative functions, as early allies serving similar goals. R. Thomas also observes that "Bucket is not the first representative of the law" in *Bleak House*, since "the most significant legal figure of the first half of the novel is the cruel solicitor Mr Tulkinghorn" ("Detection" 177). R. Thomas adds that while there are differences between "the evil, self-centered Tulkinghorn" and Bucket "as a duty-bound public servant," there is a clear transition between Mr Tulkinghorn as a representative of the legal system and Mr Bucket as an upholder of the social order (R. Thomas, "Detection" 177). Mr Bucket seems to evolve from Mr Tulkinghorn, a male professional serving a baronet's interest, to serve the protection of the social order as a whole. This social order needs protection not from a specific crime, but rather moral contamination, as critics such as Maunder and Moore have argued. Hence, the detective emerges from an urban, male professional class to eradicate moral contamination and protect the social order, even as he stands on morally ambiguous ground himself. Identification with a specific profession is a minor theme in the novel, illustrated by Richard's failure to settle down into a line of work (whether as a surgeon, lawyer, or soldier). But over-identification with a specific profession and the urban forces of self-interest (as seen in Mr Vholes) also threatens to erode personal and emotional bonds.

From cold professionalism to amiable sociability: Mr Tulkinghorn and Mr Bucket

As earlier noted, the detective is not necessarily a likeable character in *Bleak House*. In fact, the detective embodies the cool and self-calculating rationality of a male professional class, exemplifying ideals of professional conduct and also a callous disregard for others' private affairs. As Mr Bucket states, "Very strange things comes [*sic*] to our knowledge in families," an opinion that would later be echoed by Sergeant Cuff in Wilkie Collins's *The Moonstone* (Dickens, *Bleak* 749; see Chapter 9). Mr Bucket explains, "I have had the honor of being employed in high families before; and you have no idea . . . what games goes [*sic*] on" (Dickens, *Bleak* 749). The unlikability of the detective is likely less an authorial decision and more a consequence of the detective's knowledge of family secrets. The detective only manages to be less deviant himself by serving the social order, upholding patriarchal authority, and eradicating female moral threats. Despite this, his position is somewhat tenuous and he serves a narrative function, rather than standing alone as a fully fleshed character in his own right. Even when such attempts at fleshing out his character occur, these reveal writerly negotiations with making him more likeable than anything else. The detective manifests a professionalism in his investigations that confers on him a measure of respect and recognition. However, these work against the detective's acquisition of private knowledge and secrets that can be personally empowering. When Mr Tulkinghorn obtains information of Lady Dedlock's secret, the reader is led to believe that his murder is poetically justified, since Lady Dedlock suffers intolerable pressure to prevent her husband from learning about her past. Mr Bucket, as a continuation of the role that Mr Tulkinghorn played, earns less the reader's sympathy (which are instead conferred on Lady Dedlock) and more the reader's respect.

Mr Tulkinghorn employs Mr Bucket to obtain information about Lady Dedlock's past, but is also his close ally. When the reader is first introduced to Mr Bucket, he appears with Mr Tulkinghorn in the same room. Mr Tulkinghorn sits with an "impenetrable" expression, "pondering, at that twilight hour, on all the mysteries he knows, associated with darkening woods in the country, and vast blank shut-up houses in town" (Dickens, *Bleak* 326). The lawyer's capacity for private secrets indeed makes him a vehicle for detective work in later sensation novels. Mr Bucket silently enters the room, evading notice, and also sits with an "attentive face" as a "composed and quiet listener" (Dickens, *Bleak* 328). From his first appearance, Mr Bucket is associated with Mr Tulkinghorn's astute ability to penetrate through to other characters' secrets and pry into their domestic affairs. This alliance seems fitting, as Mr Tulkinghorn deals with the intimate details of family inheritance in his own right, implicating him in his clients' private affairs. The lawyer's reach into private and public affairs parallels detective work, which also uncovers private mysteries and family dramas. In his first appearance, Mr Bucket does not serve society's benefit at large, as a law enforcement officer, but rather, the specific private interests of Mr Tulkinghorn as a lawyer. It is the detective's ability to weave through private and public spheres, even as he apprehends moral culprits, that makes him an ambiguous and, at times, unlikeable character.

Mr Tulkinghorn pursues a private investigation into Lady Dedlock's past, penetrating through her claims to social status and privilege to reveal moral shortcoming. He "pursues her [Lady Dedlock] doggedly and steadily, with no touch of compunction, remorse, or pity" (Dickens, *Bleak* 423). Lady Dedlock describes him as "passionless" and "mechanically faithful without attachment, and very jealous of the profit, privilege, and reputation of being master of the mysteries of great houses" (Dickens, *Bleak* 537). Such descriptions of "mechanical" devotion would also appear in Collins's *Armadale*, where Mr Bashwood servilely follows Miss Lydia Gwilt's wishes. The detective is cast here as devoid of personal decency and sympathy, fully characterized by an unwavering allegiance to some seemingly inhuman end. Mr Tulkinghorn seems incapable of moral introspection or even human empathy. In Lady Dedlock's words, he is "indifferent to everything but his calling. His calling is the acquisition of secrets, and the holding possession of such power as they give him, with no sharer or opponent in it" (Dickens, *Bleak* 537).

Such passages reveal how the detective becomes a suspicious and ambivalent character, in part due to self-empowerment from private knowledge and family secrets, but also due to an uncanny devotion to his vocation. What kind of allegiance must the detective have to override basic principles of human decency, privacy, and compassion, in the aftermath of a momentous revelation? Mr Tulkinghorn becomes an "obdurate and unpitying watcher" of Lady Dedlock, whose security comes to depend on the tyrannical oversight of her husband's lawyer (Dickens, *Bleak* 538). Mr Tulkinghorn is a new kind of antagonist who inspires fear and respect due to his professionalism and ability to pry into family secrets. He is a male professional characterized by all exteriority and no interiority. As with Mr Nadgett, we learn little about Mr Tulkinghorn's background and he seems emptied in his distance and emotional inaccessibility. He attains an intolerable and unacceptable level of personal power over a baronet's family, guided not by moral principles or emotional attachments (as Mr Guppy may be), but by his own whims and professional calculations. Hence, even though he uncovers a woman's wrongdoing, he also becomes implicated as an antagonist. His demise is indeed poetically justified, due to the unnatural level of power he comes to hold over her and, by extension, the Dedlock family. But even after he is eliminated from the narrative, the detective's work is incomplete as there remains an equally threatening moral threat, unleashed by the revelation of Lady Dedlock's dubious past. It is not a coincidence that Miss Summerson chooses not to inform the other characters about her mother's secret, withdrawing from them as though to protect them from a contagious disease. Such moral shortcoming amounts to a contagion that must be eradicated for social order to be restored.

Mr Tulkinghorn professes to serve Sir Leicester's interests alone, but his knowledge of Lady Dedlock's secret grants him a troubling degree of personal power. As a detective character, he acts on his own personal initiative and does not seem susceptible to emotion. However, this combination of individual power and lack of external moral allegiances casts the detective in an ambiguous light. The Dedlock family is effectively at the lawyer's mercy, but the lawyer is not bound to any code beyond his profession. Dickens writes about him,

> To say of a man so severely and strictly self-repressed that he is triumphant, would be to do him as great an injustice as to suppose him troubled with love or sentiment, or any romantic weakness. He is sedately satisfied. Perhaps there is a rather increased sense of power upon him, as he loosely grasps one of his veinous wrists with his other hand, and holding it behind his back walks noiselessly up and down.
>
> (*Bleak* 603)

He reminds Lady Dedlock that her secret is "[his] secret, in trust for Sir Leicester and the family," making it a mere "matter of business" (Dickens, *Bleak* 687). Miss Summerson also views him as "a dangerous man," while Mr George vents his grievances about him as "a confoundedly bad kind of man" (Dickens, *Bleak* 635, 671). Mr George adds, "He is a slow-torturing kind of man. He is no more like flesh and blood, than a rusty old carbine is" (Dickens, *Bleak* 671). Mr Tulkinghorn resembles, much like Mr Wakem in George Eliot's *The Mill on the Floss* (1860), a man solely motivated by personal interest and unresponsive to those helpless against the legal system he represents. The moral ambiguity and professional respect for lawyers blur into the character of the detective that he is often associated with in sensation novels (see Pool 130). Even though Lady Dedlock is introduced as vain and self-indulgent, epitomizing landed privilege, she earns the reader's sympathy as she becomes the victim of a designing professional man. Even as the detective is framed against the moral contagion of female wrongdoing in this novel, he also stands on ambiguous and suspicious ground himself.

After his death, Mr Bucket takes on a more significant role, with his character development revealing negotiations over the detective's moral positioning. His professionalism earlier in the novel gives way to a remarkable sociability and even domesticity, in contrast to Mr Tulkinghorn. Mr Bucket lives with his wife and lodger at home, though he has no children. He emphasizes to Mr George and his friends, Mr and Mrs Bagnet, that happiness "must be sought within the confines of domestic bliss," rather than in public life (Dickens, *Bleak* 707). Mr Buckets appears a "sparkling stranger" and "a new and agreeable feature in the evening," capable of light and charming conversation (Dickens, *Bleak* 706). Dickens writes, "[Mr Bucket] is so friendly, is a man of so many resources, and so easy to get on with, that it is something to have made him known there" (Dickens, *Bleak* 706). These amiable and domestic qualities contrast with the cold professionalism of Mr Tulkinghorn and can be read as a negotiation into a more positive detective character. Mr Bucket has both a domestic life and public vocation, unlike Mr Nadgett and Mr Tulkinghorn, who represented exteriority at the expense of any interiority or emotional susceptibility. The stark contrasts are visually presented in the illustrations by Hablot Knight Browne (Phiz) that were published in Dickens's *Bleak House*. While Browne's visual interpretations of Dickens's characters do not necessarily reflect his authorial intentions, they do influence how the book would have been consumed and read by the literate public.[1] In Chapter 33, Browne inserts an illustration of Lady Dedlock's meeting with Mr Tulkinghorn. Mr Guppy has just risen to leave, having opened the door, when, at "that same moment, there happens to be an old man of the name of Tulkinghorn" (Dickens, *Bleak* 495). Mr Tulkinghorn comes in just as Mr Guppy turns to leave with his hand on the door handle. "One glance between the old man and the lady; and for an instant the blind that is always down flies up. Suspicion, eager and sharp, looks out. Another instant; close again" (Dickens, *Bleak* 495). In this illustration, Mr Tulkinghorn appears an old and professionally attired man, with spectacles in his right hand, indicating a man who reads and writes letters. In contrast to the stooping Mr Guppy and the seated Lady Dedlock, Mr Tulkinghorn stands with a hand on a chair for support. Lady Dedlock looks askance at him, perhaps less with cold suspicion than with misgiving and uncertainty.

Mr Bucket could not, perhaps, present a more contrasting image with Mr Tulkinghorn in the illustration for Chapter 49. He sits around a hearth with the Bagnets and Mr George, with two young girls seated on his lap. The caption reads, "Friendly behavior of Mr Bucket," and the illustration shows Mr Bagnet and Mr George with elongated pipes in their hands. A boy beside them plays a fife (similar to a piccolo) while Mrs Bagnet stands, seeming to fill a pipe. This domestic scene contrasts with Chesney Wold, aligning Mr Bucket with the simplicity of lower middle-class pleasures and social gatherings. Ousby has said that Mr Bucket may represent "the incarnation of lower middle-class respectability," and it is easy to draw this inference from this illustration alone (98).

At the same time, Mr Bucket presents "a very ordinary and a very extraordinary figure," or an ordinary character with an extraordinary talent for detection and observation (Ousby 98). In Dickens's words,

[Mr Bucket] is in the friendliest condition towards his species, and will drink with most of them. He is free with his money, affable in his manners, innocent in his conversation – but, through the placid stream of his life, there glides an under-current of forefinger [*sic*].

(*Bleak* 742)

This forefinger represents Mr Bucket's capacity to study and observe human nature. His sense of self-respect is derived from his intelligence and infallible knowledge about "so many characters, high and low," rather than his

Figure 3.1 "The old man of the name of Tulkinghorn," illustration by Phiz (Hablot
K. Browne) for Charles Dickens's *Bleak House*. Public domain
(Browne, "Old Man").

social position or profession (Dickens, *Bleak* 757). Mr Bucket is at once
identifiable with his profession, as a private detective, and also somehow
seems to transcend it in his sociable behavior. In his professional work,
he lends the impression that he is "everywhere, and cognizant of everything" (Dickens, *Bleak* 667). He is able to instill "dread power" in criminals through his assiduous observations, but also inspires "steadiness and
confidence" in those whose causes he serves (Dickens, *Bleak* 763, 832).
Mr Bucket is able to inspire Miss Summerson with trust and confidence

Figure 3.2 "Friendly behavior of Mr Bucket," illustration by Phiz (Hablot
            K. Browne) for Charles Dickens's *Bleak House*. Public domain
            (Browne, "Friendly").

through his intuition and reasoning, in contrast to Mr Tulkinghorn's
unchallenged power, which had inspired suspicion and fear. His ability
to win Miss Summerson's trust contrasts with Mr Tulkinghorn's "formal
politeness . . . [and] composed deterrence" that had transformed him into
a "dark, cold object" (Dickens, *Bleak* 604).

The shift occurs here from an exclusive emphasis on Mr Tulkinghorn's
public life, associated with self-interest (often at others' expense), towards
a closer alignment between humane qualities and the broader public interest as a whole. Mr Bucket serves not only his clients, but also, in Mr Skimpole's words, "discovers our friends and enemies for us . . . recovers our
property for us . . . [and] avenges us comfortably" (Dickens, *Bleak* 864,
italics mine). Mr Bucket is "a tamed lynx, an active police officer, an intelligent man, a person of peculiarly directed energy and great subtlety both
of conception and execution" (Dickens, *Bleak* 864). He is the antithesis
to the child-like and nonchalant Mr Skimpole, but does not fall into the
extreme category of self-interested and self-empowered individuals, such
as Mr Vholes and Mr Tulkinghorn. Miss Summerson describes Mr Bucket

as "really very kind and gentle," someone to be relied on as her own mind is "perturbed" and restless (Dickens, *Bleak* 803–4). Mr Bucket serves the social order and a collective cause, rather than the resolutely private interests that were pursued by Mr Tulkinghorn in service to his client.

Mr Bucket's character development can be read, as earlier stated, as a negotiation in the shaping of the detective as a heroic or positive literary type. He is positioned, somewhat ambiguously, between the domestic and public worlds. For the detective to emerge as a hero, the criminal must distill public anxieties and present a moral threat. But this identification of secrecy does not come without its difficulties, since such knowledge threatens to further destabilize the social order. Hence, the detective's work is twofold, namely, to uncover wrongdoing and to address the fallout. In *Bleak House*, these activities are conducted by two separate detective characters, Mr Tulkinghorn and Mr Bucket, allowing one to be punished as an antagonist and the other to emerge as a new urban hero. The task of making the detective relatable and humane also presents challenges, since the detective is supposed to be gifted with acute powers of observation. Dickens pitches Mr Bucket's language in a more relatable and common register, in contrast to the cold and self-assured tone of Mr Tulkinghorn. After his meeting with the Bagnets and Mr George, Mr Bucket suddenly turns on Mr George and arrests him as a murder suspect. Even though he is misguided in arresting him, his language reveals competing impulses. He states,

> My wish is, as it has been all the evening, to make things pleasant. . . . You and me have always been pleasant together; but I have got a duty to discharge; and if that hundred guineas [reward] is to be made, it may as well be made by me as by another man.
>
> (Dickens, *Bleak* 709)

As a private detective who is paid for his work, Mr Bucket has more relatable concerns about making a living. Mr Bucket becomes a character who "may as well" earn a reward of a hundred guineas, as any other man. He is cast as a hard-working and self-improving character, caught between the compulsions of work and the pleasures of social life.

It is possible to see the detective as caught between the cross-hairs of popular anxieties and fantasies, between social mobility and individual achievement on the one hand, and societal disintegration on the other. The detective becomes an individual who champions and protect social values through his remarkable intelligence and talent for observation. He confers the appearance of security to society, while also manifesting the more troubling desire to overcome social barriers. The detective represents individual achievement to those who aspire to social mobility as well as normative consolidation to those anxious to preserve the status quo. He remains both within and without the existent social order, transcending its boundaries and evading suspicion by apprehending more overt moral threats.

In contrast to *Martin Chuzzlewit*, detection is not necessarily accompanied by writing in *Bleak House*. Mr Bucket has "very little to do with letters, either as sender or receiver," while Mr Guppy has "learnt the habit of not committing [him]self in writing" – concerns that reveal the close connection between legal work and writing (Dickens, *Bleak* 427, 745). Writing is seen as potentially incriminating or comprising, as seen, for instance, in the decisive evidence about Captain Hawdon (masquerading as Nemo) coming about through a comparison of their handwriting. Such techniques would also recur in later sensation novels, most memorably in Collins's *Armadale*. The assiduous detective does not leave written signs or clues behind, making investigation a more psychological endeavor in *Bleak House*. Physicians also observe their patients in *Bleak House*, with Mr Allan Woodcourt drawing inferences from his friends' expressions and appearances. While closely observing Richard, Mr Woodcourt concludes that "it is not . . . his being so much younger or older, or thinner or fatter, or paler or ruddier, as there being upon his face such a singular expression" that implies "all anxiety, or all weariness; yet it is both, and like ungrown despair" (Dickens, *Bleak* 652–53). Mr Woodcourt also observes details about the lives of the poor in Tom-all-alone's, including a woman whose clothes are stained by clay, inferring that her husband must be a bricklayer (Dickens, *Bleak* 658). The difference between the physician and the detective is that the detective uses such information to resolve social disorder.[2] While the physician's eye does lift details about the working poor to the reader's awareness, such knowledge does not culminate in a heroic eradication of moral contagion or settlement of wrongdoing.

Notes

1 For more on Victorian visual culture and illustrated books, see (Maxwell; Leighton and Surridge).
2 The doctor occupied a rather "awkward" position between gentleman-practitioner and tradesman-apothecary, according to some scholars, until the 1858 Medical Act. An apothecary was a tradesman because he required no educational qualifications and made his living from selling drugs. An apothecary could not charge for giving medical advice (see Altick, *Presence* 627). The 1858 Medical Act aimed to distinguish between qualified and unqualified medical practitioners, following which doctors became known by their titles "Dr" rather than "Mr" (see Sutherland, "Explanatory" 481).

4 Detectives of the late 1850s and early 1860s

Russell, Collins, and Wood

The inspiration for Dickens's Mr Bucket, Inspector Charles Field, left the London Metropolitan Police Force by 1854 and became a "private inquiry agent" (T. Hughes 103). One of his unusual private cases culminated in the 1854 *Evans v. Robinson* trial, in which Mr Lloyd Evans sued Mr Robert Robinson for having an affair with his wife. Though Mr Evans had separated from his wife (Mary Evans) shortly after their marriage in 1850, they remained legally married and unable to divorce. Mr Evans continued to provide his wife with an annuity (250 pounds), but noticed that Mr Robinson frequented his wife's residence in London. Hiring Inspector Field, Mr Evans obtained witness testimonies from spies, whom Inspector Field installed as servants in Mrs Evans's home. On Inspector Field's advice, the cook bored a hole with a gimlet into the drawing-room door and saw "the defendant and Mrs. Evans sitting on the sofa in such a position, and with their clothes in such a state, as left no doubt of criminal intercourse taking place" ("Evans v. Robinson"). At the trial, such covert tactics attracted as much dismay and disapproval as Mrs Evans's alleged adultery. The defendant's lawyer protested, upon hearing Inspector Field testify on his honor, "You have no honour, sir!" (qtd. in T. Hughes 104). The *Daily News* concurred on 24 August 1854, remarking,

> Who is safe if the myrmidons of Scotland-yard are to keep in pay cooks and other menials, to be sent into families, armed with gimlets, for the purpose of making peeping holes through which they may watch their unconscious masters and mistresses, and who are richly remunerated if they bring any intelligence that can be turned to account by their suborners?
>
> (*Daily News*, 24 Aug. 1854)

The *Evans v. Robinson* trial ignited a debate about detectives in England, whom the *Daily News* declared "had never been a favourite with Englishmen – not even with those who admit its necessity as a means of repressing

DOI: 10.4324/9781003369622-5

felonies" (24 Aug. 1854). The *Daily News* protested the "abuse" of detectives as "agents of private vengeance – as instruments to hunt up private scandals," arguing that such a group of private spies seemed more suited to European countries, resembling "the secret police of the *ancien régime* in France" (24 Aug. 1854). According to Shpayer-Makov, the French police system was seen as highly centralized and efficient by some in Britain, but most viewed it as "invasive and aggressive and marked by censorship and the abuse of civil liberties" (29–30). The word "espionage," as critics pointed out, was French (Shpayer-Makov 30). According to the *Daily News* in 1854, detectives acting as private spies were dangerous because they infringed upon the sanctity of the domestic space – as the writer expressed, "an Englishman's house is his castle" (24 Aug. 1854). The suspicion and revulsion against detectives, when hired not in the service of the public but for private individuals, reinforced a sense of Englishness. To be English meant to have an entitlement to privacy and a private life free from state intrusion. To even imagine a person's servants were spying on oneself, in one's most intimate and private moments, was an abomination not only against individual sensibilities but also against a cultural idea of Englishness.

Hence, when the *Daily News* writer contrasted England as a free country with "the *ancien régime* in France" or with "the police in Prussia and other Continental states," they were complaining about the un-Englishness of the private spy (*Daily News*, 24 Aug. 1854). What was more horrifying than a married woman committing adultery was the idea that her trusted servants had been privately hired to surveille her in the domestic space. Such surveilling and spying activities were reminiscent of oppressive France or the "old French police," the newspaper complained, than befitting a country where there were no such "state police prosecutions" (*Daily News*, 24 Aug. 1854). This perceived abuse of power and the detective's presumed lack of decency or moral allegiance to anything other than his private interests made them suspicious and repulsive figures. The writer speculated that if detectives were to lend their services to private individuals, their skills would be "monopolised by parties possessed of great wealth or influential, social, and political station," breeding corruption and wrongdoing, rather than correcting them (*Daily News*, 24 Aug. 1854).

The *Evans v. Robinson* trial is mentioned in the preface to William Russell's collection of detective stories, *Recollections of a Detective Police-Officer* (1856). The stories were separately published in *Chamber's Edinburgh Journal*, between 1849 and 1853, making Russell one of the first English writers of detective stories. Their book publication followed the trial, with Russell noting in the preface that "notwithstanding the lofty rebuke lately administered by a dignified judge to late Inspector Field," detectives could be seen as "peace officers" or soldiers defending public order (vi-vii). In these stories, the criminals are often portrayed as foreign, particularly French. This anti-foreign sentiment is distinctive of detective and mystery stories around this period, as will later be seen in Collins's *The Woman in White*. In Russell's stories, the criminals usually speak in French, have French names (such as Levasseur, Le Breton, Dubarle, or Duquesne), or come from other European countries, like Switzerland. In contrast, the innocent victims that the detective (Mr Waters) defends are usually English gentlemen, young women, or young lovers. The effect of the detective's inquiries in these stories, then, is to purge foreign cunning and intrigue from the narrative and reinstate a sense of English identity. The detective is recruited to defend, rather than undermine an idea of English-ishness against a French threat. There is no tension between the detective's "ingenuity and boldness" and the cause of justice in these stories – partly because Mr Waters usually works within the police institution, and partly because he defends English victims from felons and fraudsters (Russell 10).

Before turning to Russell's stories, it is worth noting that this preoccupation with English identity, as contrasted with other European countries, interspersed the pages of *Chamber's Edinburgh Journal*, where the stories were first published. Russell's stories were read among pages narrating "pictures of the English, drawn by a Frenchwoman" (25 Aug. 1849), depicting "social life in France" (18 May 1850), relaying scenic travel accounts of "the North of Europe" (17 Nov. 1849), and describing the Indian Koh-i-noor diamond (28 July 1849). Collectively, these paratextual articles reveal an ongoing fascination with English identity as opposed to those of the Continent. The detective stood in this ambiguous terrain amid the formation of English identity, alternately upholding a sense of English order while employing tactics seen as inherently un-English. This ambiguity has much to do with the detective's fluidity, whether as a police officer or as a private agent, and his willingness to resort to "stratagems and disguises" that Russell justifies as "honorable *ruses de guerres*" by "Peace Officers" (vi-vii).

Russell's detective "memoirs" and observational skill

Russell published his detective stories in *Chamber's Edinburgh Journal* anonymously, and later under the pseudonym "Waters" for the book volume in 1853. The "memoirs" of a detective police-officer deliberately blur the distinction between fact and fiction. Russell was one of the first authors to write a fictional detective memoir, which proved such a successful and popular formula he would repeat it in his later works (see Saunders 122; Shpayer-Makov 234; Worthington 142).[1] While originally published between 1849 and 1853, the recalled events in Russell's pseudo-memoir date between 1832 and 1836, well before the establishment of the

Metropolitan Police detectives. By presenting his stories as factual recollections, Russell works an air of nostalgia into their narrative, recalling a time shortly after the Reform Acts and preceding Queen Victoria's ascension to the throne. Russell conjures a period of relative prosperity but also criminal activity in London. He presents his detective protagonist as a "Peace Soldier," comparable in his role to a military officer (Russell v). There is no contradiction, as earlier noted, between the detective police-officer and the public cause of justice. Nor is there any friction between the detective and the police institution in these stories, with Waters usually taking orders from his superiors and "entrusted with strictly-defined legitimate duties" (Russell vi).

The detective is dressed as a gentleman in plain clothes, but identifies himself as a police officer throughout the stories. As a police officer, Waters is not motivated by personal gain, but rather public duty. He aims to capture and bring to justice "blacklegs, swindlers, and forgers," with the provision of "legal evidence" (Russell 11, 21). He reminds the reader that he has a wife and children, identifying him as a breadwinner as much as a professional man. As Worthington observes, "the adventures that comprise his work are contained and framed by his domestic life" (143). The "small personal and domestic touches" in the stories are significant, since they align Waters with middle-class aspirations (144). As Worthington writes, "Waters [is presented] as a family man with responsibilities, fallen on hard times but using his skills to follow a profession in the hopes of bettering himself, a pattern and goal shared by a middle-class Victorian audience" (145).

Waters claims to have skills suited to detective work, particularly in observing and reading people's expressions. In the story "Guilty or Not Guilty?" he decides that a young man, who appears "a gentleman" without "the starting, nervous tremor always in [his] experience exhibited by even old practitioners in crime," must be "guiltless" (Russell 36). Based on his observations, he determines that "a diabolical plot for his destruction" has been elaborately laid by the real criminals and resolves to vindicate his innocence (Russell 36). Such elaborate guesswork based on mere observation seems foolhardy and superficial by today's standards of intelligence work. Such reading of superficial clues and expressions to determine character has a long history and is partly rooted in the since discredited "science" of physiognomy. Waters presents his observational powers as a professional skill, commenting that he is "a practised reader of the meanings of men" and has "much practice in reading the faces and deportment" of suspicious characters (Russell 225, 296). These powers of observation allow him to intuit and ascertain "some sinister design" in other characters (Russell 225). But of course, there is no self-questioning when it comes to reading criminal behavior. For instance, he observes in "Flint Jackson" that a man at a lodging-house is "a wiry, gnarled, heavy-browed, iron-jawed fellow of about sixty, with deep-set eyes aglow with sinister and greedy instincts" (Russell 221). He later ascertains, from "the sinister glances of his restless eyes," that the man has criminal intentions (Russell 227). Such seemingly objective conclusions obscure any inward reflection of his own prejudices or assumptions. But the absence of an internal thought process makes many of these stories less "sensational" than the mysteries of sensation novels. The detective depends on ambiguity to generate dramatic tension in the narrative. Altogether, the lack of such ambiguity, the apparent ease with which the detective arrives at the correct conclusion, and the absence of friction between the detective and the police, make investigative work a rather unexciting enterprise in these stories. This holds true even for the action-packed sequences in some stories, resulting in surprise or terror on the part of foiled criminals. Even with the allusions to female madness and the "cunning of lunacy," the stories seem listless and predictable in that they affirm public perceptions of criminality and foreign intrigue, decipherable by the observant individual through facial cues (Russell 255).

Despite this relative lack of gripping sensationalism, Russell's stories anticipate a later development in detective stories. The detective, through his observations, merges into the role of a narrator. His identity is fluid and he blends into the background, relating details about other characters through free indirect discourse. In "The Widow," for instance, he describes how "a stoutish, strongly-set man of forty years of age" seems to constantly follow a "widow lady" with "deep grief and sadness" in her eyes (Russell 83–84). Waters becomes convinced that the man "was in some way or other connected . . . with the young and graceful widow" (Russell 85). The detective enters the action as he converses with the man and later apprehends him for engaging in "a felonious conspiracy" to deprive the widow of her inheritance (Russell 103). This movement from observation to action renders the detective a fluid character, wavering between narrator and central character. This reveals, as will later be seen in *Lady Audley's Secret*, the close association between detective observation and interpretation – the reading and relaying of information to the reader. The detective has a privileged vantage-point, not only in his observational scope, but also in "reading" certain characters and informing the reader of his impressions. The detective becomes almost indistinguishable from the narrator, an association that would later be further experimented with in twentieth-century adaptations of the detective novel (see Yoon).

Framing criminals and masculine detection in *The Woman in White*

Two major sensation novels by Collins and Wood account for a decadelong interval between Dickens's *Bleak House* and Braddon's novels. Neither *The Woman in White* nor *East Lynne* has an identifiable detective and are only

The game is up, my good Mr. Gates : I arrest you for felony.—p. 105.

Figure 4.1 Frontispiece to William Russell's *Recollections of a Detective Police-Officer* by an unidentified artist. Public domain/scanned by University of California, digitized by Google (Russell frontispiece).

loosely mystery stories, rather than detective novels. However, they replay familiar themes in Victorian sensation novels, such as anti-foreign sentiment and the appearance of lawyers as investigators. Indeed, it would be amiss to overlook *The Woman in White* in a study of sensation novels, since the work is widely regarded as having launched the genre. Oliphant remarked after its publication that the novel had "given a new impulse to a kind of literature which must, more or less, find its inspiration in crime, and, more or less, make the criminal its hero" ("Sensation" 568; see also "Enigma novel"). Braddon is said to have confessed in a later interview that she "owe[d] Lady Audley's Secret to The Woman in White," adding that "Wilkie Collins is assuredly my literary father" (qtd. in Lycett, *Wilkie* 235). Collins is mentioned in *Lady Audley's Secret*, with the protagonist Robert Audley confessing that he had read Collins's mystery novels (see Braddon, *Lady* 342). Both *The Woman in White* and *East Lynne* center on criminality, cast here as moral shortcoming rather than illegal activity (as in Russell's stories). In *The Woman in White*, criminal intrigue is associated with Italian characters, as the antagonist Count Fosco links the narrative with Italian secret societies (see historical contexts in Chapter 1).

Collins had tried his hand at detective stories before *The Woman in White*, notably in "The Diary of Anne Rodway," published in *Household Words* in July 1856. This two-part serial introduces perhaps the first female detective, the twenty-six-year-old Anne Rodway, who investigates the mysterious murder of her friend Mary Mallinson (see Lycett, *Wilkie* 162–63; Kestner 14–16). Their sorority is replicated in *The Woman in White*, where two women present polar opposite ideas of womanhood. As I later argue, Miss Marian Halcombe's masculinity corresponds to the rationality associated with her detective work. She drives the narrative action with her astute watchfulness and intelligence, but these in turn preclude her from possessing more feminine traits. In contrast to Russell's stories and Dickens's novels, detective work in *The Woman in White* is mainly conducted by younger, unmarried characters, like Mr Walter Hartright and Miss Halcombe. Both are fatherless and play a masculine role in their families. Mr Hartright is the sole surviving son in his family and Miss Halcombe protects her half-sister, Miss Fairlie. Detective work becomes a means to procure evidence and obtain security by vulnerable and disadvantaged individuals in this novel.

A notable feature of *The Woman in White*, from the perspective of detective work, is the association between criminal intrigue and foreign outsiders. This link would be more heavily invested with imperial overtones in Collins's later novel *The Moonstone*. (The themes of imperial romance also appear in the detective stories of the *fin-de-siècle*, such as by Doyle.) Collins famously enjoyed travelling across Europe, visiting countries such as Italy, Germany, and France, and later frequenting their spas for his health. He brings elements of anti-foreign suspicion into his narrative, associating the Italians with secret societies and moral deception. The final installment of *The Woman in White* was followed by an article in *All the Year Round*, entitled "Italian Distrust." The anonymous writer argued in this article that the "bane and poison of Italian nature . . . is Distrust," though this was also reason for their "acuteness and intelligence" ("Italian" 105–6). Within the novel, a housekeeper states that foreigners like Count Fosco and his wife "do not possess our blessings and advantages; and they are, for the most part, brought up in the blind errors of popery" (Collins, *Woman* 362–63). Oliphant saw Count Fosco as, "by a very long way the most interesting personage in the book" ("Sensation" 567). She added,

> He is intended to be an impersonation of evil, a representative of every diabolical wile: but Fosco is not detestable; on the contrary, he is more interesting, and seizes on our sympathies more warmly than any other character in the book.
>
> ("Sensation" 567)

In *The Woman in White*, there is a clearer link between a sense of national identity, as an orderly and rule-abiding people, pitted against a projection of foreign disorder, moral short-sightedness, and political unrest. The detective participates in this discourse of foreign criminality *vis-à-vis* British rationality (see also Reitz).

The Woman in White, as in Collins's later novels *No Name* and *Armadale*, presents detection as initiating from a hunch or instinct. Detection may be associated with rational thought and writing, but it primarily follows a supernatural misgiving. This links the sensation novel with the earlier Gothic tradition and, indeed, Collins would return to this pattern of experiential knowledge following intuition. Mr Hartright, for instance, feels "an inexplicable unwillingness" that contrasts "so painfully and so unaccountably" with his inclination when receiving an employment offer from Frederick Fairlie (Collins, *Woman* 19–20). Upon meeting Miss Fairlie, he states, "she unconsciously gave me the key to her whole character . . . I only knew it intuitively then. I know it by experience now" (Collins, *Woman* 35).[2] Marian Halcombe also expresses "fears and fancies" about Sir Percival Glyde's character and intentions (Collins, *Woman* 482). Only later does this intuition or instinct translate into confirmed knowledge. What is helpful to note here is that there a similar tension, as seen in *Martin Chuzzlewit*, between a spiritualism (derived from the Gothic tradition) and the ratiocinative process of gathering evidence. Whereas empirical information dispels irrational fears in *Martin Chuzzlewit*, ratiocination confirms the validity of supernatural instinct in *The Woman in White*.

Earlier, *Bleak House* was described as a legal drama and there are similar overtones of a legal drama to this narrative as well. The difference is that *The Woman in White* foregrounds first-hand experience and the limitations of one's observations through its compilation of multiple written narratives. The narration is shared by different characters, ranging from Mr Hartright, to Miss Halcombe, to the Fairlie family's lawyer, to the Fairlie family's cook, to Count Fosco, and including a letter from Mrs Jane Catherick. Altogether, the narrative structure lends a strong emphasis to the relation between observation, interpretation, and behavior. There is also a strong element of legal testimony and witnessing in the novel, opening a window into the domestic sphere. As Mr Hartright states in the opening chapter, "As the Judge might once have heard it, so the Reader shall hear it now. No circumstance of importance, from the beginning to the end of the discourse, shall be related on hearsay evidence" (Collins, *Woman* 9). Such a narrative style was likely influenced, as Surridge and Tromp have argued, by the ongoing divorce court journalism following the 1857 Matrimonial Causes Act (as outlined in Chapter 1; Tromp, *Private Rod*). The reader participates in detection in this novel, piecing together a coherent narrative that assigns meaning to each character's actions and behavior. The reader gathers clues from the recovered letters, diary entries, and snippets of conversation, which renders the act of reading an active work of interpretation. Hence, the conventional narrative sequence is inverted here, since the reader is shown the outward gesture before learning of its motivation. While novels traditionally expressed a character's psychological perspective before segueing into action, this novel calls on the reader to infer motivation from outward action or written fragments.

As earlier stated, sensation novels often foreground female wrongdoing and sexual misbehavior. Even though the criminal in *The Woman in White* is Sir Glyde, his secret can also be traced to a woman's shameful past and sexual transgression. As Mrs Jane Catherick explains to Mr Hartright, Sir Glyde's mother had been previously married, but her husband had mistreated and deserted her (Collins, *Woman* 531). Sir Glyde's father had not married her for this reason, nor had he left an inheritance to his son in his will. Mrs Catherick scorns Sir Glyde's mother, even though she is also a victim of desertion and had her own adulterous affair. Sir Glyde evolves as a criminal who attempts to rectify his illegitimate birth and conceal his mother's sexual wrongdoing. Likewise, the asylum or madhouse become a site that contains female deviance and errant sexuality, a feature that would recur in later sensation novels. On the other hand, the reader is presented an image of feminine virtue in Miss Laura Fairlie, but she also seems to reveal "something wanting" in her "imperfectly impassive" behavior (Collins, *Woman* 53, 184). Mrs Catherick also has a weakness for "foolish admiration and fine clothes," showing how most women in this novel are deficient for one personal quality or another (Collins, *Woman* 466–67). The detective is framed against this image of female deficiency and sexual deviance.

Interestingly, however, the detective's masculinity is translated in non-biological terms, rendering Miss Halcombe an investigator in her own right. Miss Halcombe is subject to the constitutional weaknesses of her female body. She writes about the pressures of living in the same house as Sir Glyde and Count Fosco, stating,

> my mind seemed to share the exhaustion of my body . . . my head was giddy, and my knees trembled under me. There was no choice but to give it up again, and return to the sofa, solely against my will.
>
> (Collins, *Woman* 272–73)

Despite the susceptibility to her body's weaknesses, Miss Halcombe emerges as one of the more insightful and observant characters in the novel. She not only appears masculine – with an "almost swarthy" complexion, dark down on her upper lip resembling a moustache, and a "large, firm, masculine mouth and jaw" – she also lacks the perceived "feminine attractions of gentleness and pliability" (Collins, *Woman* 35). Count Fosco remarks that Miss Halcombe has "the foresight and the resolution of a man" (Collins, *Woman* 324). The detective is a figure of masculine ambivalence, and this ambivalence appears in non-biological terms in this novel. Count Fosco clearly respects Miss Halcombe as an antagonist, stating that, "with that woman for my enemy, I, with all brains and experience – I, Fosco, cunning as the devil himself . . . I walk, in your English phrase, upon egg-shells" (Collins, *Woman* 324). It is Miss Halcombe who directs Mr Hartright to "crush" his feelings for the engaged Miss Fairlie, telling him to "tear it out; trample it under foot like a man" (Collins, *Woman* 73). Miss Halcombe embodies determination and self-control, masculine qualities associated with detective work. In the process, she becomes voided of more feminine attributes, even as she develops as a compelling character in the novel. Her masculine appearance and ugliness ironically seem to lend credibility to her mental strengths as a detective. In precluding romantic interest or attraction, she acquires respect for her astute observations.

As stated in the previous chapter, there are close allegiances between the lawyer and the detective in mid-nineteenth-century Victorian novels, as seen in Wood's *East Lynne*. In *The Woman in the White*, however, the lawyer does not take an active role in detection, though the novel is structured as a legal drama. Mr Gilmore, the Fairlie family's lawyer, is an older man of business representing an extension of ineffectual institutions against insidious threats. As he tells Mr Hartright, "I am an old man; and I take the practical view. You are a young man; and you take the romantic view"

(Collins, *Woman* 119). Indeed, detection is related to romance in Collins's novels, rather than the reinstatement of patriarchal authority. While detective work does expose sexual wrongdoing, deviant women, and scheming foreigners, it is often conducted by younger characters in the face of indifference from the older characters. Mr Gilmore is a disinterested and well-meaning but ultimately ineffectual observer, who lacks insight into Sir Glyde's character. He lacks the uncanny intelligence of Mr Tulkinghorn, limited to his area of expertise without the imaginative or "romantic" capacity to intuit more sinister motives.

Passive detection and chauvinism in *East Lynne*

It may be unfair to read *East Lynne* alongside Collins's *The Woman in White*, as he resented the apparent differences in their quality and earnings. Collins wrote to his publisher George Smith in 1872 that he considered himself "a rather better novelist, with a rather wider reputation than Mrs Henry Wood," even though she averaged "a thousand a year profit to herself by the sale of her novels" (*Letters* II, 359). Such remarks were not hyperbole, since Wood, in spite of the perceived poor quality of her work, attained significant wealth through her novelistic success. Upon her death in 1887, her estate was valued at over 36,000 pounds, well over triple Collins's fortune left behind two years later (Jay, "Introduction" xvii).[3] Wood initially had difficulty finding a publisher for the book form of *East Lynne*, after its serialization in the *New Monthly Magazine* (owned and edited by Ainsworth) between January 1860 and September 1861. Chapman and Hall declined her manuscript based on a review by their reader, the novelist George Meredith, who stated that the novel demonstrated "foul taste" (qtd. in Jay, "Introduction" xiii). Richard and George Bentley, who published the book form, were recommended by their reader Geraldine Jewsbury to have "the grammar and the composition . . . thoroughly revised by some competent person," as Wood, in her opinion, was "not qualified for the task" (qtd. in Jay, "Note" xl). Jewsbury also noted "needless sins against good taste" in the novel and expressed skepticism over some of the novel's plot development (qtd. in Jay, "Note" xl). Oliphant dismissed *East Lynne* as a "dangerous and foolish work, as well as false, both to Art and Nature" that had nonetheless achieved "some inscrutable breath of popular liking" ("Sensation novels" 567). The journalist Eliza Lynn Linton also opined that Wood was "a very, very shallow writer, a shallow observer of society, and a puerile and a vulgar one" (qtd. in Cruse 327). Wood was clearly seen as a popular writer, rather than an intellectual or creative one.

Despite the criticism the novel received, however, *East Lynne* was likely one of the bestselling novels of the 1860s and 1870s (see S. Eliot 57). It was also the most frequently adapted sensation novel, with two stage productions in New York and two stage productions in London within five years of its book release (see Adams, *History* 203; Maunder, "I Will Not Live"). By the end of the nineteenth century, *East Lynne* had sold over 430,000 copies and was among the most popular novels in circulating and public libraries (Altick, *English* 385; Tromp, "Mrs. Henry Wood" 257). The combined sales of the book, in its three-volume format, have been estimated to have reached around one million by the end of the nineteenth century (Liggins and Maunder 150).[4]

The novel is difficult to read for modern readers, not because of its language – indeed, its language has been described as "racy" and "slang-ridden" (Jay, "Note" xli) – but because of its overt chauvinism and double gender standards even for a sensation novel. The novel is profoundly con-servative and stages a triumphant reinstatement of the patriarchal order. More so than even other sensation novels, married women are treated as children, susceptible to their emotions and superstitious beliefs, while male ignorance and miscalculations are freely pardoned. About half of the novel concerns Lady Isabel making penance for her sin of adultery against her husband. The second half of the novel sees Lady Isabel horribly disfigured, reduced from an earl's daughter to a mere governess, with her youngest son killed in a train accident. She initially represents an ideal of virginal womanhood, which was why Mr Carlyle fell in love with her. But it is because of her child-like behavior that Mr Carlyle fatally withholds the secret of Barbara Hare's brother from her. Nor does Mr Carlyle reflect on his own actions that may have contributed to her flight, even as Lady Isabel is cruelly forced to suffer for her wrongdoing. As critics have noted, the novel seems to court a male audience, as explained by the "predominantly masculine tone" of the *New Monthly Magazine* in which it was serialized, and indeed, the dominant reading of *East Lynne* is as a story of "Victo-rian bourgeois triumphalism" (Jay, "Introduction" xv, xxx; see Kaplan 78; Riley 175; Kucich 162).

Mr Carlyle is the undisputed hero of the novel and also a competent lawyer. He is a man of business with "noble qualities," who runs for public office to represent his town in London (Wood 297). He is unscathed by the scandal of Lady Isabel's affair and Barbara comments that he is "one of the very few men, so entirely noble, whom the sort of disgrace, reflected from Lady Isabel's conduct cannot touch" (Wood 553). His ascendence in the novel parallels Lady Isabel's demise, as he becomes the parliamentary representative for West Lynne (Wood 553). He sees himself as a potentially "good and efficient public servant . . . his talents were superior; his ora-tory was persuasive, and he had the gift of a true and honest spirit" (Wood 436). Mr Carlyle is aware of the moral ambiguities of the legal profession, but steers clear of any compromising transactions. Overall, the legal estab-lishment represents an extension of patriarchal authority in its disciplining of male criminality and female disobedience. This is apparent not only in Mr Carlyle's success in the novel, but also in the witness room where Aphrodite "Afy" gives her testimony. The testimony is presided over by none other than Justice Hare, the father of the man whose affections she had spurned and who stands suspected of murder. Justice Hare "thunder[s]" at Afy to testify, reducing her vanity to humiliation and leaving a stain on her public character (Wood 542).

Mr Carlyle, as a lawyer, does not investigate other characters so much as receive information and take credit for their observations. This distances him from the moral dilemma of prying into the private lives of other characters. Women often make discoveries and intuit answers (such as Barbara), but men take the glory of "solving" a mystery. For instance, Barbara suspects early on that Sir Levison is Captain Thorn, whom her brother identified as the real murderer. By the time she has gathered enough courage to confess as much to her husband, Mr Carlyle already knows this and has received corroborating evidence from male witnesses (see Wood 484). What a woman correctly suspects can only be ratified or legitimized by men in the public domain. Hence, John Kucich suggests that Mr Carlyle is a "passive detective" and that "clues [that his second wife] Barbara grasps intuitively seem to elude him" (186). When read as a novel that reorganizes "social order around middle-class moral values" (Kucich 162), Mr Carlyle cannot stoop so low as to be involved in the detective process of secret observation and investigation. Nonetheless, he takes full credit for the trial's outcome, representing a promising middle-class ascendency and the moral authority of a professional elite. *East Lynne* explores a new kind of bourgeois dignity and masculinity at the expense of weak and frivolous women. It is in the domain of business, as sanctioned by the law, that men achieve recognition and success. Such success, however, cannot be compromised by the ambivalence that covert detective work entails.

Notes

1 The 1860s and 1870s saw a spate of similar detective pseudo-memoirs, including those written by James McLevy and James McGovan (see also Chapter 8).
2 Mangham has argued that Mr Hartright's "detective work has much in common with the perceived analytical skills of nineteenth-century psychiatrists" ("What Could I Do" 118).
3 According to Elizabeth Jay in her introduction to the Oxford edition of *East Lynne*, Wood's estate was valued at £36,393 in 1887, compared to Collins's estate at £10,831 in 1889. Anthony Trollope had left behind £25,892 upon his death in 1882 (Jay, "Introduction" xviii).
4 Wood's literary reputation also seems to have improved towards the end of the century (see Liggins and Maunder 149–50; Riley 165).

5 Early detectives in Braddon's *The Trail of the Serpent* and *The Black Band*

In recent decades, scholars of Victorian sensation fiction have drawn attention to Braddon's work, particularly her best-known and most successful novel, *Lady Audley's Secret*. Beller has observed that Braddon has "undoubtedly . . . received the preponderance of attention" in studies of Victorian sensation fiction ("Fashions" 467). But, as Jessica Cox points out, Braddon's early fiction has been "relatively unexplored" and "critically overlooked" ("Introduction" 2, 12). Braddon's early works include her first novel, *The Trail of the Serpent*, first serialized as *Three Times Dead* in penny weekly parts (a "penny blood") in the short-lived journal *The Welcome Guest* in 1860. The novel was revised and republished in volume form by Maxwell the following year to capitalize on the success of *Lady Audley's Secret*, reputedly selling a thousand copies in its first week (see Pykett, "Mary Elizabeth Braddon" 125; Pedlar 187; Tomaiuolo, *In Lady* 115n16). Braddon's early fiction also includes another mystery novel, *The Black Band*, which briefly features two London detectives unable to foil the culprits at the heart of an international criminal organization. While critics have read important clues to Braddon's novelistic development in *The Trail of the Serpent* (see Ferguson; Bennett; Mangham, "Murdered"; Mangham, "Drink It Up"; Louttit; Sussex 85–89), there has been scant critical attention to *The Black Band*. Overall, Braddon's early fiction has largely been dismissed as "artistically immature" commercial hackwork leading up to her most successful novel (Tomaiuolo, *In Lady* 115n16).

The Trail of the Serpent and *The Black Band* both feature detectives to varying degrees. *The Trail of the Serpent* reveals Braddon's growth as a writer, since she was specifically commissioned by the printer to write a serial with "the human interest and genial humor of Dickens [combined] with the plot-weaving of G. W. R. [*sic*] Reynolds" (Sussex 85; Pykett, "Mary Elizabeth Braddon" 124–25; see Braddon, "My First Novel").[1] Braddon's first novel follows more closely in the footsteps of Dickens and Ainsworth, authors of *Oliver Twist* and *Jack Sheppard* respectively, rather

DOI: 10.4324/9781003369622-6

than in the mold of Collins's psychological drama *The Woman in White*. Both Dickens and Ainsworth are explicitly mentioned in the novel (see Braddon, *Trail* 299, 341), and there is a Dickensian approach to depicting the urban landscape in the novel. For instance, the narrator often focuses on an unnamed character wandering the streets who gradually becomes more distinct against a blurry background. There is a self-conscious attempt to be literary, even where the plot is sensational and fast-paced, and even if Braddon later recalled that she had written the novel "with all the freedom of one who feared not the face of a critic" ("My First Novel" 25). Braddon noted that the novel was received as the product of "a pen unchastened by experience," though she would pare down many of the literary and descriptive elements by her third novel *The Black Band* ("My First Novel" 25). *The Trail of the Serpent* helps bridge the gap between the urban crime novels of the 1830s and the domestic melodramas of the 1850s and 1860s within the trajectory of developing detective fiction. It replicates many of the themes in Dickens's novels, particularly his attention to urban crowds and the potential for self-reinvention in the city, while introducing the elements of sexual control and male "scientific" inquiry in Victorian sensation fiction.

Detection in the city: *The Trail of the Serpent*

While the majority of the action in *The Trail of the Serpent* may not be set in London, the fictional town of Slopperton-on-the-Sloshy seems, at times, consciously modelled on London. References to the impoverished Blind Peter's Alley in Slopperton-on-the-Sloshy paint a "labyrinth of tumble-down houses, pig-styes, and dog-kennels" that has become a "refuge for crime and destitution" (Braddon, *Trail* 116). Blind Peter's Alley "looked very much like a London alley which had been removed from its site and pitched haphazard [*sic*] on to a Slopperton mountain" (Braddon, *Trail* 81). Mark Bennett points out that the river Sloshy, which runs through Slopperton, seems "inextricably linked with a cyclical flow of bodies" and is "repeatedly described as being saturated with the corpses of the suicidal and the drowned" (41). The people in Slopperton have heard of "many murders" in the city, which seems infected with a sense of moral decay and deception, as reflected in its urban filth and pollution (Braddon, *Trail* 106). Slopperton is "so dark a blot" on the "face of such a fair and lovely earth" that it serves as a metaphor for moral contagion and undetected crime (Braddon, *Trail* 115). While the narrative is also partly set in London, relocating there halfway through the novel, and in France and Liverpool, it begins and ends in this crowded city of Slopperton, associated with unseen criminality. Jabez North is a product and epitome of the city's association with crime, as we shall later see.

In Dickens's and Ainsworth's novels of urban crime, the London setting was integral to the atmosphere and enactment of crime. One could even argue that detective stories, as they evolved in Victorian England, can hardly be imagined without the parallel urbanization and industrialization of the nineteenth century. The metropolis provided an inhabited space in which individuals could freely reinvent their identities, while allowing them to mingle with members of the aristocracy, the middle class, and the working class. There is simultaneous fascination with the spectacle and chaos of London in *The Trail of the Serpent*, as the narrator marvels at its "emporiums of splendour" and the "crowds of excited pedestrians, and such tearing and rushing, and smashing of cabs, carts, omnibuses, and parcel-delivery vans, all of them driven by charioteers in the last stage of insanity" (Braddon, *Trail* 290). These crowds create both a sense of excitement and action, but also allow for secret crimes. The city engenders both a sense of possibility about the heightened visibility on the streets and an anxiety about the private lives of individuals in the crowd. Together, these urban experiences foster the fantasy figure of a detective who, through his powers of acute observation, can pierce through deceptive appearances and discern a person's hidden identity.

In *The Trail of the Serpent*, the anxiety of a potential mismatch between a respectable public appearances and secret (even criminal) intentions are overlaid in the character of Jabez, the principal antagonist and a master manipulator of identities. He is, as announced when finally exposed, "Jabez North, *alias* Raymond Marolles, *alias* the Count of Marolles" (Braddon, *Trail* 425). By all appearances, Jabez seems "a good young man; a benevolent young man; giving in secret, and generally getting his reward openly" (Braddon, *Trail* 6). He has an "excellent nature" and "every citizen of the borough praised and applauded this model young man" (Braddon, *Trail* 6). But as the novel reveals, this teacher of French and mathematics is secretly a licentious, murderous, and remorseless man, with a "wicked heart . . . so much more foul and so much bitterer a poison," in the words of his deceived lover (Braddon, *Trail* 40). Intent on self-betterment, Jabez desires, in his own words, "a long life of wealth and luxury, with proud men's necks to trample on, and [his] old patrons to lick the dust off [his] shoes" (Braddon, *Trail* 79). In Mangham's words, Jabez is "a wicked social climber" who ironically also "represents the mid-Victorian self-made man" ("Murdered" 29, 31). Jabez also exemplifies the capacity to remake and refashion one's identity in the crowd, aided in part by the appearance of his rediscovered twin brother, Jim. Jabez exploits the capacity for disguise and self-reinvention in the crowd, moving through London and Liverpool under new identities. Braddon criticizes the hypocrisy and preoccupation with public appearances, noting that even after his murderous crime, he seemed a "superior and intellectual man," with a "truly benevolent character" (*Trail* 88–89).

Simultaneously, the anxiety over an individual's ability to reinvent their identity in a rapidly changing urban environment exposes another, deep-seated skepticism about the effectiveness of institutions to trace and tackle crime. Such skepticism had earlier been seen in the general disregard for police competence (see Chapter 2), but is also seen in this novel. In *The Trail of the Serpent*, the legal system is unmatched by the criminal's superior capacity for deception. Earlier, in Dickens's *Bleak House*, there had been a similar skepticism that the legal system was capable of or adept at dealing with deep-seated moral decay and cunning. These concerns also appear in *The Trail of the Serpent*, where Richard Marwood is falsely accused and incarcerated for his uncle's murder. This skepticism in institutions gives rise to a parallel fantasy in the popular imagination that a resourceful and observant individual could detect the criminal's wrongdoing. The detective is molded into the shape of this fantasized figure, acting outside the stifling bureaucracy of institutional constraints, while simultaneously bearing the legitimacy and authority of the legal system. Ironically, as an individual, the detective is a self-made man, rather than the product of an incompetent system, whose skill and intelligence can remedy (albeit temporarily) the ineffectuality of the criminal justice system. His ambivalent position stems not only from his resemblance to or reflection of the criminal (as a self-made individual), but also in his ability to both resist institutional constraints while relying on its conclusive authority.

As earlier noted, the narrator in *The Trail of the Serpent* introduces characters on the Slopperton streets as they seem to emerge from a hazy background (as "a man" or "a woman"), observing their movements well before disclosing their personal histories. The reader becomes an observer, one who initially has little access to the secret or private thoughts of the observed individuals. This process mimics the pattern of detection, which is primarily visual and observational. The detective Mr Joe Peters concludes, for instance, that Richard is not guilty because his "colour never changed" when apprehended at the train station, while Jabez had "the look of a man as is guilty of what will hang him and thinks he's found out" (Braddon, *Trail* 273, 276). The Indian servant Mujeebez likewise testifies, "[Richard] did not look like a murderer. . . . A black heart will make strange lines in the handsomest face, which are translatable to the close observer" (Braddon, *Trail* 310). Even Richard's friends state "there's something unmistakable about [Jabez's] pale thin face" that belies his "calm, aristocratic, and serene" demeanor (Braddon, *Trail* 301). To be sure, this reliance on acute powers of observation is pseudo-scientific and potentially prejudicial, revealing a fantasy about the visual manifestation of secret criminality. Braddon never discredits the phrenologists who suggest that Jabez's "head and face . . . bespoke a marvelous power of secretiveness" (*Trail* 78). These powers of observations are marked not only as specifically masculine, but also as bearing a veneer of scientific or mathematical legitimacy. As Mr Peters remarks about his conclusions of the characters' respective expressions, "what a detective officer's good at, if he's worth his salt, is this 'ere – when he sees two here, and another two there, he can put 'em together . . . and make 'em into four" (Braddon, *Trail* 274).

Here, the suggestion is that the detective (and the criminal, as we shall see) lays claim to a higher and more modern form of authority that supersedes tradition or institutions. The claim to scientific authority is, as earlier stated, exclusively masculine and hinges upon an apparent method of reasoning or calculation. Braddon repeatedly refers to Jabez as a "mathematician" who likens his scheme for wealth to a game of cards (*Trail* 141). As will also be seen in *Lady Audley's Secret*, the rational male thinker is contrasted with the emotional female actor, whose "mind is easily influenced by others" (Braddon, *Trail* 194). As Jabez states to Valerie,

> You have passion, genius, courage . . . but you have not that power of calculation, that inductive science, which never sees the effect without looking for the cause, which men have christened mathematics. I, mademoiselle, am a mathematician. As such, I sat down to play a deep and dangerous game with you; and as such, now that the hour has come at which I can show my hand, you will see that I hold the winning cards.
>
> (Braddon, *Trail* 194)

Jabez contrasts himself, as an embodiment of "inductive science" with a mathematical "power of calculation," to Valerie, who may have "passion, genius, [and] courage," but not the infallibility of scientific reasoning. Their contest of wills, in Jabez's mind, is one in which female emotion and cunning are dimly held against the flame of "mathematics," which guarantee Jabez a "winning" hand. Jabez lays claim to the upper hand in their "deep and dangerous game" through the male discursive authority of science and mathematics.

To a modern reader, the tendencies to infer from appearance, draw hasty conclusions from observations, and make lucky guesses can hardly be described as "scientific" or "mathematical." But what matters here is not whether such actions amount to legitimate scientific practice, but how male individuals lay claim to a sense of superiority or authority emerging from such claims, particularly over women. Braddon reprises the conventional view that women, as constrained by their bodily processes and emotions, are more easily swayed and manipulated by male schemers and thinkers. Valerie becomes "a pitiful puppet in the hands of a master fiend" (Braddon, *Trail* 343). It is not a man's claim to title or wealth that assures his superiority or authority over her, but his powers of intellect and reasoning, which (compellingly enough) are theoretically accessible to men of all social ranks. Jabez plays an intricate game of mental "cards" with Valerie, in which he has "nothing but [his] brains for weapons in the great fight" (Braddon, *Trail* 194). As he later confesses, he had "a will as indomitable as the stars" and has taken his own road, "unloved, unaided, unprayed for, unwept; motherless, fatherless, sisterless, brotherless, friendless" (Braddon, *Trail* 443). Jabez's reliance on his mental powers reconfigures the Romantic hero into a self-made man, who secures his position in the world through his tenacious will and reasoning capacity.

As noted, this "science of mathematics" grants the self-made man some authority over women, even of higher social ranks (Braddon, *Trail* 196). Jabez feels this power most acutely when Valerie breaks out in "rage and hatred" against him, as he senses "his calculating brain and icy temperament made him her superior" (Braddon, *Trail* 203). What distinguishes him from the detective, however, is his inability to feel any emotion or humanity that could render him more relatable. In this sense, he resembles Mr Tulkinghorn in *Bleak House*, who is all cold intellect and rationality without any recognizable humanity. Jabez states that he is incapable of understanding that "weakness of the brain, which men have christened love" (Braddon, *Trail* 203). He is incapable of feeling remorse, despite playing a hand in multiple murders and deaths. Jabez attracts suspicion for his excessive rationality or adherence to science, which could be deemed monstrous. As Mangham observes, Jabez's "house of cards, a symbol of his social aspirations, is built using the sexual passions and indiscretions of the woman as its raw materials" ("Murdered" 31). Similarly, the spiritualist and chemist Laurent Blurosset inspires abhorrence for his inhumanity and exclusive devotion to "the pursuit of science" and the "study of the great laws of cause and effect," making him unresponsive to pleas of pity or mercy (Braddon, *Trail* 207, 347). Even here, his practices in supernaturalism and occultism are falsely paraded as a "science," which are, in actuality, intended to deceive and manipulate a woman (Braddon, *Trail* 169).

In contrast, the detective Mr Peters is a mathematician *and* a philanthropist, who takes into his care a young girl named Kuppins and an abandoned baby named Slosh (later revealed to be Jabez's illegitimate son). Mr Peters is "rather soft-hearted" about babies by his own confession and enjoys visiting the leisurely Rose-Bush tea gardens with Kuppins and Slosh (Braddon, *Trail* 278). Even though he is not, in his words, "a marryin' man, and [is] by no means likely ever to 'av a family of [his] own," Mr Peters still enjoys the modest comforts of the domestic and private sphere (Braddon, *Trail* 279). As a single gentleman and philanthropist, his home is like an "indoor Eden" on the quaint-sounding "No. 5 Little Gulliver Street" (Braddon, *Trail* 114). Like Mr Nadgett, he is inconspicuous since he is unable to speak, but like Mr Bucket, he inspires Kuppins with a sense that he is "the law and the police in person" (Braddon, *Trail* 119). As a professional man,

"He sees that the young and beautiful girl is prepared to give him battle."—P. 146.

Figure 5.1 Frontispiece to Braddon's *The Trail of the Serpent* by an unidentified artist in an edition published by Ward, Lock, and Tyler in 1866. Public domain/scanned by University of Illinois at Urbana-Champaign, digitized by Google (Braddon, *Trail* frontispiece).

he is a distinguished detective possessing "such a degree of tact, triumphing so completely over the difficulties he labours under" that he earns both a better position in the police force at Slopperton and a higher salary (Braddon, *Trail* 113). Despite this, Mr Peters craves a mental challenge, revealing that while he is a man who works within the established institution of the police force, he is also a capable and gifted individual with comparable powers of reasoning and calculation as the criminal.

But even here, there remains some ambivalence in the distinction between the detective and the criminal. Mr Peters notes, for instance, that the eight-year-old Slosh (who has grown from a baby) would make an accomplished detective because, like his father Jabez, he has little emotional attachment to his family. Mr Peters muses that the "under-current of his father" in Slosh's character will "make him the glory of his profession" (Braddon, *Trail* 298). Mr Peters continues that this unscrupulousness, even callousness, will serve him well as a detective, since "soft-heartedness has been the ruin of many a detective, as has had the brain to work out a deep-laid game, but not the heart to carry it through" (Braddon, *Trail* 298). The implication here is that qualities that make a criminal successful are also what make a detective competent. The comparison between mental exertion and a game of cards extends from Jabez's criminal scheme to the work of detection. In another scene, the detective is able to apprehend the criminal partly due to the anonymity afforded by the crowd, even as the criminal is also a symptom of the crowd's heterogeneity. Both the criminal and the "amateur band of police, formed for the special purpose of the detection" of Jabez (the Cheerful Cherokee Society) act outside the boundaries of the established legal system (Braddon, *Trail* 301). The Cherokees, or "Daredevil Dick's secret police," act as an extrajudicial force outside a corrupt and incompetent legal system (Braddon, *Trail* 305). The crowd provides cover both for anonymity and for private investigation. The criminal may also be observed and followed, as when Jabez is pursued by Slosh through Blind Peter's Alley.

There are other, less developed elements of sensation novels and detective stories in *The Trail of the Serpent*, such as the use of opium, Orientalist insinuations of the East, accusations of insanity, the mental asylum, the unfeeling father, occultism, Italian intrigue, and references to distant colonies. As in other sensation novels, laudanum is a widely available drug but also widely accessible poison in *The Trail of the Serpent*. The theme of the doppelganger, as seen in the sudden appearance of Jabez's twin brother, foreshadows the doubling that would take centerstage in Collins's *Armadale* – or even later, in Robert Louis Stevenson's *Strange Case of Dr Jekyll and Mr Hyde* (1886). The reader is, unlike in Braddon's subsequent novel, given more than a passing glimpse of life inside a mental asylum, rendered more comical and absurd than the restrictive and regimented madhouse in

Lady Audley's Secret. But perhaps the more significant development in this novel is the association between investigation (both detective and criminal) and scientific legitimacy. This assertion of masculine superiority, based on a claim to scientific authority, would be further explored in *Lady Audley's Secret*, continuing to gender detective work in Victorian fiction.

Gothic criminality in *The Black Band*

If the majority of the action in Braddon's first novel took place in the fictional English town of Slopperton-on-the-Sloshy, modelled in part on London, Braddon's third novel *The Black Band* takes place across Britain and continental Europe, in cities such as London, Paris, Venice, Naples, and remote regions of Scotland. The style of Braddon's *The Black Band*, better characterized as a mystery novel about crime rather than a detective story, is also more rapid and sensational than her first novel. Published anonymously in 1861 as a weekly penny serial (also known as a "penny blood"), much of the action in *The Black Band* is crudely thought out and appear as mere sketches of ideas, rather than as a fully developed narrative. The reader stumbles across two marriage proposals within the first fifteen pages and two secret marriages within the first thirty-two pages. While the novel features two detectives, Inspector Martin and Sergeant Boulder, they are outmatched by the extent of criminal intrigue and secret societies spanning Europe and Britain. Even "two of the cleverest detectives in London" are thrown into "hopeless confusion and disappointment" in unravelling their crime (Braddon, *Black Band* 105, 117). Inspector Martin and Sergeant Boulder may be practitioners in "that wonderful science which tracks the dark pathways of crime with such marvelous success," which has led the public to "look upon the detective police officer as the magician of civilized life," but even they are confounded by the sprawling skein of crime and deception woven by the Black Band (117).

Braddon confessed around the time she wrote *The Black Band* that she often had to resort to stories of crime and treachery in the *Newgate Calender* ("Devoted 158; see Thomas, "Detection" 173–74). Writing to her friend and mentor Bulwer-Lytton in 1862, she wrote, "The amount of crime, treachery, murder, sow poisoning, & general infamy required by the Half penny reader is something terrible. I am just going to do a little paracide [*sic*] for this week's supply" (Braddon, "Devoted" 11). As a prolific writer, Braddon wrote, by her own confession, "an immense deal of work" for cheap half-penny and penny journals while serializing her longer novels, like *Lady Audley's Secret* and *Aurora Floyd*. Braddon's *The Black Band* more closely resembles Collins's *The Woman in White* in its depiction of Italian secret societies that take justice into their own hands. The central premise is based on an international organization of criminal intrigue and blackmail, led by the Austrian Colonel Oscar Bertrand, who has a political interest in thwarting the Italian resistance. But the ideas that would appear in her later novels also appear in *The Black Band*, specifically the focalization on a ruthlessly manipulative female character, who is "worldly," "ambitious," "heartless and mercenary," and willing to romance multiple men to secure her fortune (Braddon, *Black Band* 31–32, 49). The theme of bigamy is introduced in *The Black Band*, as Edith Vandeleur becomes simultaneously Lady Edith Merton and the Marchioness de Montebello. Even the antagonist, Colonel Oscar Bertrand, attributes his moral downfall to a Frenchwoman's deception, without whom he might have been "an honest man" (Braddon, *Black Band* 142). The narrative devices of madness, asylums, chemical drafts, and Italian intrigue recur throughout the novel (Braddon, *Black Band* 203). Against this far-reaching network of crime, led by a criminal mastermind with "sinister and invincible power," even "the detectives . . . that wonderful police" are unable to solve their mysteries (Braddon, *Black Band* 25, 97). Bennett has said that Colonel Bertrand "repeatedly recalls the supernaturally endowed diabolic tempers, popular within a range of contemporary working-class fictions," such as Mephistopheles, with whom he is explicitly compared in the novel (47). In this sensation novel, the sense of the Gothic or the supernatural overrides the modern science of detection.

Colonel Bertrand resembles the detective only in that he appears to have supernatural knowledge of other characters' secrets and actions. He tells the baronet Sir Frederick Beaumorris that he had "followed [him] step by step" from London, prompting him to indignantly accuse him of "play[ing] the spy" (Braddon, *Black Band* 74). In a dramatic twist, Colonel Bertrand reveals that the young girl that Beaumorris had been pursuing is actually his niece. The colonel uses such incriminating information against his victims to blackmail them into submission and loyalty to his international network of crime. He plays both the hero and the villain, but is ultimately unmasked as a self-serving and powerful criminal. Colonel Bertrand even seems at times to simultaneously be in both France and Scotland, as he appears in alternating chapters that take place across the Continent. He has become "too deeply steeped in crime, and . . . too long familiar with guilt, not to have become a stranger to both remorse and terror" (Braddon, *Black Band* 139). In his own words, his life has been "one long calculation, based on the weakness and wickedness of men" (Braddon, *Black Band* 160). Colonel Bertrand operates and conducts his business outside the purview of the law, but ultimately loses his far-reaching intelligence when he unknowingly drinks a chemical draft that renders him into an "idiot" (Braddon, *Black Band* 203). As Braddon describes, "the man whose powerful intellect had ruled the souls of his fellow-men," succumbs to the drug, which "slowly rots away the brain of him who tastes it" (Braddon, *Black Band* 203–4).

This humiliating demise means that Colonel Bertrand becomes "helpless, feeble, decrepit, idiotic . . . [sinking] lower than the animals that grazed in the valley" (Braddon, *Black Band* 206). Colonel Bertrand falls beyond the need for fear or revenge as a result of his pride.

Beyond Colonel Bertrand, there are other parallels between *The Black Band* and contemporary iterations of the London detective. Inspector Martin has an "insignificant appearance," much like Mr Nadgett in Dickens's *Martin Chuzzlewit*, such that he "might pass unnoticed anywhere, by reason of that very insignificance of appearance" (Braddon, *Black Band* 150). Both Inspector Martin and Sergeant Boulder rely on the since-discredited science of physiognomy, examining a suspect's face with "that peculiarly searching glance known only to [detectives] – a glance in which the clever detective can read the inmost secrets of a man's soul" (Braddon, *Black Band* 110). Other characters also intuit a person's character through their expression, such as Robert Merton's friend, Arthur Danvers, to whom "the face was always an index to the mind – a key by which he could often read the secret workings of the heart" – an idea earlier seen in *The Trail of the Serpent* (Braddon, *Black Band* 32). But it is not only the detectives who seem ever-observant and omnipresent in the crowd. Members of the Black Band also drive vehicles across the city, with "houses of resort in every quarter," and are able to navigate "all the byeways [*sic*] of London" (Braddon, *Black Band* 391, 93). They are brought to justice, not through the legal establishment or detective force, but through facing the consequences of their treacherous actions, turning mad, or being thwarted in their murderous plots.

Note

1 While outside the scope of this study, Reynolds's *Mysteries of London* series has also been read as early detective fiction.

6 Between gentleman and detective

Masculine negotiations in *Lady Audley's Secret*

Braddon's *Lady Audley's Secret* has seen a surge of critical interest since the 1970s, contributing to a wider exploration of the sensation fiction genre (see Beller, "Fashions"). The novel has also been seen as "contribut[ing] to the development of the detective novel," with Vicki A. Pallo arguing that Robert Audley "mov[es] closer to the manner of the typical detective" in the narrative (468, 473). Pallo correctly observes that Robert finds himself in "a position of power over Lady Audley" through his investigations, as detective work becomes associated with social discipline and control (473). Other critics have seen "important distinctions between Robert and the traditional detective" (Gilbert, *Disease* 96; see also Dunbar; Auger). But what such critics have tended to overlook is the predominance of uncertainty and vacillation in the novel. Robert does evolve into a detective who pursues a woman, in contrast to the more dispersed forces of control and surveillance in Collins's *The Woman in White* and Wood's *East Lynne*. Such work is individualized, but detective work is also hedged with an air of disrepute, which means much of the narrative revolves around Robert's interior self-questioning and self-doubt about his role as a detective. Even as Robert intuits that Lady Audley harbors a concealed past, he hesitates to justify such a personal pursuit and exposure of this secret. Tellingly, he reveals his own disdain for detective officers, who seem, in his view, "stained with vile associations, and unfit company for honest gentlemen" (Braddon, *Lady* 343).

Studies of detective fiction tend to take a one-dimensional approach to power and control, as though the detective embodies a singular force of dominance and surveillance. What is often overlooked is that the detective was not seen as "gentlemanly" and indeed occupied an ambivalent status in the social imagination. On the one hand, as Robert states, detective officers had "vile associations" with criminals and spies. On the other hand, detection becomes a vehicle through which other moral threats (such as self-promotion and deceit, as represented by Lady Audley) are exposed and eliminated. The ambivalence of detective work means that much of the

DOI: 10.4324/9781003369622-7

novel becomes a complex negotiation of hesitations and justifications until the final revelation. These hesitations signal not only Robert's character development, but also gesture to the moral ambivalence associated with detective work.

Even though *Lady Audley's Secret* presents an individual process of investigation, staged between a male investigator and a female suspect, these individuals are also socially embedded in their family relationships. The difficulty of eradicating Lady Audley as a moral threat stems from the very gender ideology that she appears to subvert. As B. Griffin explains, explains, the Victorian patriarchal ideology depended on a view of marital unity, with traditionally religious values. The marital unity subsumed the woman's identity under the husband's will, rendering a woman's submission the condition for domestic happiness (B. Griffin 46–48). The deceit practiced by Lady Audley does not extricate her from her familial ties. She fully understands the protection of the patriarchal order into which she has married. As she declares to Robert, "Those who strike me must strike through him [Sir Michael Audley]" (Braddon, *Lady* 186). Again, she states, "my husband shall protect me from your [Robert's] insolence" (Braddon, *Lady* 232). Hence, Robert struggles to find a justification for the exposure of her past because it will not only mean her demise, but also deliver a damaging blow to his uncle's family and reputation. There is significant pressure in the novel for Robert to set aside his investigation and to leave secrets unexplored in the absence of a compelling justification for such disruption. Much of the novel explores possible justifications for such detective work, without staining Robert's character or status as a gentleman.

In this chapter, I outline the idea of the gentleman (contrasting with Robert's notion of the detective), Robert's evolution into a detective, three justifications for his detective work, his masculine method of reasoning, and, finally, the role of female deviance *vis-à-vis* detective work. I argue that detective work amounts to a method of reading or interpreting events, which reconstitutes and upholds the patriarchal order.

The idea of the gentleman and Robert's character

Lady Audley's Secret had an unusual publication history, originally appearing in the weekly journal *Robin Goodfellow* between July to September 1861. The journal was owned by Maxwell, with whom Braddon bore six children and eventually married after his wife's death. After the magazine closed, Braddon set the novel aside to work on her next novel *Aurora Floyd*, which appeared in Maxwell's *Temple Bar* between January 1862 to January 1863. *Lady Audley's Secret* continued serialization after its interruption in the monthly *Sixpenny Magazine* between January to December 1862, overlapping with its book publication in three volumes in October 1862. Within two months, the book had reached its eighth edition. The novel was re-serialized, following a slightly revised book form, in *London Journal* in 1863. George Eliot envied the novel's success, writing that she "sicken[ed] again with despondency" when comparing the sales of her recent novels with those of Braddon (309; see Sussex x).

Before discussing Robert's development as a character, it is worth taking a closer look at the idea of the gentleman. Gilmour's study *The Idea of the Gentleman in the Victorian Novel* (1981) remains the best-known of such studies, but it also helps to look at contemporary definitions and sources. Around the turn of the nineteenth century, the *Encyclopaedia Britannica* had defined the gentleman as a man of social rank, "all [those] above the rank of yeomen, whereby noblemen are truly called *gentlemen*" (3rd ed., 631). Hence, a gentleman was usually one "who, without any title, bears a coat of arms, or whose ancestors have been freemen" (3rd ed. 631). Around the mid-nineteenth century, however, such ideas of the gentleman became more elastic to incorporate moral qualities, sometimes irrespective of social rank. By the mid-1850s, the male protagonist in Elizabeth Gaskell's *North and South* (1855) was complaining that he was "rather weary of this word 'gentlemanly,' which seems to . . . be often inappropriately used, and often, too, with such exaggerated distortion of meaning" (164). In 1856, a writer in *Chamber's Journal* commented that "almost everybody had a particular and private account of [a gentleman] to give," and that the term was usually "applied by the lower classes to those of their superiors who are most lavish and extravagant" ("What is a Gentleman" 399–400). Generosity was one feature of the gentleman, but so also were the moral qualities of a gentleman practicing "what is right and just . . . whose conduct is regulated by a true principle of honor," according to the 1856 edition of the *Encyclopaedia Britannica* (8th ed., 456). By the mid-nineteenth century, a gentleman was defined by "self-respect and intellectual refinement," rather than outward claims to rank or lineage (*Encyclopaedia* 8th ed., 436). As Gilmour observes, the idea of the gentleman revealed "social ambiguity" but also a strong "moral component" (3).

Even as the idea of the gentleman evolved in the nineteenth century, it increasingly came to evoke social respectability and moral principles. By 1862, the *Chamber's Encyclopaedia* defined the gentleman as distinguished either "by birth" or "by profession and social recognition" (687). By 1910, the *Encyclopaedia Britannica* suggested that the definition of the gentleman had become increasingly relative, "but it always implies some sort of excellency of manners or morals" (11th ed., 606).[1] Reflecting this shift in the perception of a gentleman from aristocratic rank to moral values, Samuel Smiles wrote in his 1860 book *Self-Help* that "the poor man may be a true gentleman – in spirit and in daily life"

(349). The quality of being a gentleman consisted, according to Smiles, in "gentleness" and "a consideration for the feelings of others," which served as "the best test of gentlemanliness" (355). Again, Smiles wrote that the test of gentlemanliness was "a respect for [others'] self-respect" and gentleness towards "his inferiors and dependants [*sic*] as well as his equals" (355). Smiles proclaimed, "He who bullies those who are not in a position to resist may be a snob but can not be a gentleman" (355). The gentleman, Smiles argued, is "honest, upright, and straightforward," does not enjoy exercising power over others, and "scrupulously avoid[s] mean actions" (354–55, 348). The status of a gentleman was accessible, therefore, to men across social ranks.

Gimour argues that the idea of the gentleman could not definitively be reduced to either social rank or moral qualities, but instead remained "neither a socially exclusive nor an entirely moralized concept" (12). On closer inspection, a poor man could hardly be a gentleman by sheer force of character, as his actions would also have to be associated with generosity and leisure. Certain gentlemanly pursuits and interests remained beyond the reach of the working class, in spite of Smiles's claims to the contrary. The gentleman remained an aspirational ideal, even a middle-class fantasy, since he always remains outside the realm of competition and labor, but within the social networks of mutual respect. He enjoyed the pursuits of a wealthy society, without submitting to its economic pressures. To borrow Gilmour's words, he represented "respectability and independence within the traditional social hierarchy," enjoying the respect of the middle and working classes, while also retaining recognition from the landed society (7–8). As Gilmour writes, the idea of the gentleman "answered to the conflicting needs of the nascent middle classes in the eighteenth and nineteenth centuries, their desire to be accepted by the traditional hierarchy and at the same time to make their impact upon it" (9).

Hence, when Robert states that a detective is "stained with vile associations, and unfit company for honest gentlemen," he aims to create distance between a morally ambivalent figure and his own claims to gentlemanly status. Robert is the heir presumptive to Sir Michael Audley's baronetcy and estate, but is a barrister by training (though he does not practice law). He represents a fluid upper-middle class, with claims to aristocratic rank. As Rae scoffed in his 1865 review of the novel, Robert's "favorite amusements are smoking German pipes and reading French novels," while "he is a barrister by profession, and briefless by choice" (183). The two words most commonly associated with Robert in the novel are "lazy" and "gentleman." He is introduced as "a handsome, lazy, care-for-nothing fellow, of about seven-and-twenty; the only son of a younger brother of Sir Michael Audley" (Braddon, *Lady* 32). He is not ambitious, self-interested, or designing, in contrast to Lady Audley, who comes to represent the vices of selfishness, personal ambition, and lack of empathy associated with the vulgar working class. Robert is described as having "the lymphatic nature of [a] gentleman," perpetually idle with a "listless, dawdling, indifferent, irresolute manner" (Braddon, *Lady* 33–34). Robert is, Braddon writes, "a man who would never get on in the world; but who would not hurt a worm" (Braddon, *Lady* 33).

Robert represents a gentlemanly character, at odds with the more morally suspect figure of the detective, because he embodies, to borrow Gilmour's words, "respectability and independence within the traditional social hierarchy" while "challeng[ing] the dignity of the work which made the new industrial society possible" (7). Put differently, Robert has claims to both the respect of the landed class, as well as the middle and working classes, but exudes a leisurely idleness that represents freedom from economic constraint. He may not be morally excellent, but he seems far too lazy to be the mean or tyrannical bully that Smiles argued was the antithesis of the gentleman. Robert has an air of professionalism and indeed claims to derive his deductive process from the legal profession, despite being a non-practicing barrister. He maintains distance from the demands of actual work, manifesting a bourgeois ideal of professional achievement alongside leisurely satisfaction. In shifting towards a detective role, he casts himself as "an idle *flâneur* upon the smooth pathways that have no particular goal," rather than a determined investigator (Braddon, *Lady* 372). Hence, the "social ambiguity" of the gentleman also ironically allows for the fluid movement of the detective (Gilmour 3). While the work ethic of a detective evokes labor, dubious connections, and moral ambivalence, Robert aims to maintain a distance from these inferior associations, even as he emerges as a knower of compromising secrets.

Before discussing how detective work reveals contradictions in Robert's character, it is worth noting that it is only because Robert is a *flâneur* and idle gentleman that he has the time and resources to travel across England to investigate Lady Audley's past. As a member of the professional class, he can project authority in urban, working-class neighborhoods, such as Brigsome's Terrace and Crescent Villas. He can visit Grange Heath and the pier at Wildernsea, as his comfortable income and freedom from work grant him greater mobility to investigate Lady Audley's history. As a man of social status, he is able to talk with and question strangers in a way that indeed no respectable woman would have been able in mid-nineteenth-century England. Even as he pursues clues into Lady Audley's past, however, he complains about the disruption to "the usual lazy monotony of his life . . . broken as it had never been broken before in eight-and-twenty tranquil, easy-going years" (Braddon, *Lady* 86). What matters even more than credible detective work is the maintenance of a self-contained and gentlemanly aura, as Braddon likely sensed in her novel.

Justifications for dubious detective work

As earlier noted, Robert hesitates and struggles to justify his pursuit into Lady Audley's past. He torturously questions,

> Should I be justified in doing this? Should I be justified in letting the chain which I have slowly put together, link by link, drop at this point, or must I go on adding fresh links to that fatal chain until the last rivet drops into its place and the circle is complete?
>
> (Braddon, *Lady* 135)

Part of the reason for Robert's hesitation is the anticipated rupture in his uncle's family and, by extension, a destabilization of the social order. Robert understands that his investigations will lead to "sorrow and disgrace" among those whom he loves (Braddon, *Lady* 181). But he is also averse to "the office of spy, the collector of damning facts" that would bring his uncle to ill repute (Braddon, *Lady* 222). Without an external justification, Robert potentially becomes a disruptive force, severing social bonds in an antagonistic and troublesome way. He becomes the antithesis of the gentlemanly character as sketched above. To investigate a married woman's private life, without the consent of her husband, is also more befitting of a "scoundrel" in the words of one character in Collins's *Armadale* (441). As this character states,

> if a man made private inquiries into a lady's affairs, without being either her husband, her father, or her brother, he subjected himself to the responsibility of justifying his conduct in the estimation of others; and if he evaded that responsibility, he abdicated the position of gentleman.
>
> (Collins, *Armadale* 423)

Clearly, there is a tension between Robert's claims to gentlemanly status here and the narrative compulsion for him to conduct detective work, even if it means surveilling a married woman, who is normatively and legally under her husband's protection. Braddon locates this justification in three "duties." The first duty is Robert's friendship and attachment to his missing friend, George Talboys, who is also described as a "gentleman." Even in accounts about his desertion of his wife, he is related as a "gentleman [who] ran away to Australia, and left the lady, a week or two after her baby was born" (Braddon, *Lady* 208). Such references betray the definitional looseness of the word "gentleman," but they contribute to a juxtaposition between a socially mobile, female threat and a simultaneously amorphous but recognizable group of "gentlemen." Again, Luke Marks states his impression of George as a gentleman in similarly vague terms. Luke says, "There was something' in the way he spoke that told me he was a gentleman, though I didn't know him from Adam, and could see his face" (Braddon, *Lady* 360). The social mobility and leisureliness of the gentleman is framed against a bigamous female threat, as such opportunistic behavior and deceit must be reinscribed under the patriarchal order. The social bond and trust between the gentlemen Robert and George become homosocial, with George confessing at the end of the novel that he had "yearned for the strong grasp of your hand, Bob; the friendly touch of the hand which had guided me through the darkest passage of my life" (Braddon, *Lady* 378).[2] But this justification for detective work remains insufficient, since it does not seem to warrant a disruption of the social order and intrusion into his baronet uncle's private affairs.

A second duty that justifies detective work arises with the appearance of George's sister, Clara Talboys, with whom Robert Audley becomes infatuated and later marries. Robert's loyalty to Clara means that detective work transforms into a heavy-hearted acceptance of moral duty, rather than prying or mischievous behavior. The astute reader sees a contradiction here in Robert's character in the midst of justifying detective work. While Robert had been cast as almost immune to feminine charms, such that the idea of his falling in love seems "preposterous," his affection for Clara seems to surmount his idle indisposition (Braddon, *Lady* 53). He becomes obsessed with the "sublime" image of Clara, resolving to "keep [his] promise" to her and seek her brother's revenge (Braddon, *Lady* 193, 204). His emotional attachment to Clara seems more narrative necessity, rather than consistent with his initial character. Despite his apparent desire to extricate himself from the mystery, Robert finds himself recalling Clara's pleading expression. Braddon writes, "Could he stop now? For any consideration? No; a thousand times no! Not with the image of that grief-stricken face imprinted on his mind. Not with the accents of that earnest appeal ringing on his ear" (*Lady* 193). Robert becomes inconsistently susceptible to ideas of divine duty and providence, intuiting "God's hand in this strange story" and envisioning Clara, "with an imperious gesture, beckon[ing] him onwards to her brother's unknown grave" (Braddon, *Lady* 216). She appears, in a moment of sheer coincidence, to spur him to his purpose, appealing, "You will not suffer my brother's fate to remain a mystery . . . I know that you will do your duty to your friend" (Braddon, *Lady* 222). These contradictions in Robert's character development arise from the unwieldly alliance between a gentleman acting as a detective, or, put differently, the moral ambivalence of the detective. The detective does not have the same claims to respectability and moral principles that the gentleman has, and, in attempting to fashion Robert as both gentleman and detective, Braddon allows for such inconsistencies in his behavior. As earlier noted, Robert requires an external motivation and duty to perform such morally questionable work, even where it means the exposure of a covert moral threat.

The third duty that Robert subscribes to in his justification of morally ambivalent detective work is Lady Audley's increasingly dangerous, erratic, and mentally unstable behavior. Lady Audley comes to represents the combination of "the three demons of Vanity, Selfishness, and Ambition," which must be purged from the social body (Braddon, *Lady* 253). She is driven by "the horrible egotism of her own misery," unable to feel even the redeeming impulse of maternal affection (Braddon, *Lady* 263). As she exclaims,

> I can feel nothing but my own misery. . . . I am selfish still – more selfish than ever in my misery. Happy, prosperous people may feel for others. I laugh at other people's sufferings; they seem so small compared to my own.
>
> (Braddon, *Lady* 295)

More damningly, she confesses that she "did not love" her son, who had been "left a burden upon [her] hands" (Braddon, *Lady* 300). Again, as in *Bleak House*, one sees a clear double standard between uncaring fathers (such as Mr Talboys) and uncaring mothers (like Lady Audley). But Braddon prevents Lady Audley from becoming a victim in her own right, like Lady Dedlock of *Bleak House*, by casting her as mentally unstable. Leveraging the taboos and misconceptions surrounding mental illnesses at the time, Braddon has Lady Audley diagnosed by a male doctor within a ten-minute interview. Doctor Mosgrave concludes, "The lady is not mad; but she has the hereditary taint in her blood. She has the cunning of madness, with the prudence of intelligence. . . . She is dangerous!" (Braddon, *Lady* 323). Adding to his medical assessment, he states, "as a physiologist and as an honest man I believe you could do no better service to society" than by sending her to an overseas sanatorium, "shut[ting] her from the world and all worldly associations" (Braddon, *Lady* 324). Robert's detective work becomes a "service to society," sanctioned by science, to contain the moral and pathological contagion that Lady Audley represents.

Even as he conducts an investigation into Lady Audley's past, he repeats that he does so not out of malicious intent or corrosive curiosity. He states that it is his "destiny" and that he is "relentlessly . . . carried on" (Braddon, *Lady* 147, 172). Robert says, "It is not myself; it is the hand which is beckoning me further and further upon the dark road whose end I dare not dream of" (Braddon, *Lady* 147). Again, he says, "A hand which is stronger than my own beckons me on. . . . I must go on; I must go on" (Braddon, *Lady* 148). These pretensions to helpless passivity are at odds with Robert's earlier idle and leisurely character. But Robert must at least claim that he is not initiating the detective inquiry, but that he is following an externally determined and pre-ordained fate, to avoid criticisms of troublesome behavior. In order not to be cast as unlikeable, Robert must claim that "this awful responsibility has been forced upon [him]" (Braddon, *Lady* 313). But this does not detract from the feeling of power, as pointed out by other critics, that he relishes from uncovering Lady Audley's secret and from "reading" her as he would a book (Braddon, *Lady* 185). Lady Audley concedes defeat when she declares, "you have conquered, Mr Robert Audley. It is a great triumph, is it not? a wonderful victory! You have used your cool, calculating, frigid, luminous intellect to a noble purpose" (Braddon, *Lady* 294). As the narrator underscores, in this intellectual game of cards, "[Lady Audley's] opponent's hand had been too powerful for her, and he had won" (Braddon, *Lady* 316). Whatever protestations Robert may make to the contrary, detective work becomes a political contest that involves an inferior reading of the other.

Altogether, Braddon uses various claims to duty – ranging from Robert's obligation to his friend, his infatuation with Clara, and society's protection against a "dangerous" woman – to legitimize an investigation that would otherwise render Robert a morally ambivalent character (Braddon, *Lady* 323). Robert continues to worry about the fallout, recognizing that he would become the agent by whom "the most important personage in the parish of Audley" would be disgraced (Braddon, *Lady* 222). The convoluted negotiations involved in this narrative may have prompted Braddon to outsource such detective work to a professional detective in her subsequent novel, *Aurora Floyd*, due to its morally dubious and suspicious associations. But eventually, Robert becomes a patriarchal authority in his own right by the novel's end. With the separation between his uncle and Lady Audley, and the withdrawal of Sir Audley from the narrative, Robert becomes the *de facto* patriarch of Audley Court. Sir Audley regards him as his son and leaves the estate in his care. Robert also remains heir presumptive to Sir Audley's baronetcy and estate, unthreatened by any issue that Lady Audley might have otherwise had. (This may also have been another reason why his detective work might have seemed potentially self-serving and ungentlemanly.) By the end of the novel, Robert has become a husband and father, reinstating a sense of domestic tranquility in the place of familial separation and disruption. Braddon makes a series of compromises and negotiations in this novel that undermine the consistency of Robert's character, but salvages him from the morally dubious associations with detective work, even as he emerges triumphant from his discoveries.

Detection as discursive interpretation

A major development in the detection process in *Lady Audley's Secret* is a method of circumstantial reasoning that reinforces the detective's authority. While considerations of time and space had been evident in *The Woman in White* – a novel that Braddon later described as an inspiration for her novel (see Lycett, *Wilkie* 235) – the process of deduction in *Lady Audley's Secret* becomes much more clearly associated with a set of material facts. The culmination of "infinitesimal trifles" may reveal "the whole secret of some wicked mystery, inexplicable heretofore to the wisest upon the earth" (Braddon, *Lady* 107). These trifles may range from

> a scrap of paper; a shred of some torn garment; the button of a coat; a word dropped incautiously from the over-cautious lips of guilt; the fragment of a letter; the shutting or opening of a door; a shadow on a window-blind.
>
> (Braddon, *Lady* 107)

In contrast to *The Woman in White*, Robert in *Lady Audley's Secret* asserts this methodical process of reasoning, from material evidence, as a form of power and interpretation. What emerges is the identification of an empirical mode of reasoning that becomes distinctively masculine. The forging of a "chain of circumstantial evidence" aims to constrain a woman, whose own excess of mental activity seems to threaten her sanity (see Braddon, *Lady* 188, 214, 221).

This methodical process of reasoning, based on circumstantial evidence, is derived in part from Robert's legal profession. Even though Robert has, by his confession, "never practiced as a barrister," he lays claim to its principles of deduction and inductive reasoning (Braddon, *Lady* 106). He derives the "theory of circumstantial evidence" from legal practice and examines characters as if they were potential witnesses in a "cross-examination" (Braddon, *Lady* 107, 117–18). As earlier noted, there runs a consistent parallel between the legal profession and detective work in the sensation novels. Robert declares that "a thousand circumstances" can become "links of steel in the wonderful chain forged by the science of the detective officer" (Braddon, *Lady* 107). He claims to be "able to draw a conclusion by induction," intuiting from rather obvious clues that his cousin Alicia has received a marriage proposal (Braddon, *Lady* 110). As earlier noted, Robert lays claims to the prestige and merits of his legal profession, even as he maintains a distance from its labor and constraints. Robert is a gentlemanly *flâneur* not only in his perspective on life, but also in conveniently treading the boundaries between the professional class and more leisurely aristocracy.

What emerges from this elevated mode of reasoning is a particular discursive and framing strategy. Robert attempts to "read" Lady Audley, prying into her thoughts as though she were a compliant book (Braddon, *Lady* 185). Similarly, Lady Audley tries to "read the innermost secrets" of Robert's mind, which builds a narrative tension between them (Braddon,

Lady 220–21). Detective work and reading are closely allied in this novel, as Robert collects documents and material evidence in his pocket-book, and stores them in a pigeon-hole in his office desk. He takes notes during his investigations in a memorandum-book, leaving observers with an impression of the "solemnity and importance which pervaded [the] business" (Braddon, *Lady* 208). But reading and documentation also extend to interpreting the other, framing them within a desired context. The gathering of clues and rearrangement of signs gesture to an attempt to authoritatively interpret a person, and to scrutinize and subject them to a knowing gaze. As Sally Shuttleworth points out,

> detective fiction . . . is premised . . . on a form of symptomatic reading: the skilled eye of the detective, like that of the doctor, unlocks of the details of external form invisible to the untrained eye, which reveal the secret history hidden below.
>
> (46)

Yet Robert cannot succeed in his investigation, while protecting his reputation and likeability as a character, without Lady Audley's compliance and confession. He can only weave a coherent narrative from circumstantial evidence *with* her concession and acknowledgment about his truth and authority. Lady Audley must admit defeat and accept Robert's authority for him to emerge as a hero. She eventually concedes, "you have conquered – a madwoman," owing to his "cool, calculating, frigid, luminous intellect" (Braddon, *Lady* 294). This contrasts with Sir Audley's earlier assessment that Robert was "a little stupid" and Alicia's criticism that he is "a sluggish ditch-pond of an intellect," but these contradictions show the variable pressures on Robert's character as he evolves as a detective (Braddon, *Lady* 243, 281). Robert's intellect in this case is contrasted with Lady Audley's cunning, as she reflects that her "worst wickednesses [*sic*] have been the result of wild impulses, and not of deeply-laid plots" (Braddon, *Lady* 253). The process of forcibly reading and framing a character through detective work leads to what Caroline Reitz has called the "acquisition and centralization of 'local knowledge'" in Victorian detective stories (xxii–xxiii). As R. Thomas has also said, "lawyers [may] literally write the terms in which 'questions of identity' can be asked and answered" (*Detective* 63). The detective embodies masculine rationality, with a veneer of scientific legitimacy, framed against female madness and mental incapacity. Hence, the novel follows the same trajectory noted earlier in Dickens, namely, the vindication and reassertion of male authority over miscreant deviance.

Lady Audley is cast as a child-like character, innately "selfish" and "sensuous," and incapable of sustained rational calculation (Braddon, *Lady* 271). By casting Lady Audley as a child-like character, Braddon

seems to anticipate her discipline through the reinstatement of the patriarchal order.[3] Her excessive self-interest justifies her incarceration and isolation, perhaps more so than her attempted crime. Lady Audley must be
removed from society because she does not display the moral or feminine
virtues of maternal care, selflessness, and devotion. The detective not only
reveals criminal behavior, but also punishes moral deviance and casts out
scapegoats. The criminalization of a self-promoting woman in *Lady Audley's Secret* points to the cultural force of the Victorian ideology, as shaping market trends and literary output. But even though Braddon suggests
that madness is associated with great intellect – Sir Audley states that "it's
generally your great intellects that get out of order" (Braddon, *Lady* 243) –
Lady Audley's insanity is depicted as moral weakness and overextended
mental activity. After her confession to Sir Audley, Lady Audley begs to
be taken away to sleep as her "brain is on fire" (Braddon, *Lady* 311).
She describes "the blood surging up to [her] brain" in moments when she
devises criminal schemes (Braddon, *Lady* 304). Her face glows with an
"unnatural crimson" and her eyes with "unnatural luster" as she resolves
on action (Braddon, *Lady* 266). This mental disintegration contrasts with
Robert's mental skill in deducting and refining inferences based on circumstantial evidence. The detective process is uniquely posited as masculine
activity, in contrast to and to counterbalance feminine hysteria.

But if detective work amounts to an authoritative act of interpretation,
there are also other, obscured ways in which to read Lady Audley's character. An alternative narrative is indeed hinted at by another male professional, Doctor Mosgrave, who states that Lady Audley had "found herself
in a desperate position" and "employed intelligent means" to escape her
situation (Braddon, *Lady* 321). In this more sympathetic reading of her
past, he says that "she carried out a conspiracy which required coolness
and deliberation in its execution. There is no madness in that" (Braddon,
Lady 321). Doctor Mosgrave later revises his assessment after a private
interview with her, but this is certainly a credible reading of her character.
As Sussex notes, "every crime of Lady Audley's stems from a perfectly
sane self-interest" (91). Taylor and Crofts also note that "her crimes . . .
are committed for the sanest of motives," and that her mental illness reads
as "a *deus ex machina* solution" (xxv). In this alternative reading of her
past, Lady Audley may be interpreted as a resourceful, if unscrupulous,
woman born into poverty. Robert demonstrates little sympathy for the
poor, even as he traverses the impoverished neighborhoods of Brigsome's
Terrace and the Crescent Villas. Visiting such places does not afford him
with insight into Lady Audley's character or determination, even as he
sees "the poverty-stricken locality" and the "hopeless masses of stone and
plaster on every side" in these areas (Braddon, *Lady* 139, 194). Robert
expresses little regard for Lady Audley, even though she had been deserted

by her husband and left to live as "a slave allied for ever to beggary and obscurity" (Braddon, *Lady* 300). As Lady Audley rightly states, "You and your nephew, Sir Michael, have been rich all your lives, and can very well afford to despise me; but I knew how far poverty can affect a life" (Braddon, *Lady* 299).

Lady Audley pointedly adds that, after three years' absence, she had "a right to think that [her first husband was] dead," and divorce laws in the early 1860s would have indeed allowed this as a basis for a formal separation if she could have afforded the procedure (Braddon, *Lady* 301). Emma Griffin points out that "desertion, as opposed to death, was so serious" for working-class families because it "closed down the possibility of remarriage" (*Bread Winner* 151). As Griffin points out, "bigamy carried heavy penalties" and could result in prosecution in addition to public shame (E. Griffin, *Bread Winner* 152). Lady Audley's pleas for sympathy under these circumstances fall on deaf ears, however, as the conservative inclination in this sensation novel tends towards the cleansing of social deviants. Detective work interpretatively frames and morally situates perceived miscreants to shore up the interests of a particular group (in this case, upper- and middle-class men). Robert assumes that Lady Audley can conveniently "run away," but Lady Audley realizes that she has nowhere to run to and no money (Braddon, *Lady* 181). Ultimately, Lady Audley's mental illness becomes a scapegoat for Robert and Sir Audley to maintain their emotional distance and withhold sympathy.

As demonstrated, there are other ways of reading and interpreting Lady Audley's character, but Robert, as a detective, frames her as selfish, deceptive, and manipulative. Such an account is presented as objective and impartial, based on empirical evidence, rather than a construction of knowledge reinforcing existent power structures. The gender double standard, seen in earlier novels, is also evident in *Lady Audley's Secret*. Sir Audley does not attract suspicion for falling in love with a "childish" and "capricious" woman who appears little "more than seventeen," at his age of fifty-five (see Braddon, *Lady* 50–54). Nor is there any acknowledged irony in Sir Audley appearing to have been willingly deceived by her, through a "voluntary confidence in involuntary distrust" (Braddon, *Lady* 300). Neither is George chastised or punished for having deserted his wife and newborn son, without sending her any letters for three years. Instead, the entire case is, in Robert's words, "all women's work from one end to the other" (Braddon, *Lady* 178). George is cast as the victim of a cruel and heartless woman, while Robert declares himself the helpless agent of "another woman," Clara (Braddon, *Lady* 178). Robert makes overtures to objective knowledge while covertly asserting his interpretative version of events. He guides the reader in how the narrative should be read and understood, maintaining that Lady Audley was "the most detestable and despicable of her sex – the most pitiless and calculating of human creatures" (Braddon, *Lady* 228–29). Male culpability is condoned, while blame is conveniently shifted to self-interested women. Male characters assume little responsibility and instead complete glory for the restoration of the social order.

The selective framing of the narrative and free indirect discourse support the interpretative authority of the detective. Throughout the novel, the reader is made privy to Robert's thought processes, while they are effectively shielded from Lady Audley's apparently insane impulses. In the moments when Lady Audley seems to act impulsively, the reader is shown only her outward features. The reader sees her complexion change and the "overpowering excitement" in her appearance, but they are kept at a safe distance from her mental processes (Braddon, *Lady* 266). The reader gains an understanding of Robert's "hundred doubts and perplexities," but they are encouraged to view Lady Audley as a dangerous and mentally unstable character (Braddon, *Lady* 220). Lady Audley's apparent madness interposes an even greater distance, as she becomes incomprehensibly other to the reader. When she attempts to murder Robert, Lady Audley's removal and confinement becomes justified, just as her separation from Sir Audley becomes a social and moral necessity. Detective work entails a gymnastic feat of contradictions and tensions, as confronted by Robert, but allows for the convenient scapegoating and expulsion of a deranged and sexually experienced woman. The method of circumstantial reasoning plays into this discursive strategy, which elevates the detective's mental authority over female irrationality.

Notes

1 For studies of the Victorian gentleman in the late nineteenth century, from 1870 to 1901, see (Waters).
2 For more on male homosociality in *Lady Audley's Secret*, see (Nemesvari).
3 For more on Lady Audley's child-like depiction, see (Taylor and Crofts vii; Russett 55).

7   Oriental mystique and spying servants in Braddon's *Aurora Floyd*

In *Lady Audley's Secret*, Braddon had negotiated contradictory tensions over her main character, Robert Audley, to cast him both as a detective and as a gentleman. While both the detective and the gentleman were fluid and socially ambiguous figures, the gentleman was distinguished from the detective in his recognized claims to respectability and trustworthiness. In *Aurora Floyd*, written alongside the serialization of *Lady Audley's Secret*, Braddon effectively delegates the morally compromising work of investigation to a professional detective, Mr Joseph Grimstone of Scotland Yard. But Mr Grimstone does not feature as a major character nor as a hero in the novel. While Mr Grimstone gathers information and evidence to reveal a servant as a murderer, it is another male character, Mr Talbot Bulstrode, who claims the heroism of sudden revelation. As Braddon writes, "Talbot Bulstrode had been the captor" of the murderer in his physical confrontation with the humpback servant Stephen Hargraves (*Aurora* 459). *Aurora Floyd* shines light on the development of the detective, even as it significantly casts criminality through an imperial lens. The novel recasts the representation of wrongdoing and transgression against the social order through the imbrication of imperial and patriarchal discourses.

Aurora Floyd appeared in Maxwell's monthly magazine *Temple Bar* between January 1862 and January 1863, overlapping with the serialization of *Lady Audley's Secret* in the *Sixpenny Magazine* between January to December 1862. The book form of *Lady Audley's Secret* appeared in October 1862, followed only three months later by the book publication of *Aurora Floyd* in January 1863. *Aurora Floyd* received praise from critics, including Oliphant, who described it as "a very clever story . . . well knit together, thoroughly interesting, and full of life" ("Novels" 263). Oliphant wrote that the novel was "certainly not of a high description, but . . . genuine in its way," adding that "few people with any appreciation of fiction could refuse to be attracted by a tale so well defined" ("Novels" 263).[1] One of the more striking features about *Aurora Floyd* is its allusions to the Indian Mutiny of 1857, as the novel imaginatively welds the image

DOI: 10.4324/9781003369622-8

of a bigamous wife with imperial anxieties.[2] To be sure, spying servants also feature in other sensation novels (see Trodd, *Domestic Crime* 45–68), but the difference in this sensation novel is that their disobedience and treachery are given colonial overtones. In casting the bigamous wife and the scheming servants as dissenters, *Aurora Floyd* evokes the recent memory of the Indian Mutiny to dramatic effect.

The initial threat posed to the social order is Aurora Floyd, who is cast as an Orientalized, Eastern character, even though she is racially English. Aurora is repeatedly exoticized in Eastern terms, varyingly described as "Cleopatra," "a black-eyed queen," a "tartar," a "Sultana," an "Egyptian goddess," an "Assyrian queen," and the Babylonian queen Semiramide (Braddon, *Aurora* 67, 129, 217, 260, 386).[3] She is described as an untamed force of nature, a mystical being, akin to a "black-eyed sorceress" (Braddon, *Aurora* 152). Such stylizations were obviously influenced by Braddon's earlier sensational work and theatrical background (see Pedlar), but this exoticization of a female threat to the patriarchal order reveals how sensation novelists intuited the commercial potential of layering imperial anxieties with domestic social concerns. Such imperial nuances would also appear in subsequent sensation novels, most notably Collins's *The Moonstone*, but also Doyle's *fin-de-siècle* story *The Sign of the Four*. Against this exoticized and mythized figure, Mr Bulstrode stands as a bastion of English masculinity. He not only resists Aurora's charms, which threaten to "enslave" him, but also defeats the murderer Hargraves (see Braddon, *Aurora* 33). In defeating this treacherous servant, Mr Bulstrode is cast as "the heir of all the Bulstrodes, the commander of squadrons of horses, the man who had done battle with bloodthirsty Sikhs" (Braddon, *Aurora* 454). He is simultaneously heir to a wealthy line of Cornish baronets and also an experienced fighter in imperial wars. Though he is not a detective hero, the culmination of a detective's discovery legitimizes his triumph over a social threat.

The subsequent threat posed to the social order, after Aurora, stems from two household servants, Mrs Walter Powell and Hargraves. Even though Aurora is initially depicted as suspicious and rebellious, she becomes subsumed within the patriarchal order after her exposure and humiliation. The first detective characters in the novel are these two servants, who act as spies within the Mellish family household. Mrs Powell's detective work is privately motivated by envy and hatred for Aurora and her husband. Mrs Powell "[gropes] in mazy darknesses which baffled her utmost powers of penetrations" to find the "clue to the mystery" of her mistress's past (Braddon, *Aurora* 199). She tries to find "some link in the mysterious chain she was so anxious to fix together" through clues in Aurora's behavior (Braddon, *Aurora* 203). Altogether, detective work underscores Mrs Powell's "ignorant and soulless and low-minded and vulgar" character, tainted with a "diseased curiosity" (Braddon, *Aurora* 51, 183). Rachel Smillie points out that that Mrs Powell seems to bear an "unnatural, animalistic quality [that] positions her as an almost monstrous figure," since she undermines the Victorian domestic ideology through her "household espionage" (12). Mrs Powell's desire for private knowledge and incriminating details about her employer decisively casts her as a troublesome, self-serving, and suspicious antagonist. Similarly, Hargraves is motivated by resentment, "nursing discontent and hatred" against Aurora for banishing him from Mellish Park (Braddon, *Aurora* 141). Hargraves represents a mortal threat to patriarchal authority, embodying a chorus of discontent that seems to match "the slanderous tongues of a greedy public . . . swelling into a loud and ominous murmur against the wife John [Mellish] loved" (Braddon, *Aurora* 450).

The similitude between the servants and the spy in the novel highlights an uncomfortable anxiety of the Victorian middle-class household. As Trodd points out, the Victorian middle-class depended on domestic service drawn from the working class.[4] Trodd writes in *Domestic Crime in the Victorian Novel* that "servants were necessary to define the household's status" in the mid-nineteenth century (51). This sat uncomfortably with the middle-class values of privacy and separation from the working class. In *Aurora Floyd*, Braddon explores a mutiny of class distinctions, drawing particularly on the anxiety that live-in servants could double as spies on their employers. Trodd observes that servants could be "perceived as the weak link in the maintenance of the privacy of the home, both as internal intruders and as publicists to the outside world" (*Domestic Crime* 8). Domestic servants ironically made the middle-class aspiration a possibility, but also implicated the family in a wider social network that could potentially involve morally compromising connections. The transformation of servants into spies in *Aurora Floyd* plays on the anxiety that the middle-class household might not be as insulated from external social influences as they might have wished to believe. Simultaneously, the novel reveals how, through their very inclusion in the narrative as agentive characters, the middle-class ideal depended on the invisibility of domestic workers in the functioning of the household. In an ideal middle-class household, servants do not bear mentioning. As Trodd notes, "servants do not in general play prominent roles in Victorian novels; the one area of fiction where they routinely assume high visibility is in plots and sub-plots involving crime" (*Domestic Crime* 46). Their very inclusion as agents in *Aurora Floyd* exposes the contradiction on which the middle-class ideal was premised, namely, the concealment of working-class labor and inter-class social relations.

In *Aurora Floyd*, the professional detective Mr Grimstone helps resolve the narrative ambiguity before the novel stages Mr Bulstrode's triumph over Hargraves. Mr Grimstone is a detective from the Metropolitan Police

Force, who appears to have little private interest in divulging secrets at Mellish Park. He has a "business-like composure in his manner . . . entirely different to the eager curiosity of a scandalmonger and a busybody" (Braddon, *Aurora* 412). The detective exhibits a professionalism distinguished from the servants' prying manner. Braddon sings the praises of London detectives, writing that "these men are very clever; some significant circumstance, forgotten by those most interested in discovering the truth, would often be enough to set a detective on the right track" (Braddon, *Aurora* 417). Yet the detective is principally a mercenary and functional character in the narrative, whose primary interest is a "sublunary reward," rather than "love of justice" (Braddon, *Aurora* 436). Indeed, it is Mr Bulstrode (rather than Mr Grimstone) who discovers Hargraves attempting to steal money from Mellish Park, even though he "liberally" rewards the detective for his work (Braddon, *Aurora* 459). Braddon resolves the moral ambiguity of detective work by separating the investigative work from its heroic resolution. Braddon chooses not to compromise her main male character, distancing him from investigative work even as she allows him to take full credit for the crime's resolution.

In what follows, I explore the exoticized representation of a female threat and the corresponding English identity that offsets such social destabilization. I outline the ways in which Aurora is exoticized and Mr Bulstrode is cast as an English hero, before turning to the detective work conducted by the servants. Such investigations were imbued with the memory of the recent Sepoy Rebellion (of which more in Chapter 1), which reinforces contact-points between the imperial discourse and patriarchal ideology. While this study does not principally delve into representations of femininity and womanhood in sensation novels (which have already been covered by numerous other scholars), the construction of the Other shapes the sense of English identity. The masculine hero does not exist in a vacuum, but responds to and counteracts the effects of the deviant other. In this case, the bigamous wife also becomes an exoticized threat. Even though there is no consistent detective hero in this novel, *Aurora Floyd* reveals ambivalent aspects of detective work, simultaneously aligned with treachery and professionalism. The ambivalence of detective work means that the masculine hero, as in Wood's *East Lynne*, benefits from the revelation and punishes the criminal, without sullying his own hands in the process of tracing and questioning characters. Detective work is separated between its morally ambiguous (but necessary) process and the final, triumphant resolution.

An exoticized female threat and male English rationality

In the early chapters of the novel, Aurora is depicted as an "Eastern empress" who threatens to undermine Mr Bulstrode's reason (Braddon,

Aurora 41). Aurora not only behaves like an Eastern empress, but also dresses like one. She wears a "diamond bracelet, worth a couple of hundred pounds" given by her father, as well as an opera cloak of "a voluminous drapery of soft scarlet woollen stuff" (Braddon, *Aurora* 35, 67). Her father, Mr Archibald Floyd, is said to have "very nearly as much money as Aladdin" and could produce "dishes of uncut diamonds" (Braddon, *Aurora* 215). Even though she does not appear racially different from other English women, she is constantly described as a "Cleopatra" (Braddon, *Aurora* 65, 131, 213), a "jewel beyond all parallel" (Braddon, *Aurora* 131), a "dark-haired goddess" (Braddon, *Aurora* 42), and "the wicked enchantress, the soulless siren" (Braddon, *Aurora* 152). Her black eyes are her most distinctive feature, which are dramatized through such descriptions of her as "the black-eyed sorceress" (Braddon, *Aurora* 152), "a black-eyed queen" (Braddon, *Aurora* 260), and a "black-browed divinity" (Braddon, *Aurora* 399). Aurora is also described as an "Assyrian queen, with . . . flashing eyes and the serpentine coils of purple-black hair" (Braddon, *Aurora* 217). She is cast as a tragic, imperious, and mythical figure, drawing upon theatrical representations of the East. Braddon indeed compares her to prominent actresses, such as Louisa Cranstoun Nisbett, Lola Montez, and Nell Gwyn (*Aurora* 47). Aurora also represents an uninhibited force of nature, seeming like "some beautiful, noisy, boisterous waterfall; for ever dancing, rushing, sparkling, scintillating, and utterly defying you to do anything but admire it" (Braddon, *Aurora* 74–75).

The effect of this Eastern empress on Mr Bulstrode is to almost enslave his masculine rationality. Mr Bustrolde fights an inner battle between reason, which recognizes Lucy Floyd's suitability as a wife, and his instinctive fascination with Aurora. Braddon writes, "The very battle [Mr Bulstrode] was fighting kept [Aurora] for ever in his mind, until he grew the verist slave of the lovely vision, which he only evoked in order to endeavor to exorcise" (*Aurora* 55). His initial infatuation with Aurora reminds him of an Indian drug (possibly cannabis), that he had previously tasted, which was said to make "the men who drank it half mad" (Braddon, *Aurora* 33). Mr Bulstrode compares the allure of Aurora's beauty with "the strength of that alcoholic preparation; barbarous, intoxicating, dangerous, and maddening" (Braddon, *Aurora* 33). From early in the novel, Aurora represents a threat to English masculinity, threatening to undermine its integrity and rationality. Braddon makes clear that Mr Bulstrode's "strength of brain lay in the reflective faculties," compared to John Mellish's (Aurora's eventual husband) strong "power of perception" (*Aurora* 142). Mr Bulstrode stands, as critics have noted, as "the exemplar of tradition and power" (Schroeder and Schroeder 81), but he is also conscious of threats to his family prestige should his future wife have him "dragged through the mire of a divorce court" (Braddon, *Aurora* 33). He is keenly aware of the danger that a future wife could wreak on his values of family pride and respectable lineage. Later, Braddon has both John and Aurora Mellish turn to Mr Bulstrode for moral support and guidance, reinforcing the conservative tendency of the novel. The implication is that Mr Bulstrode represents a stoic and traditional English morality that has almost come undone by, but resisted Aurora and her secret past. Aurora's Oriental exoticization is primarily meaningful in that it threatens to undo Mr Bulstrode's traditional values and morality. Mr Bulstrode's path to heroism thus requires him to withstand Aurora's charms and marry her character opposite, Lucy, since in doing so, he preserves his masculine authority and superior rationality.

In the novel, Mr Bulstrode represents stoic English morality as a man of "Saxon extraction," who seeks nothing less than to protect and uphold his "pride of birth" (Braddon, *Aurora* 31, 68). He also reveals, shortly before wrestling Hargraves, that he served as a military commander in colonial India. He had been "accustomed to deal with refractory Sepoys in India" and had "done battle with bloodthirsty Sikhs," direct references to the Sepoy Rebellion of 1857 (Braddon, *Aurora* 454). As part of his masculine heroism, Mr Bulstrode claims that he has also "struggle[d] with a tiger before," when pitted against the "savage terror" of Hargraves, who seems "more repulsive, than the ugliest of the lower animals" (Braddon, *Aurora* 453–54). Mr Bulstrode is not only "Captain of Her Majesty's 11th Hussars," he is also heir to a long-established Cornish baronetcy (Braddon, *Aurora* 30). Despite his infatuation with Aurora, he refuses to marry a woman who might compromise his morals or traditional values. Even as he finds Lucy "pretty [and] inanimate," he recognizes that she is "exactly the sort of woman to make a good wife" (Braddon, *Aurora* 48, 64). Indeed, when Lucy marries Mr Bulstrode, she is (in contrast to Aurora) submissive and unopinionated, considering "whatever Talbot did [to be] right" (Braddon, *Aurora* 93).

One sees here the themes of Eastern mysticism and intrigue working their way into sensation fiction and early detective fiction. The themes of drugs and their effect on psychology are alluded to here, without taking on the extensive imaginative scope of Collins's *The Moonstone*. In *Aurora Floyd*, the trauma of a colonial uprising is reimagined, not only to suggest the dangers of a woman's concealed past, but also the fear of potential social disintegration. As Saverio Tomaiuolo has pointed out, Aurora is specifically associated with India, which, only a few years before the novel's serialization, had witnessed a rebellion. Tomaiuolo observes that the Indian Mutiny was also represented as a feminized threat, especially through the figure of Rani Lakshmi Bai of Jhansi, the queen of a North Indian state (see also Tange, "Picturing"). The Sepoy Rebellion correspondingly inspired fears of "unchecked female sexuality," which in turn "reinforced the patriarchal attempt at controlling and managing improper manifestations of femininity *inside* . . . Victorian Britain" (Tomaiuolo, "Sensation" 121, italics in original). Hence, Aurora in this novel is presented as "a (potentially) corrupting Oriental woman," evoking memories of the colonial uprising (Tomaiuolo, "Sensation" 122). This reading of Aurora as a colonial force is supported by Nayder's observation that there were perceived similarities between the married Englishwoman and the colonial native. Nayder argues that the Englishwoman's "lack of property rights and legal autonomy [was] similar to that of a subservient or rebellious native," meaning that the "feminized" native could be "protected and exploited much like a Victorian wife" ("Empire" 450, 452, 445). Novels like *Aurora Floyd* could explore, through a "domestic betrayal within respectable English homes," the traumatic event of the Sepoy Rebellion (Nayder, "Empire" 450, 452).

After marrying John, Aurora continues to behave as an empress at Mellish Park. Unlike Mr Bulstrode, who comes from a long line of Cornish baronets, John is a "Yorkshire gentleman and landowner" whose estate spans "far-away farms, upon wide Yorkshire wolds and fenny Lincolnshire flats," bringing him an income of "something between sixteen and seventeen thousand a year" (Braddon, *Aurora* 89, 144). As "queen" of this estate, Aurora orders her husband to heed her wishes (Braddon, *Aurora* 260). On one occasion, she directs her husband to take her to London, with a "haughty toss of her beautiful head, and one bright flash of her glorious eyes, which seemed to say, 'Slave, obey and tremble!'" (Braddon, *Aurora* 213). Mr Mellish follows her "meekly, wonderingly, fearfully; with terrible doubts and anxieties creeping, like venomous living creatures, stealthily into his heart" (Braddon, *Aurora* 213). As the novel progresses, however, Aurora becomes increasingly infantilized into the image of a foolish and ignorant school-girl. She confesses that she had had a "school-girl's sentimental fancy" and a "school-girl's frivolous admiration" for James Conyers, her first husband and her father's former groom (Braddon, *Aurora* 352). Mr Bulstrode reflects on Aurora's earlier "school-girl's foolish delusion" (Braddon, *Aurora* 360), tempering his view of her as a woman "whose worst fault had been the trusting folly of an innocent girl" (Braddon, *Aurora* 399). Aurora is reduced to a "passionate, impetuous, spoiled child of fortune and affection" who desires only John's love and protection (Braddon, *Aurora* 415). Unlike Lady Isabel in Wood's *East Lynne*, Aurora is given a second chance, since, in becoming the prime suspect in Conyers' murder, she bears the moral punishment for her "curse of disobedience" (Braddon, *Aurora* 310). Aurora comes to accept that she is better protected under patriarchal authority as represented by her husband. She is reintegrated into the patriarchal order when she penitently realizes her vulnerability and her husband's generosity.

Aurora's motherless upbringing mitigates some of her childish actions. Mr Bulstrode imagines and pities her "in her childish ignorance, exposed to the insidious advances of an unscrupulous schemer [Mr Conyers], and his heart bled for the motherless girl" (Braddon, *Aurora* 353). Braddon writes that even though Aurora was born with an "allegorical silver spoon in her mouth, she was poorer than other girls, inasmuch as she was motherless" (*Aurora* 45). The absence of a mother implicitly makes Aurora more susceptible to male advances and intrigue as she lacks sufficient moral guidance. Hence, even though Aurora's secret is shameful, Victorian readers are encouraged to accept her remorse. Aurora is herself aware of the emotional currency of motherhood, as she appeals in her first conversation about her past to Mr Bulstrode, "I was motherless from my cradle . . . Have pity upon me" (Braddon, *Aurora* 104). Interestingly, John had also lost his mother as a child and later his father, which had left "none to restrain his actions" (*Aurora* 59). In contrast, Mr Bulstrode is cautioned early on by his mother, Lady Raleigh Bulstrode, against marrying a woman with a questionable secret in her past. In contrast, Mangham argues that Mrs Powell "lives up to the mid-Victorian ideal of post-menopausal women as brooding, infectious, and gorgon-like relics," though, in fairness, Braddon does not give a clear indication of her age (*Violent Women* 124). The most information given about Mrs Powell is that she has "straight light hair" and that her husband, an ensign, had died within six months of their marriage (Braddon, *Aurora* 51).

Aurora's moral restitution occurs when she also becomes a mother and gives birth to "a black-eyed child – a boy," with the novelistic expectation that maternal feeling will now curb and restrain her dominating impulses (Braddon, *Aurora* 458). It is Aurora's transition to motherhood that fully secures her within the patriarchal order. Rae mocked this narrative development, noting in 1865 that, "curiously enough, Aurora has no child by either husband till after the clearing up of the mystery which surrounds her" (Braddon, *Aurora* 188). As in Wood's *East Lynne*, Aurora finds validation and meaning in motherhood, as she transitions from a child-like woman, raised without a mother, into a maternal figure in her own right. In contrast to *Lady Audley's Secret*, where Lady Audley does not become a mother, and Collins's *The Woman in White*, where Jane Catherick has a child but seems monstrously devoid of maternal feeling, Aurora's transition to motherhood here redeems her and reinscribes her within the social order. One might be reminded of Linton's words as late as 1891, when she wrote that

> the *raison d'être* of a woman is maternity. For this and this alone nature has differentiated her from man, and built her up cell by cell and organ by organ. The continuance of the race in healthy reproduction, together with the fit nourishment and care of the young after birth, is the ultimate end of woman as such.
>
> (161)

Braddon leaves her reader with a final image of Aurora, "a little changed, a shade less defiantly bright . . . bending over the cradle of her first-born," as the Mellish family's reputation is salvaged by the punishment of the real murderer (*Aurora* 459).

Private spies and a professional detective

As the threat to rationality and patriarchal authority presented by Aurora is defused, a new threat arises from among the servants of the Mellish household. As earlier mentioned, Mrs Powell and Hargraves are the first detectives in the novel, as neither Mr Bulstrode nor Mr Mellish attempt to uncover Aurora's secret. Aurora describes Mrs Powell as a "spy" in her household, who actively tries to besmirch the Mellish family name (Braddon, *Aurora* 330). Mrs Powell exults in her power over Aurora as she discovers, with "a thrill of savage [and] horrible joy," clues about Aurora's past (Braddon, *Aurora* 204). She exclaims, "They're [Mr and Mrs Mellish] in my power – they're both in my power; and I'm no longer a poor dependant [*sic*] to be sent away, at a quarter's notice, when it pleases them to be tired of me" (Braddon, *Aurora* 337). Detective work here resembles the search for "link[s] in the mysterious chain" that Robert had also sought in *Lady Audley's Secret* (Braddon, *Aurora* 203). The difference here is that detection becomes a covert means to assert power over one's social superiors to allay resentment and envy. There is an irony, as Smillie observes, in the begrudging access granted to the professional detective in the family home, and the "near unlimited access" given to servants who must "neither observe nor interpret the secrets, or traces of crime, they encounter" (12). Detective activities are reprehensible when conducted by servants, since it flouts not only a basic sense of trust and decency, but also threatens to undermine the social order and the middle-class ideal. Detective work is villainous when conducted to nurse a personal grudge or achieve a personal advantage particularly over one's social superiors. Detection may be useful for the power it confers on the knower, as Mr Bulstrode discovers towards the novel's end, but in the wrong hands (especially those of an inferior social class), it can be damaging and destabilizing.

The extent of detection's destabilizing influence culminates in a near reversal of positions. Mrs Powell exults in her power over John and Aurora, revealing how detection can blur into blackmail. Even though she is a servant, she says she "would fain have boxed John's ear, had she been tall enough to have reached that organ" (Braddon, *Aurora* 268). Detective work allows for arrogance and misbehavior, as servants ignore their proper places. Again, this translates into a counterbalancing hyper-masculinity that Braddon toys with but ultimately eschews, writing,

If Mrs Powell had been a man, she would have found her head in contact with the Turkey carpet of John's dining-room . . . as she was a woman, John Mellish stood looking her full in the face, waiting till she had finished speaking.

(Braddon, *Aurora* 344)

Mrs Powell's near-omniscient presence in the house and her ever-watchful gaze render her a distinctly unlikeable character, especially as she leverages such knowledge to harm her mistress. Her detections have the potential to ruin Aurora's reputation, as symbolically conveyed when Mrs Mellish passes Hargraves a letter for Mr Conyers, while Hargraves carries a gun in his pocket. The private knowledge contained in the letter is carried away by the same person who steals a gun from the Mellish home.

Mrs Powell is effectively ejected from the narrative after her confrontation with Mr Mellish, but insidious disobedience and defiance remain on the premises, not least in Hargraves. Hargraves is depicted as a hump-back inspiring "instinctive dislike," who resembles "some ugly animal at bay" (Braddon, *Aurora* 134–35, 453). He is more akin to "some viperish creature, some loathsome member of the reptile race," than an Englishman (Braddon, *Aurora* 169). He is "a poor half-witted hanger-on" embodying brooding treachery and scheming discontent, who eventually attempts to murder Mr Bulstrode with a Sheffield blade (Braddon, *Aurora* 387, 454). Both Mrs Powell and Hargraves are cast as "hawks" who prey on Mr and Mrs Mellish as figurative "pigeons . . . plump and nice-eating for [their delectation]" (Braddon, *Aurora* 371). Detective work, spying, and surveillance are the means by which they whet their predatory appetites.

Detective work when conducted by servants is all the more reprehensible for the tacit trust between the master and mistress, and their employees. Again, this connects with the trauma of the Indian Mutiny, restaging the uprising within the domestic sphere. But Braddon deliberately amplifies such suspicions of intrigue, telling her reader that

your servants listen at your doors . . . and watch you while they wait at table, and understand every sarcasm, every innuendo, every look, as well as those at whom the cruel glances and the stinging words are aimed.

(Braddon, *Aurora* 177)

Scandal-mongering and gossiping among servants are heightened into active investigation in this novel, with servants depicted as "feverishly inquisitive" about their employers' secrets (Braddon, *Aurora* 177). The inconspicuous surveillance in the London streets of *Martin Chuzzlewit* is transformed in this sensation novel into domestic surveillance, as seen earlier in Collins's *The Woman in White*. More broadly, crime threatens to transform into a social contagion, "slowly percolat[ing] through insidious channels" (Braddon, *Aurora* 256). Crime and "evil deed[s]" move through the social body like "the germ of a foul-running weed, whose straggling suckers travel underground beyond the ken of mortal eye, beyond the power of mortal calculation" (Braddon, *Aurora* 256). Detecting crime results in a purge of perceived deviants from the social body, but the process involves surreptitious means that could also seem morally ambivalent.

The servants' intrusive investigations contrast with the activities of the policeman, Mr William Dork, and the professional detective, Mr Grimstone. Mr Dork is cast as "a simple rural functionary," who does not pursue information or clues with rigorous attention to detail (Braddon, *Aurora* 313). In the interim between the murder and its investigation by Mr Grimstone, the newspapers comment on and speculate about the identity of the murderer. Mr Grimstone appears in the final chapters of the novel, making him more of a convenient plot device, rather than a central character or hero. He is recognizable as a detective by his behavior, as he takes in "one brightly rapid and searching glance . . . the most minute details" (Braddon, *Aurora* 411). Mr Grimstone fits the prototype of a detective, as earlier identified by Dickens, as watchful and highly observant. At the same time, it is his business and "the principle of his life to avoid observation" himself, following suspects like Hargraves undetected (Braddon, *Aurora* 428).

For all Mr Grimstone's resourcefulness, however, he does not emerge as a moral hero in the novel. Indeed, Braddon seems to rely on his intervention only to reveal evidence about the murder without compromising her main characters. Braddon seems to delegate to Mr Grimstone the work of following and questioning characters, which would be a morally ambiguous process when conducted by private individuals. She also makes clear that while Mr Grimstone has an "almost miraculous" knack for obtaining information, he is not without his own personal failings (Braddon, *Aurora* 432). He is motivated by personal gain and a "sublunary reward," which leads him to work alone, rather than by a "love of justice" (Braddon, *Aurora* 436). It is this professionalism that sets Mr Grimstone apart from the idle scandalmonger, but that also makes him a calculating and self-interested character. He does not emerge as the hero, nor even as the principal "criminal hunter" in the narrative, though his detections resolve the disorder and confusion left in the wake of the rebellious servants' departure (Braddon, *Aurora* 444). This shows how, in *Aurora Floyd*, detective work may be seen as both necessary and morally complicated. While detective work restores social stability (in contrast to the disruptive investigations by the servants), the detective himself remains a marginal and ambivalent figure that nonetheless eases the narrative tension towards resolution.

Notes

1 Oliphant reserved her negative criticism for Braddon's later novels, while also recognizing Braddon's central role in the rise of sensation novels.
2 Marlene Tromp also notes Aurora's Eastern exoticization, but does not link this characterization with the Sepoy Rebellion ("Dangerous Woman").
3 See (Braddon, *Aurora* 65, 131, 213) for Cleopatra references.
4 For a fascinating study of domestic service as working-class employment (especially among young women), see (E. Griffin, *Bread Winner*).

8   Female detectives

Ware (Forrester), Hayward, and
Collins's *The Law and the Lady*

While several sensation novels studied today were originally serialized in journals, other sensational stories were published as cheap railway books. These paperback books often had eye-catching illustrations on glazed coverings and became known as "yellow-backs" after 1855 (see Altick, *English* 299). Mansel wrote in 1863 that such railway paperbacks offered "their customers something hot and strong, something that may catch the eye of the hurried passenger, and promise temporary excitement to relieve the dullness of a journey" ("Sensation" 485). While market forces influenced and cultivated the rise of sensation novels, changes in transportation and social transformations also created a new market for cheap and sensational stories. The stories in yellow-back paperbacks could be read quickly, rather than extending for months or years over serial publication. Yellow-back stories were sensational, but they were usually much more condensed than their counterparts in the periodical press.

Few of these yellow-back books continue to be read today, but they provide a glimpse into the public perception of detectives in concise and even blunt terms. Two yellow-back books of the 1860s featuring detectives are Ware's *The Female Detective* and Hayward's *Revelations of a Lady Detective*, both published in 1864. Hayward published his book anonymously, while Ware wrote under the pseudonym Andrew Forrester. Collins appears to have read *The Female Detective*, as he sent a copy to his mother in September 1867, mere months before the first serial of *The Moonstone* (Lycett, *Wilkie* 274). As the titles indicate, both books feature a female detective and are comprised of short stories. These were not the only books to feature female detectives, who also appear in Braddon's dramatic novel *Eleanor's Victory* (1863) and Collins's *The Law and the Lady* (1875), the latter of which is discussed at the end of this chapter.[1] But the yellow-back novels by Ware and Hayward reveal dominant perceptions of the detective force and its imagined extension to female investigators. The protagonist in Ware's *The Female Detective* states plainly, "I know well that my trade is despised. . . . My trade is a necessary one, but the

DOI: 10.4324/9781003369622-9

world holds aloof my order" (Forrester 2). She continues, "I am quite aware that there is something peculiarly objectionable in the spy, but nevertheless it will be admitted that the spy is as peculiarly necessary as he or she is peculiarly objectionable" (Forrester 2). The tone here marks a sharp contrast from the praise for detectives as "peace officers" in Russell's 1856 detective stories. There is also a clearer distinction in these books between the individual detective and the police institution. Equally, detectives are prone to "atrocious" failures and are more clearly motivated by monetary incentives (Forrester 115).

In the same year, James Fitzjames Stephen wrote an essay in *The Saturday Review* condemning "detective-worship" in fiction. Stephen expressed exasperation about their fanciful and heroic characterizations, stating that real detectives operated through the systematic collection of evidence. The idea that detectives relied predominantly on individual sagacity or even "guesswork," rather than "the rules of evidence," amounted, in Stephen's words, to "one of the silliest superstitions that ever were concocted by ingenious writers" (713; see also Smajić 108–9). Ware criticizes such fantasies in *The Female Detective*, writing that it is a mistake to believe "that a detective is never hoodwinked" or that "a detective is not to be taken in" (Forrester 97, 113). Ware also dismisses the suspicion that "the English detectives were in the habit of prying into private life . . . as though no citizen were free from . . . a system of spydom" (Forrester 116). Ware's stories also complicate the detective's role of resolving trouble and restoring the social order. Indeed, the first story in *The Female Detective* ("Tenant for Life") turns on a revelation of fraud, uncovered by the female detective, that threatens to create more social injustice than rectify wrongdoing.

There is an ambivalence at work in these stories, not least because they anachronistically feature middle-aged women as detectives, well before the official recruitment of female detectives in the London Metropolitan Police Force from 1883.[2] On the one hand, such detective stories play on the appeal of individual ingenuity, but on the other hand, they also depend on attendant police officers to resolve their plots. The ambiguity of the female detective plays into the moral ambivalence of the detective. As a police supervisor states in *Revelations of a Lady Detective*, "a woman is more likely to be successful" in covert detective work, "because men are thrown off their guard when they see a petticoat" (Hayward 57). Saunders observes that the imagined lady detective could "pass unnoticed and unsuspected," which "allowed the reader to safely accompany the detective into even more diverse and inaccessible places" (124). Thus, featuring a woman as a detective was not a recognition of her mental or intellectual powers *per se*, but rather, a dramatization of foiled expectations and accentuation of the detective's association with the mistrusted spy. Mrs Paschal, the female detective in Hayward's stories, is able to call on "histrionic powers" that are implicitly female and describes herself as "an accomplished actress" on the stage of reality (3, 76). Casting a woman as a detective is an extension of the errant femininity explored in other sensation novels, especially when they disguise themselves as household servants to spy on their targets. For instance, Mrs Paschal is able to take on a range of inconspicuous roles (whether as a wife or a domestic servant) in her detective investigations. Featuring female detectives plays on the pre-existent ambivalence of the detective, further amplifying their moral ambiguity by casting a seemingly trustworthy middle-aged woman as a covert spy.

Another dominant theme in these books is anti-foreign sentiment, which remained largely intact since the publication of Russell's detective stories about a decade prior. The detectives in these stories, however, are more independent and less constrained by institutions. The female detectives also reveal a moral relativism in their detective stories. Even though foreigners are cast as criminals and young lovers are presented as victims, the female detective does not emerge as a hero because she aims to achieve mental superiority over the criminal, rather than the restoration of the social order. The female detective's willingness to engage in subterfuge and deception renders her a morally slippery character, in spite of her apparent ingenuity. For instance, Mrs Paschal takes advantage of her appearance as "remarkably innocent, simple, and hardworking" to deflect suspicion and even betray the trust of ordinary townspeople (Hayward 34).

Female detection as deceptive spying in Hayward's stories

In the 1860s, casting a young attractive woman as a detective would have defied belief and also presented narrative difficulties, since she would have attracted rather than deflected attention while walking in the streets. Hence, Mrs Paschal in Hayward's *Revelations of a Lady Detective* is cast as a widow approaching forty years old, who describes herself as having been "well born and well educated" (Hayward 3). These qualities render her "an accomplished actress" for the little-known group of female detectives, supervised by Colonel Warner (Hayward 3). She states that her "brain was vigorous and subtle" and is anxious to fulfil her duties, on which she depends for her living (Hayward 3). Contradictions appear in her character throughout the narrative, such as when she states that she had formerly worked as a barmaid at a railway station (Hayward 276). Detective work in these stories is conducted for personal and professional reputation. As Colonel Warner explains to her, "You are like a gold-digger at Ballarat who is in luck; you have an auriferous claim, and it only requires work and perseverance to bring out the nuggets" (Hayward 268). This remark takes place within the context of an open case with the prospect of a liberal reward. Later, Mrs Paschal notes that "many detectives have more than one piece of employment on their hands at one time, because they are tempted by the rewards" (Hayward 95). Detectives are prone, from Mrs Paschal's view, to "cupidity and grasping after money," which often leads them into failure (Hayward 95). She distinguishes herself from these other detectives by restricting herself to a single case at a time, through which she hopes to "prov[e her]self cleverer than they turned out to be" (Hayward 96).

The perception of detectives here differs here from Russell's *Recollections of a Detective Police-Officer*, since there is open acknowledgement, as in Ware's stories, of public suspicion and disdain for detectives as mercenary spies. Mrs Paschal, while exulting in success over her unsuspecting targets, remains as morally ambivalent as her personal background is opaque. She gains entrance into domestic spaces by taking on unassuming roles, such as a housekeeper in "The Mysterious Countess," a domestic servant in "Incognita," and a nun in "The Nun, the Will, and the Abbess." Indeed, she states that "the necessity" for masquerading as a domestic servant "often" arises in her work (Hayward 275). Mrs Paschal states that "men are less apt to suspect a woman if she play [*sic*] her cards cleverly and knows thoroughly how to conduct the business she is instructed to bring to a successful termination" (Hayward 43). As stated earlier, casting a woman as a detective is less a recognition of her mental powers or intelligence, and rather hinges on her capacity for deception. Mrs Paschal expresses no remorse for those she dupes in the process of investigation, nor does she seem to show sympathy for innocent victims. Instead, Mrs Paschal seems more motivated by the satisfaction of success and her reputation, rather than subscribing to higher moral or social values. She also exhibits a greater independence from the police or legal institutions than was seen in Russell's stories.

There are similarities between Russell's and Hayward's stories, however, especially in the stereotypical characterization of criminals as European foreigners or minorities. These criminals are usually Italians ("The Secret Band"), Catholics ("The Nun, the Will, and the Abbess"), Jews ("The Lost Diamonds"), gypsies ("Which is the Heir?"), or scheming women ("Incognita" and "Fifty Pounds Reward"). The category of perceived social suspects here is broadened to include not only Catholic foreigners, but also women and minorities in England. "Fifty Pounds Reward" and "Incognita" bear perhaps the strongest resemblance to sensation novels in casting women as undermining the social order. In the former story, a female friend persuades an impressionable young wife to fraudulently sign her husband's cheque, weakening their marital unity and his male authority. In the latter story, an already married woman tries to persuade a young heir to marry her, while concealing her past and previous marriage through skillful "tricks of the trade" (Hayward 290). In both stories, the sanctity of the domestic sphere is undermined by female culpability and moral weakness.

There are also hints of the imperial romance (which would be amplified in late Victorian detective stories), such as in the depiction of a subterranean maze leading to a bank's vaults in "The Mysterious Countess" and in the theft of Indian diamonds in "The Lost Diamond."

Despite her discoveries, however, it is difficult to characterize Mrs Paschal as a gifted individual, since she relies on blatant guesswork, random assumptions, and judgments based on people's appearance (such as their apparent brain size). On the thinnest of assumptions, Mrs Paschal determines that an Italian patriot has "unquestionably" murdered Signor Mantuani in "The Secret Band" (Hayward 56). She states that the Italian patriot "possessed great determination, and was a man of unlimited plans and experiences," despite having only held a single conversation with him (Hayward 57). In "The Lost Diamonds," Mrs Paschal recognizes a male character "in an instant," despite never having met him before (Hayward 110). Similarly, in "The Nun," she sees "at a glance" that an imprisoned girl at the abbey is the heiress Evelyn St. Vincent, despite also never having met her before (Hayward 161). In "Found Drowned," she identifies a man as Stephen Bardsley based on her "conception" of his appearance (Hayward 202). Mrs Paschal is often guided by "a vague presentiment" in her investigations, rather than basing her conclusions on compelling evidence (Hayward 160). The elaborate guesswork and sheer luck in these detective stories conveniently accelerate the process of detection and maximize those features likely seen as their strongest appeal. Ironically, they also undermine a woman's perceived capacity for rational thought and intelligence.

Featuring a woman as a professional detective, then, did not so much disentangle the close association between masculinity and rational thought, as leverage women's perceived capacity for intrigue and deceit. Casting a woman as a detective underscored the moral relativism of detective work, rather than emphasizing female contributions to the wider social good. Hayward's female detective is fully aware that she appears an inconspicuous, middle-aged woman as she engages in disguise and deception. As a widow approaching forty years old, her presence in other people's homes or on the London streets does not attract attention or raise questions. Hayward's stories derive their dramatic effect from such a woman unmasking criminals within the seemingly safe spaces of their homes. The reader is invited to participate in the vicarious excitement of intruding in characters' private lives from the perspective of a concealed spy, whose tactics inspire ambivalence and discomfort. In this context, Mrs Paschal appears little more than a talented actress or spy.

To reiterate, casting a female detective is less an acknowledgement of women's capacity for rational deduction and more a stylized rehearsal of their ability to engage in deception. In both longer sensation novels and in Hayward's stories, women conceal and fashion their identities. In Hayward's stories, Mrs Paschal uses her arts of acting, performance, and disguise to catch criminals. She is able to call upon "histrionic powers" that are implicitly female to conduct her investigations (Hayward 76). She even describes herself in the opening pages as "an accomplished actress" whose dramas are of "real life, not the mimetic representation . . . on the stage" (Hayward 3). Critically, however, she relies on "masculine strength" and assistance to apprehend criminals after the moment of revelation (Hayward 35). Male policemen wait for her signal as she confronts the criminal, reminding the reader that she is physically powerless. Hence, she is usually assigned cases relating to concealed mysteries (even those that lack a legal basis for investigation), rather than violent crimes. The process of detection relies heavily on mental shortcuts and dramatized acting, which only point to the moral ambiguity of such investigative work.

Moral ambivalence in Ware's *The Female Detective*

Writing under the pseudonym Andrew Forrester, Ware's stories about a female detective reveal even less about their protagonist than Hayward's stories. Set in 1855, the opening words of the book are: "Who am I? It can matter little who I am" (Forrester 1). The female protagonist, who goes by the initial "G.," hints that she may be "a widow working for [her] children" or "an unmarried woman, whose only care is herself" (Forrester 1). She reveals even less about her financial position, though she states that she "had for some years earned good money, and had laid by a trifle" (Forrester 1). As seen earlier in Dickens's *Martin Chuzzlewit*, the detective investigates others even as he (in this case, she) remains unessentially unknown in these stories. Ware's female detective identifies herself as a member of the "secret police" or as "a police officer in petticoats" (Forrester 78, 240). She consults and collaborates with lawyers, though she observes that detectives are more open to "risk and audacity" than lawyers (Forrester 41). Ware's female detective begins with the caveat that she understands that detectives are "despised" and that "the world would still avoid the detective as a social companion" (Forrester 2). She repeats that she is "quite aware that society looks upon the companionship of a spy as repulsive," even as she justifies that "we detectives are necessary, as scavengers are called for" (Forrester 3). Again, she concedes that a female detective may be "regarded with even more aversion" than male detectives, though she argues that there is equally a demand for "female detective police spies" (Forrester 3). As seen in Hayward's stories, Ware states that "the woman detective has far greater opportunities than a man of intimate watching," and it is indeed the woman's capacity for "intimate watching" and as "family spies" that animates both books (Forrester 4).

Figure 8.1 A cover illustration by an unidentified illustrator for Hayward's *Revelations of a Lady Detective*. Public Domain/The British Library ("Revelations").

As in Hayward's stories, Ware's female detective acknowledges that most detectives are motivated by a monetary reward. Detectives are motivated by "the probabilities of profit" as well as "some distinction which shall carry them to the top of their particular tree" (Forrester 42, 238). Here, as in Hayward's stories, detectives are more often self-interested gatherers of information, rather than officials serving the public good. Ware states, "detectives are as much excited by one of these rich government rewards as . . . a ladies' school by the appearance of a new and elegant master" (Forrester 153). As in Hayward's stories, Ware's female detective sees a mercenary and performative element in her work, noting that "we detectives are like actors, or singers, or playwrights," who aim to enhance their reputations (Forrester 42). Even when Ware's female detective claims to be motivated by "duty," such aspirations ring hollow as when, for instance, she misidentifies a murderer in "The Judgment of Conscience" (Forrester 165). While she states that "the end of the detective's work is justice," her own investigations thwart moral resolution and social justice (Forrester 55). The moral ambiguity of detective work is made clear in "The Unknown Weapon," where the female detective states that if "evil-doing is a kind of lie levelled at society . . . it is to be conquered . . . on the side of society, through its employes [*sic*], by similar false action" (Forrester 258).

The detective's moral ambiguity is made clear from the first story, "Tenant for Life." Here, the female detective discovers evidence of fraud of her own volition, without having been privately hired or directed. As a consequence of this revelation, made to the selfish baronet Sir Nathaniel, his virtuous relatives face destitution. The discovery of fraud benefits a profligate and "miserable tyrant" at the expense of his well-intentioned relatives (Forrester 88). The female detective excavates legal fraud but sets into motion a moral crisis, where vice threatens to conquer virtue. She manufactures a crisis that would have better been left unexplored, resulting in consequences of which she becomes "ashamed" (Forrester 77). She "hung her head in sorrow and regret," as she hears that she has "done a wretched thing" in transferring the entire estate to a cruel and profligate man (Forrester 80, 86). When conducted without legal validation, sympathy, or compassion, private investigations reinforce the sense that the detective is a mischief-maker and troublemaker, rather than a hero. The narrative is only resolved when Sir Nathaniel opportunely succumbs to a fatal heart disease at the climactic moment. The association between the detective and the troublemaker reappears in "The Unknown Weapon," when the female detective's intrusive prying leads a housekeeper to burn down "one of the oldest [and] most picturesque" estates in the midland counties to avoid arrest (Forrester 303). Unlike in Hayward's stories, Ware's female detective does not follow orders from a supervisor, but rather seems to voluntarily interfere in other people's affairs as she hunts for evidence of wrongdoing or crime.

As in other detective stories, Ware's stories are replete with anti-foreign and anti-Catholic sentiment. In "The Unraveled Mystery," Ware writes that crimes are often committed among foreign refugees hiding in London. Ware writes, "London is the resting-place of many determined foreigners," which has "at all times been that sanctuary for refugees" and "foreign malcontents" (Forrester 124). Consequently, "London has always been the centre of foreign exiled disaffection," which has led to secret assassination attempts (Forrester 124). Foreigners become the prime suspects for mysterious crimes, as in Hayward's stories, while a criminal mentality is associated with Catholicism. There are ominous references to a "foreign mask" in "The Unknown Weapon," where the housekeeper (as a manslaughter suspect) seems to have "almost Spanish nations of family honour" (Forrester 272, 302). The instrument that kills Squire Petleigh in this story is a wooden shaft with an iron arrow, "such as are used by picadors in Spanish bull-fights" (Forrester 301). These allusions to foreign criminality or intrigue often bode ill for English characters and families in these stories.

Overall, the female detective is not only an undesirable social companion, but also a social nuisance in Ware's stories. She not only belongs to a professional group resembling "scavengers," but she is also prone to disastrous missteps and miscalculations (Forrester 3). By her own admission, the detective force is "certainly as far from perfect as any ordinary legal organization in England" (Forrester 115). Detectives are prone to "atrocious" failures and may accept "a plain and straightforward statement" at surface value (Forrester 115, 236). While most detectives are motivated by monetary rewards, Ware's female detective apparently subscribes to abstract notions of justice and duty. She states in "Tenant for Life" that "the end of the detective's work is justice," even as her investigations seem to thwart social justice and moral resolution (Forrester 55). The female detective also claims to be doing her "duty" when she misidentifies a murderer who is later proven to be innocent (Forrester 165). Such abstract appeals to justice or duty ring hollow, since they are unattached to any clear validation and seem to serve instead as mere justifications for intrusive spying. While not perhaps the most thrilling of detective stories, Ware's *The Female Detective* throws into relief the contradictory and ambivalent views of detectives in the mid-nineteenth century. Detectives are not necessarily infallible or gifted individuals, but may intrude into others' private affairs in morally compromising ways. Detection allows for a vicarious exploration into characters' private lives, but also inspires revulsion and disdain for their tactics and occasional miscalculations. The integration of detectives in popular literature could become a double-edged sword, since their discoveries could lead to social disruption and involve the deception of innocent individuals.

Exploring female agency through detection in Collins's *The Law and the Lady*

As a sensation novel published in 1875, *The Law and the Lady* falls outside the mid-century timeframe of this study. However, it is valuable to compare the female detective in this novel with the earlier two yellowbacks because *The Law and the Lady* carry similar themes into the more recognizable terrain of sensation fiction. Valeria Woodville in the novel can be more accurately described as a woman investigating her husband's affairs, since she is not a professional detective in the sense of either Ware's or Hayward's novel. Despite this, Valeria's investigations are also cast as expressions of deviant (or defiant) femininity, rather than a recognition of her rational capabilities. For instance, Valeria's early discovery of her husband's secret is orchestrated like a child's play, with Major Fitz-David peeping through a chink to watch her rummage through his study for clues.

In contrast to *Aurora Floyd*, in which a woman harbors a secret from her husband, Valeria is tasked with living with a secret held by her husband (see Chapter 7). The mystery of his past challenges her to live up to her duty as a wife, which her mother-in-law alludes to. Mrs Macallan advises her, "Be satisfied with your husband's affectionate devotion to you. If you value your peace of mind, and the happiness of your life to come, abstain from attempting to know more than you know now" (Collins, *Law* 43). While such remarks may be intended to shield Valeria from compromising knowledge about her husband, they also gesture to her duty as a wife to remain willfully ignorant and satisfied. As her husband later informs her, "It was possible for you to live with me happily, while you were in ignorance of the truth. It is *not* possible, now you know all" (Collins, *Law* 112, italics in original). In investigating her husband's past, Valeria grapples with the limits of what is socially acceptable for a wife to know about her husband's affairs. Whereas a husband is entitled to full disclosure from his wife – in Talbot Bulstrode's words to Aurora, "as your future husband, I have a right to ask for an explanation" (Braddon, *Aurora* 103) – a woman does not enjoy the same privilege.[3] A secret held by a husband is not hedged with the same restraints of duty as a secret held by a wife, though Collins's novel later subverts these expectations.

In contrast to John Mellish's mute acceptance of Aurora's secret and Mr Bulstrode's blunt rejection of such a secret held by his future wife, Valeria in *The Law and the Lady* refuses to live with her husband's secret. Such curiosity is cast as distinctly feminine and as a mark of insubordination. Valeria is, in her own words, "a doubting, discontented, depressed creature" whose "mind is in a bad way" about her husband (Collins, *Law* 50). Her husband reprimands her, much like a child, to "control [her] curiosity" (Collins, *Law* 54). As he continues, "I thought I had married a woman who was superior to the vulgar failings of her sex. A good wife should know better than to pry into affairs of her husband's with which she has no concern" (Collins, *Law* 54). Valeria's decision to resist her husband's admonitions coincides with a scene where she is made up with "a box of paints and powders" to wear "a false fairness . . . a false colour . . . a false brightness" (Collins, *Law* 57). In falsely accentuating and parading her femininity, Valeria comes to resemble a commercial actress even as she relies on her womanhood to grant her intimate access to knowledge held by men.

That such inquisitiveness is distinctly feminine, or a perversion of vulgar femininity, is evident in the character shift or the "extraordinary inconsistency" in Valeria's character (Collins, *Law* 68). Valeria acknowledges that she seems "in some strange way to have lost [her] ordinary identity" in pursuing the secret of her husband's past (Collins, *Law* 58). Yet such heightened curiosity is attributed to her womanly nature, consistent with her characterization as a child-like creature alternating between pride, petulance, and impudence. She insists, for instance, that "[her] husband owes [her] an explanation" and that she cannot endure "perpetual misgiving and perpetual suspense" (Collins, *Law* 62–63). She states that "women are strange creatures; mysteries even to themselves," as the investigation tests the limits of her inner resilience (Collins, *Law* 88). The female detective in *The Law and the Lady* is presented, much like in *No Name*, as yet another exploration of deviant femininity, manifest in rebellious and insubordinate women who remain inconsistent and enigmatic even to themselves. Their actions defy the reader's credulity, and their investigations are rendered as (ironically necessary) mischief-making, as they flout codes of decency and social respectability. In refusing to submit to the domestic ideology, namely, to be ignorant and happy, they are caricaturized as unreasonably defiant, high-strung, nervous, and unable to control a "diseased curiosity."[4]

If Valeria's pursuit of her husband's secret was a defiant expression of insubordinate femininity, her "headstrong" determination to reject advice and prove his innocence is also a mark of female "obstinacy" (Collins, *Law* 283–84). Valeria marvels at her own stubbornness, reflecting that "women are contradictory creatures" and that she could "listen to nobody who advises [her]" (Collins, *Law* 285). She remarks to her father's faithful clerk Benjamin, "I have tried, tried hard, to be a teachable, reasonable woman. But there is something in me that won't be taught" (Collins, *Law* 285). Her investigations, while falling short of professional detective work as in Ware and Hayward's stories, serve as a foil to explore female deviance and independence. Through testing the limits of female respectability, whether in meeting men alone for private conversations or resorting to the use of paints, Valeria attempts both to attain restricted knowledge and to redeem her marriage through detective work. The initial mischief is caused by her heightened curiosity and it is resolved by her defiance of patriarchal authority in pursuing the investigation. In the process, she resorts to such unseemly behavior as, in the words of a vicar, "roaming about the country, to throw [her]self on the mercy of strangers, and to risk whatever rough reception . . . in the course of [her] travels . . . With nobody to protect [her]" (Collins, *Law* 121). The justification for such unconventional conduct, defying standards of decency for a young married woman, ostensibly lies in Valeria's higher devotion to "the man she love[s]" (Collins, *Law* 122). This higher allegiance to her husband ironically allows her to undermine patriarchal authority, placing a primacy on personal conviction (a mark of "the new generation," according to Benjamin) rather than mute obedience (Collins, *Law* 285).

Hence, while Valeria may not be a professional detective and is, instead, a resolute woman who refuses to remain ignorant or obey injunctions to caution, detective work in *The Law and the Lady* similarly functions as a means to explore female identity and agency. Under expressed fidelity to her husband, Valeria engages in subterfuge, "conceal[ing her] identity . . . to present [her]self, in the character of a harmless stranger," and taking advantage of male pliability to a young woman (Collins, *Law* 188). Detective work, rather than confirming a woman's capacity to engage in professional work through ratiocination, becomes a means to explore alternate expressions and modes of female identity in a patriarchal society. Valeria's investigations are ostensibly sanctioned by her emotional attachment to her husband, demonstrating a youthful impetuosity in defiance of social conventions.

As if to underscore the performative nature of detective work in *The Law and the Lady*, Valeria's discoveries are gleaned from eyebrow-raising conversations with the latent lunatic, Miserrimus Dexter. These morally compromising interactions risk Valeria's dignity as a married woman, since Mr Dexter develops an obsession with her, "put[ting] his arm around her waist" and "devour[ing her hand] with kisses" in one scene (Collins, *Law* 299, 320). Valeria's discoveries are attained amid moments of agitation and "paroxysm[s] of emotion" by Mr Dexter (Collins, *Law* 331). As an investigator, Valeria does not apply her powers of rational inference from clues, but rather leverages her position as a young, attractive woman with the ability to catch men off their guard. She is unable to see the import of Mr Dexter's remarks and reactions without the calm interpretation, social connections, and professional acumen of her husband's lawyer, Mr Playmore. Detective work allows Valeria to take on a range of guises, test the limits of the socially acceptable, and experiment with female agency, rather than allowing to assert her capacity for intellectual thought or investigative activity. Restricted as she is from the legal profession (and as a legal nonentity), Valeria works with the tools that she has, namely, her femininity and emotional sensitivity. In her investigative work, she is guided by her emotions, impulses, and jealous suspicion. "Being only a woman," Collins writes, Valeria "yield[s] to the compassionate impulse of the moment," instead of remaining steadfastly cool-headed in conversation with Mr Dexter (*Law* 299). As a woman, she is not always, in Mr Playmore's words, "in full possession of [her] excellent common sense" (Collins, *Law* 290). In this sensation novel, female detective work becomes an experiment in the range of a woman's identity and agency, extending rather than resisting popular notions of female manipulation and emotional susceptibility.[5]

Notes

1 *Eleanor's Victory* is not discussed in this chapter as it falls outside the generic range of sensation fiction with its identifiable themes and motifs.
2 Hence, in *Revelations of a Lady Detective*, characters express surprise at meeting a female detective. One criminal remarks, "Why, I should as soon have thought of seeing a flying fish or a sea-serpent with a ring through its nose" (Hayward 260; see also Kestner 7–14; Saunders 123).
3 Mr Bulstrode also tellingly declares to Aurora, "the past life of my wife must be a white unblemished page, which all the world may be free to read" (Braddon, *Aurora* 105).
4 The phrase "diseased curiosity" appears in Braddon's *Aurora Floyd* in reference to Mrs Paschal (183).
5 Nor is it a coincidence that her husband Eustace is entirely feminized and stripped of agency in the novel. It is also worth noting that Valeria is pregnant through most of her investigations.

9 From ambivalence to rationality

Detection in Collins's *Armadale* and *The Moonstone*

Collins's *The Moonstone* was identified by T. S. Eliot as "the first and greatest of English detective novels," and recent critics have also credited the novel with the rise of detective fiction (377). Lara Karpenko notes that *The Moonstone* "abounds with male detective figures," while observing that detection appears "a solely (and almost universally) masculine activity" in the novel (138). In *The Moonstone*, detective characters range from Sergeant Cuff, Gabriel Betteredge, Ezra Jennings, to Mr Bruff, with Karpenko arguing that all these characters "function as detective at some point in the story" (141). Peter Ackroyd similarly describes *The Moonstone* as "the true source and spring of the English detective mystery," dramatically reconstructing a mysterious theft on a fateful evening (164). Robert Louis Stevenson expressed admiration for the novel at age seventeen, praising *The Moonstone* as "frightfully interesting" with a "prime" detective in a letter to his mother (144–45). *The Moonstone* was also the first mystery novel by Collins to feature a detective in a major role. While he had cast a professional detective as a minor character in his earlier novel *Armadale*, Sergeant Cuff in *The Moonstone* is a more fully thought-out character. Sergeant Cuff may not be infallible, but he does claim heroic status towards the end of the novel as he helps resolve the fallout of the mystery. He reappears at the end of the novel to claim his place as "the greatest policeman in England" (Collins, *Moonstone* 296).

Detection and binaries in *Armadale*

Detective characters had earlier featured in Collins's novels, such as *No Name* and *Armadale*, though these may more properly be described as domestic melodramas, rather than detective narratives. Mrs Lecount in *No Name* acts as a detective, investigating Magdalen Vanstone's concealed past. But while Mrs Lecount is a Swiss widow, she is not a foreign nemesis like Count Fosco in *The Woman in White*. Instead, she inspires respect among English characters for her loyalty, tact, manners, and intelligence.

DOI: 10.4324/9781003369622-10

As Magdalen observes, Mrs Lecount is "a lady of mild ingratiating manners; whose dress was the perfection of neatness, taste, and matronly simplicity" (Collins, *No Name* 275). There are no associations between secret societies and Mrs Lecount in this novel, as this female character fiercely protects her English employer from a designing and deceitful Englishwoman. It is Magdalen who is cast as "one of the most reckless, desperate, and perverted women living," in the words of an English lawyer (Collins, *No Name* 591). Likewise, Captain Wragge is repeatedly described as a "scoundrel" with no sense of loyalty, engaging in a battle of wits with his counterpart, Mrs Lecount.

In *Armadale*, the novel preceding *The Moonstone*, Collins casts a biracial character in a prominent role. Ozias Midwinter wavers between the moral poles of good and evil, struggling for redemption, as he feels caught between fatalism and freedom. The central tension in the novel occurs between "the paralyzing fatalism of the heathen and the savage" and the belief in free will (Collins, *Armadale* 622). Midwinter obsessively fears that he will repeat his father's crime, as a "hereditary impulsion," in spite of his own love for Allan Armadale (whose father was killed by Midwinter's father) (Collins, *Armadale* 622). Collins uses Midwinter's biraciality to place him between two opposing cosmological worldviews. Midwinter struggles against an inherited disposition and against "heathen and savage" superstition, as he attempts to save the blond and blue-eyed Armadale, who is indissociable from the good. Midwinter has a doubly tarnished background, with his "mother's negro blood in [his] face], and [his] murdering father's passions in [his] heart" (Collins, *Armadale* 105). This "savage blood . . . inherited from his mother" is associated with primitive rage and unchecked emotion (Collins, *Armadale* 757). *Armadale* becomes a narrative about "Allan the Fair" and "Allan the Dark," as their identities and destinies intertwine throughout the narrative (Collins, *Armadale* 511).

While the lead characters are not detectives in *Armadale*, Collins experiments with scientific ideas (notably, Darwinian theories of inheritance) and imperialism in the novel, which foreshadow themes in *The Moonstone*. Collins often held conversations with scientists like G. H. Lewes, whose interests in the 1860s included human psychology and the relation between the body and the mind (see Lycett, *Wilkie* 247). Collins may well have drawn inspiration from contemporary debates, not only about evolution and inheritance, but also epistemology and psychology. But Collins importantly undercuts the assumption that science can resolve deep ambiguities and mysteries about the human mind. This appears not only in the persistence of instinct and intuition in *No Name* and *Armadale*, but also in the central plot devices of sleepwalking and laudanum. In *No Name*, Admiral Bartram's somnambulance destabilizes the mastery of the mind over the body, an idea that would recur in *The Moonstone*. Both novels feature laudanum, mirroring Collins's own addiction to the pain-relieving substance. Collins had earlier included laudanum in his detective story "The Diary of Anne Rodway," serialized in *Household Words* in July 1856. In this story, Mary Mallinson informs her friend that laudanum is only poison "if you take it all . . . and a night's rest if you take only a little" (Collins, "Diary: Chapter the First" 1). Mary adds, "sleep won't come to me unless I take a few drops out of that bottle," underscoring the pervasive use of laudanum for an assortment of medical (and non-medical) maladies in the nineteenth century (Collins, "Diary: Chapter the First" 2; see also Berridge and Edwards).[1] The mind's rational capacity depends on the body's physical processes, revealing a slippery terrain between reason and unreason. Magdalen observes these contradictions in the appearance of the sleep-walking Admiral Bartram, noting an "awful death-in-life [in] his face – the mystery of the sleeping body, moving in unconscious obedience to the dreaming mind" (Collins, *No Name* 668).

A professional detective does appear in *Armadale*, who helps reveal details about the antagonist Miss Lydia Gwilt's past. James Bashwood is a private investigator at the Private Inquiry Office in Shadyside Place, London, whose father enlists his services in uncovering Miss Gwilt's background. James has a "smoothly-deceptive surface" beneath which he behaves as "the vile creature whom the viler need of Society has fashioned for its own use" (Collins, *Armadale* 627). His investigations into Miss Gwilt's history are made even more morally ambiguous by his father's sexual obsession and infatuation with her. James is incapable of feeling "a touch of human sympathy" or "a sense of pity or a sense of shame," even towards his own father (Collins, *Armadale* 627). Instead, he is motivated by monetary gain and personal power, exhibiting the "first expression of a genuine feeling" when granted an opportunity to demonstrate "his own cleverness" (Collins, *Armadale* 632). Collins presents the detective for the reader's unapproving gaze –

There he sat – the necessary Detective attendant on the progress of our national civilization; a man who was . . . the legitimate and intelligible product of the vocation that employed him; a man professionally ready on the merest suspicion (if the merest suspicion paid him) to get under our beds, and to look through gimlet-holes in our doors; a man who would have been useless to his employers if he could have felt a touch of human sympathy in his father's presence; and who would have deservedly forfeited his situation, if, under any circumstances whatever, he had been personally accessible to a sense of pity or a sense of shame.

(Collins, *Armadale* 627)

The reference here to the gimlet-holes alludes, of course, to the 1854 *Evans v. Robinson* trial mentioned at the start of Chapter 4. But the detective is a "necessary" by-product, in Collins's words, of "national civilization." At the same time, the detective is unable to feel remorse or emotional compunction, even in a family member's presence. He is incapable of "a sense of pity or a sense of shame," which precisely renders him well-suited to his unscrupulous profession.

The professional detective in *Armadale* conducts his investigations with no interest in their moral or social value. Detectives exchange information for money, insensitive to the fallout or disruption caused by such revelations. Earlier in the novel, Mrs Oldershaw also hires a "Confidential Agent" to learn about matters at Thorpe Ambrose, recruiting "a regular Jesuit at a private inquiry," who, unlike "all the Popish priests [she had] ever seen . . . has not got his slyness written on his face" (Collins, *Armadale* 195). This private spy obtains information through underhand and deceptive means, conjuring an almost Catholic air of intrigue. Similarly, Major Milroy protests Armadale's recruitment of a private spy, stating that such surveillance of a woman was reprehensible and, implicitly, un-English. Such actions are better suited to a "scoundrel" than to a gentleman, in the absence of a clear rationale or personal connection to the surveilled person (Collins, *Armadale* 441).

Collins had intuited before *The Moonstone* the ambiguities, moral slipperiness, and unpopularity of detectives among his readers. But the detective also represents an independent masculinity, amid the weakening of traditional forms of authority. As in *The Woman in White*, male characters in *Armadale* navigate a world without a stabilizing father figure. Traditional hierarchies no longer hold in this novel, as male characters seek advice from other male professionals (like Mr Pedgift), who are better able to observe attempts at social self-promotion. *Armadale*, like other sensation novels, rehearses a negotiation of values where traditional sources of authority give way to a transforming social landscape and their attendant moral ambiguities. Hence, a scheming woman exerts a destabilizing and dramatic influence over men, and threatens to undermine the social order. The resultant conflict amplifies the stakes for male characters, forcing them to negotiate new forms of authority corresponding to an age of social mobility. The detective is an ambivalent and independent articulation of masculinity, in that he has no moral allegiances to family or the domestic sphere. He is wholly self-interested, but in this regard, also impervious to the destabilizing effect of manipulative women. The detective cannot emerge as a hero, however, since his individualistic professionalism and masculinity do not contribute to social reproduction. His investigations may help repair the social order, but the detective does not properly inhabit a stable or domestic sphere. Rather, the detective is more closely associated with the endless entropy of the public sphere and infinite potential for self-invention in the city.

The rational detective in *The Moonstone*

There are a few differences between *The Moonstone* and Collins's earlier novels *No Name* and *Armadale*, not least the vindication of female wrong-doing and a new focus on male deception in *The Moonstone*. *The Moonstone* continues to rely heavily on foreign mystique and social outsiders like *Armadale*, but it ultimately casts blame neither on the principal male character, Mr Blake, nor on female or marginalized characters. The reader is invited to explore such possibilities, before they are discounted in the ultimate revelation. At the end of the novel, it is Mr Godfrey Ablewhite, a vice-president and manager of women's charities, who is revealed to have led a sexually immoral lifestyle, rather than a bigamous or deviant woman. For his own part, Sergeant Cuff believes that both Rachel Verinder and Rosanna are the prime suspects, who may have collaborated on a "deeply planned fraud" (Collins, *Moonstone* 167). As in Dickens's later *The Mystery of Edwin Drood*, Collins's *The Moonstone* posits that male hypocrisy is at the heart of a mystery that only seems shrouded in exotic or colonial mystery. *The Moonstone* also departs from other sensation novels studied thus far in foregrounding two objects as centerpieces to the dramatic narrative, namely, the yellow diamond and opium. While foreign jewels and laudanum had earlier featured in sensation novels, *The Moonstone* draws specific attention to these objects, which at times seem to possess a supernatural or otherworldly influence over human actions.

Another difference between *The Moonstone* and *Armadale* is that the binarism earlier seen in *Armadale* transforms into a revised relationship between the known and the unknown in *The Moonstone*. Binaries relating to the mind and the body, to the exotic East and England, give way or are at least complicated in *The Moonstone*. The binarism between freedom and fatalism in *Armadale* opens up in *The Moonstone* to project a wider horizon of the unknown, whether this relates to the mind's receptivity to chemical influences, to Eastern superstition, or to a person's secrets. These unknown elements becoming a definitive undercurrent in *The Moonstone*, generating and amplifying the sense of mystery until its final revelation at the novel's end. The mystery is no longer construed around a predictable set of binary choices, but is instead left more open-ended, hinting at secrets that have yet to be discovered and divulged. *The Moonstone* marks a greater openness, in this regard, towards empire and the imperial imagination, as the feeling of mystery is turned outwards. The process of detection becomes less a balance between two seemingly irreconcilable values and more a process of discovering and charting the unknown. The sense of mystery lingers at the end of the novel, with the reader suspecting that more could lie undivulged between the surface of respectable social appearances. In the novel, detection transforms from a process of uncovering deviant individuals to one of revealing the secrets of ordinary characters.

Collins prefaces *The Moonstone* with an intention to "trace the influence on character on circumstances," possibly responding to criticism that his earlier novels had focused on plot at the expense of credible characters (liii). Yet Collins does craft significant character idiosyncrasies and peculiarities to account for the unlikely developments in the plot. For instance, Rosanna has an "absurd" obsession over Mr Franklin Blake, who also exhibits "queer contradictions and uncertainties in his character" (Collins, *Moonstone* 59). Rosanna, Limping Lucy, and Mr Jennings are crucially associated with the diamond's disappearance or discovery, but are marginalized or misfit characters (as shall be further explored). Yet Collins manages to elevate the work of detection above any single individual. This is most plainly seen when Gabriel Betteredge confesses to have caught a "detective-fever," comparing the feverish excitement of participating in an investigation to an infection or disease (Collins, *Moonstone* 121, 129, 300). While acknowledging this desire to uncover secrets as "very disgraceful," Betteredge states that "a curious and stupefying restlessness got possession of [him]" (Collins, *Moonstone* 154). The mystery narrative is, in part, driven by a pervasive sense of such an "infection" surrounding not only the investigation, but also emanating from the aura of colonial intrigue (Collins, *Moonstone* 185). Sergeant Cuff is directly responsible for leaving behind the fever of investigation, as Betteredge states after the detective's departure: "Sergeant Cuff had left his infection behind him. Certain signs and tokens, personal to myself, warned me that the detective-fever was beginning to set in again" (Collins, *Moonstone* 185).

Sergeant Cuff in *The Moonstone* is instantly recognizable by Londoners as "the hero of many a famous story in every lawyer's office" with an "illustrious name" commanding attention (Collins, *Moonstone* 435, 441). This transformation from a minor character to near-heroic status in *The Moonstone* does not come without its own ambiguities. Sergeant Cuff is greeted with suspicion and even open disdain in the Verinder house, where he appears after the Moonstone's disappearance. Mrs Verinder complains, "There is something in that police-officer from London which I recoil from," sensing a "presentiment that he is bringing trouble and misery with him into the house" (Collins, *Moonstone* 105). During his presence at the Verinder house, it is as though his investigation into the crime may entail more troublesome consequences than the diamond's actual disappearance. Mrs Verinder shudders as Sergeant Cuff passes her and her daughter, Rachel, who also protests "the odious presence of a policeman under the same roof with herself" (Collins, *Moonstone* 109, 136). Both Mrs Verinder and the steward Betteredge lose their tempers at Sergeant Cuff. In one scene, the steward seizes the detective by the collar and dramatically pins him against a wall when Sergeant Cuff casts suspicion on Rachel (Collins, *Moonstone* 133, 158). During his inquiries, Sergeant Cuff is described as moving like a "snake in the grass" and behaving in an "underground way" (Collins, *Moonstone* 113, 137). Even as Sergeant Cuff becomes an inspiring character in the novel, he remains fraught with moral ambiguities and suspicion. Sergeant Cuff provokes ambivalent reactions to his methods and his inferences. Nowhere are these contradictions more apparent than when Betteredge states, "I had got by this time . . . to hate the Sergeant. But truth compels me to acknowledge that, in respect of readiness of mind, he was a wonderful man" (Collins, *Moonstone* 136). Again, he confesses, "I own I couldn't help liking the Sergeant – though I hated him all the time" (Collins, *Moonstone* 179).

Despite the detective's minute observations, he reaches the wrong conclusion, delaying the mystery's final revelation. Sergeant Cuff does not account for the body's influence over the mind, namely, the effect of laudanum on Mr Blake. He assumes, in his investigations, that the characters behave consciously and rationally, which Collins later undercuts. But Sergeant Cuff notes towards the end of the novel that detectives are not always infallible or correct, stating that "it's only in books that the officers of the detective force are superior to the weakness of making a mistake" (Collins, *Moonstone* 434).[2] Despite this confession, Sergeant Cuff is reputed to be without peer or equal in England when "unravelling a mystery" (Collins, *Moonstone* 95). He enters the narrative as a substitute for the incompetent and "muddle-headed" police officer Superintendent Seegrave from the local Yorkshire force (Collins, *Moonstone* 93). Sergeant Cuff arrives from London, exhibiting a professionalism and delicacy that contrasts with Superintendent Seegrave's brute inquiries.

The main distinction between Superintendent Seegrave and Sergeant Cuff is that the latter aims to reassure and win over the members of the Verinder family. Considering Superintendent Seegrave to have caused "a world of harm" in "set[ting] the servants' backs up," Sergeant Cuff aims to quickly "smooth them down again" (Collins, *Moonstone* 102, 107). In reassuring the members of the Verinder household, Sergeant Cuff obtains insights about their actions and motivations. He professes some experience in dealing with "family difficulties" and "cases of family scandal," a claim that also carries its own moral ambiguities (Collins, *Moonstone* 132, 163, 166–67). In contrast to the spies and detective of Collins's earlier novels, Sergeant Cuff operates by reading into character. Through his "roundabout ways," he attempts to read into Miss Verinder and Rosanna's personal motivations for crime (Collins, *Moonstone* 116). Hence, detective work becomes more character-based and psychologized in this novel, with Sergeant Cuff acting as a master manipulator of people's sentiments. To borrow James Eli Adams' words, Sergeant Cuff is the professional man who "depends crucially on strategies of persuasion or charismatic self-presentation designed to convince an audience" (*Dandies* 6). Betteredge confesses, while watching Sergeant Cuff at work, that he sat as though "enjoying a stage play" (Collins, *Moonstone* 125).

On his first appearance, Sergeant Cuff is introduced as "a grizzled, elderly man" appearing "so miserably lean that he looked as if he had not got an ounce of flesh on his bones" (Collins, *Moonstone* 96). His face is sharp, his skin "yellow and dry," while his eyes are tellingly "steely light grey" (Collins, *Moonstone* 96). Adding to his steely appearance, he has a soft walk, a melancholy voice, and "long lanky fingers [that] were hooked like claws" (Collins, *Moonstone* 96). In contrast to this hawkish (almost predatory) appearance, Sergeant Cuff professes an ardent passion for roses. He retires halfway through the novel to a cottage in "the little town of Dorking" to cultivate his rose garden (Collins, *Moonstone* 354). He reappears towards the end of the novel as an "innocent country-man," who looks as though he might have "lived in the country all his life" (Collins, *Moonstone* 433). Such contrasting details about his character reveal a negotiation between the detective's shrewd professionalism and a desire to render him more domestic. By allying Sergeant Cuff with the domestic sphere and the idlest of gardening pursuits, Collins presents his detective not only as a cool-headed, rational, and calculating professional man, but also as a domestic creature. Sergeant Cuff is almost feminized in his passion for roses, particularly as they decorate and beautify a rural cottage. Collins shields his detective from criticism that he is a purely disruptive force, destabilizing the domestic sphere through his investigations, by associating him with the homeliest of rural and domestic pleasures. Sergeant Cuff becomes an alternative iteration of domestic masculinity, in contrast to the patriarchal provider and father.

Another reason why Sergeant Cuff can evolve as a heroic character, conferring narrative justice and restoring confidence in reason, is due to the presence of exotic and foreign others in the novel. Sergeant Cuff enters the narrative to resolve the mystery of the missing diamond, constantly reminding the reader of the original cause of disruption. Crucially, Sergeant Cuff declines payment for his services, stating that his task was to "throw the necessary light on the matter of the missing Diamond" (Collins, *Moonstone* 160). The diamond, associated with Indian mystique, is repeatedly described as "cursed" and as "poison[ing the air] with mystery and suspicion" (Collins, *Moonstone* 66, 82, 181, 296). The Moonstone diamond seems to unleash a dulling and deadening influence over the dinner attendants, as though to bewitch their senses and weaken their reason. As Betteredge recalls, "the Devil (or the diamond) possessed that dinner-party" and the diamond may have "cast a blight on the whole company" (Collins, *Moonstone* 66, 69). The Moonstone is tainted with "the wicked Colonel's legacy," and its exotic origins cast its disappearance as a "romance" (Collins, *Moonstone* 76, 274).[3] Such an imperial mystery allows Collins to work on his reader's credulity with greater license than would have been feasible if the events have been restricted to England. The destabilizing effect of the diamond counterbalances the intrusive investigations of Sergeant Cuff, particularly as he is allied with the domestic sphere through his passion for roses.

The novel is also populated by unusual characters and social outsiders, even where they are not foreigners. As earlier noted, the characters most closely associated with the diamond's disappearance are peculiar outsiders. Mr Blake has "foreign sides [to] his character" and exhibits "twenty different minds about the Diamond in as many minutes," reflecting his patchwork education across France, Germany, and Italy (Collins, *Moonstone* 59). Rachel has unusually firm "ideas of her own" and a "stiff-necked" independence (Collins, *Moonstone* 52). Her "secret, and self-willed; odd and wild" ways contribute to the delay of the mystery's revelation (Collins, *Moonstone* 217). Rosanna is most clearly marked as an outsider at the Verinder house, with her "deformed shoulder" and "ugly" appearance (Collins, *Moonstone* 23, 113). Together with Limping Lucy, who has a lame foot, they are presented as "deformed girls" with "a kind of fellow-feeling for each other" (Collins, *Moonstone* 124).[4] Similarly, Ezra Jennings, who helps shed light on the diamond's disappearance, is described as startlingly "ugly" with "a gipsy darkness" in his complexion (Collins, *Moonstone* 319, 410). Mr Jennings is socially mistrusted and disliked, with piebald or "parti-colored" hair signifying his biraciality (Collins, *Moonstone* 331, 364).[5] He not only harbors a secret addiction to opium (reflecting Collins's own dependence on opium), but also seems to have a "female constitution" and melancholy disposition (Collins, *Moonstone* 369). When excited, his whole appearance becomes even stranger, as Mr Blake relates, describing his "gipsy complexion [as having] altered to a livid greyish paleness; his eyes [having] suddenly become wild and glittering" (Collins, *Moonstone* 373). One could argue that Mr Jennings's remarkable strangeness counteracts and deflects attention from the strangeness of Mr Blake's own actions under the influence of opium. These marginal characters and the exotic mystique of the diamond divert attention away from a morally ambiguous detective towards a more dispersed sense of mystery.[6] Collins brings home to England the mystique and exotic allure of the East, incorporating Indian characters who knock on the door of an English family's rural home. Collins stages a colonial drama daringly close to the English domestic sphere and a young couple. By opening the narrative towards a colonial encounter, the detective becomes less of an ambivalent character than one of many mysterious characters in a narrative imbued with imperial mystery.

As with other sensation novels, *The Moonstone* is about concealed identity, but departs from earlier novels of the sensation genre in incriminating male wrongdoing and criminality, in contrast to female deceit and bigamy. In the closing chapters, the reader learns through Sergeant Cuff's investigations that Mr Ablewhite, a barrister and philanthropist, had led two different lives. Mr Ablewhite had presented "to the public view . . . the spectacle of a gentleman," while concealing "the side [that] . . . exhibited this same gentleman in the totally different character of a man of pleasure, with a villa in the suburbs . . . and with a lady in the villa" (Collins, *Moonstone* 448). Mr Ablewhite appears to be a vice-president of women's charities, but is later revealed to have led a sexually illicit lifestyle. The mysterious narrative may depend on the moral ambivalence of women, on characters with physical deformities, and on racial others, but ultimately vindicates these characters. The novel achieves its twist through revealing Mr Ablewhite as an unlikely antagonist, even as it relies on ambivalent others to maintain its suspense and float the question of the criminal's identity.

Detective work here corresponds not only with the mystery's revelation and moral vindication, but also with narrative justice. The reader is withheld details in the narrative that are ultimately revealed and explained by the detective. Despite his failure to deduce the thief, Sergeant Cuff re-emerges in the narrative to explain in detail how Mr Ablewhite had likely stolen and deposited the diamond with a London money-lender. He elucidates not only the events of the fatal night and their consequences, but also allows the reader to trace the diamond's return to the Hindus in India. Sergeant Cuff restores faith in rational comprehension, thereby dispelling the destabilizing and mystical aura of the diamond. The detective offers a sense of narrative justice by explaining events that bridge a sense of narrative disruption and discontinuity. If the diamond hinted at the threat of colonial disorder and the unleashing of the unknown, Sergeant Cuff represents the restoration of reason and the mind's ability to penetrate even into the myth-shrouded heartland of colonial India. Hence, the reader is left with statements addressed to Sergeant Cuff and the lawyer Mr Bruff about the diamond's safe return to "its wild native land" (Collins, *Moonstone* 466).

In a partnership anticipating Sherlock Holmes's friendship with Dr Watson, Betteredge acts as a sounding-board and "assistant" for Sergeant Cuff (Collins, *Moonstone* 166). As a domestic man, Betteredge becomes the unwitting foil for Sergeant Cuff's investigations and also negotiates contradictory reactions to the ambivalent detective. Betteredge is the counterpart to the detective's calculating rationality in his devotion to the Verinder family, his oddly patriarchal views, and his desire for rural simplicity. He bridges the detective with the reader, observing Sergeant Cuff studying others. Sergeant Cuff, however, always remains a step ahead of Betteredge, meaning that while the reader glimpses his thought processes, the detective remains elusive and out of reach. The reader does not learn, for instance, how Sergeant Cuff correctly predicted that Betteredge would hear from the money-lender Mr Septimus Luker (Collins, *Moonstone* 178). Nor does the reader access the evidence for Sergeant Cuff's prediction that the three Indians would soon reappear. The detective remains partly shrouded in mystery and it is unclear whether his inferences are based on individual ingenuity or on evidence. By concealing the process of his own detections, the detective emerges as a distinctive and gifted (if somewhat ambiguous) individual. But detective work is not isolated to a single individual in this novel. As earlier noted, there are other characters who fulfil the role of the detective (such as Mr Bruff) in Sergeant Cuff's absence. More generally, detective work – or "detective-fever," as Betteredge terms it – is characterized by the compulsion to know and comprehend (Collins, *Moonstone* 121, 129, 300). Sergeant Cuff not only reinstates the social order against deviant others, but he also restores a sense of narrative continuity and cohesion. He restores faith in rational comprehension, even as the diamond and opium threaten to subordinate the mind to irrational or bodily forces.[7]

Notes

1 Laudanum could be consumed as poison to commit suicide, as was chosen by Fanny Imlay, Mary Wollstonecraft's illegitimate daughter, in 1816. While poison was not a popular method of suicide, opium consumption was the preferable option in such cases. In 1865, the suicide rate from opium was twice as high among men than among women, despite their more frequent association with women in popular culture (see Berridge and Edwards 80).

2 A similar sentiment had earlier been expressed in Ware's *The Female Detective*, which Collins had sent to his mother mere months before the first serial of *The Moonstone*.

3 Interpretations of the diamond abound, including (Roberts 168; Carens 240; Taylor, *In the Secret Theatre* 195; Mangham, *Violent Women* 82; Free; Hutter 184; Gruner 230; Heller 247; Park, "Empire" 133–44).

4 For more on representations of disability and "the abnormal body" in *The Moonstone*, see (Mossman).

5 For a postcolonial reading of Mr Jennings and his hybridity in the British imperial context, see (Willey).

6 For readings of imperialism in *The Moonstone*, see (Manavalli; Free; Carens; Mukherjee 166–88).

7 For more on opium in *The Moonstone*, see (Hayter 256–59).

10 After sensation novels

Imperial themes and detectives in Dickens's *The Mystery of Edwin Drood* and Doyle's stories

Dickens's final and unfinished novel develops the themes of hidden identity and jealous conspiracy that were earlier seen in *Our Mutual Friend* (1865). But critics generally agree that *The Mystery of Edwin Drood* was largely written in response to and inspired by Collins's *The Moonstone*. Sue Lonoff notes that Dickens "resolved to improve on Collins by writing a mystery of his own," as *The Moonstone* had outperformed sales of Dickens's *Great Expectations* in his journal *All the Year Round* (163). Jerome Meckier observes a long-running literary rivalry between Dickens and Collins, as they mutually "appropriate[d] and revise[d] each other's ideas" (197; see also Nayder, *Unequal*). Between 1868 and 1869, critics also observe a weakening in their friendship, likely aggravated by Kate Dickens's unhappy marriage to Collins's younger brother, Charles. Upon its first serial, Dickens praised *The Moonstone* as "a very curious story – wild, and yet domestic" and perhaps as Collins's best work (*Letters* III, 534). The following year, however, he wrote to his friend William Henry Wills that *The Moonstone's* "construction was wearisome beyond endurance" with a "vein of obstinate conceit in it that makes enemies of readers" (Dickens, *Letters* XII, 159). For his part, Collins saw Dickens's literary powers on the decline, suggesting that *The Mystery of Edwin Drood* was possibly "the last laboured effort, the melancholy work of a worn-out brain," incomparable to his earlier novels, like *Oliver Twist* (qtd in Nayder, *Unequal* 13; see Meckier 199; Johnson II, 259).

There are similarities – and differences – between *The Moonstone* and *The Mystery of Edwin Drood*, but Dickens's stylization of the detective narrative demonstrates that the market and public appetite for mysteries remained strong, even after the popularity of sensation novels. As public tastes shifted from domestic melodramas to complex mysteries, Dickens's novel extended social anxieties and imperial themes beyond the domestic sphere. Like Collins, Dickens casts his main antagonist as an Englishman (though the manuscript remains unfinished), but the prime suspect is an Oriental outsider. Tellingly, Dickens read *The Moonstone* as simultaneously

DOI: 10.4324/9781003369622-11

"wild, and yet domestic," a contradictory balance that he replicates in *The Mystery of Edwin Drood*. Dickens's unfinished novel is overt in its racial appropriation and use of foreigners as scapegoats in the narrative. Collins has varyingly been characterized as a feminist and sympathizer for colonized people (at least in the Victorian context), but *The Mystery of Edwin Drood* opportunistically presents a temperamentally flawed foreigner as the prime suspect for murder. If *The Moonstone* explores the return of a stolen diamond to a colony and the idea of the "good native," Dickens's novel casts Neville Landless as a suspect for his "lamentable violence of temper," despite the absence of any credible circumstantial evidence (Dickens, *Mystery* 84). Neville is denied access to the domain of Englishness due to his "vindictive and violent nature," which casts him as an outsider to English male respectability (Dickens, *Mystery* 146).

Conventionally, critics have seen Dickens as exploring criminal psychology within respectable society, rather than as a foreign influence. Meckier suggests that Dickens saw "society's evils [as] aris[ing] from deep within itself," exploring "the evolution of the criminal mentality . . . now ensconced within a reputable member of a society" (155, 183). This may have been an idea that Dickens acquired from *The Moonstone* and he indeed completed the opening chapters to his novel within two months of *The Moonstone*'s final serial (Johnson II, 1114). More recently, critics have taken the opposite stance, with Nayder arguing that Dickens "orientalizes his English villain" through the association of opium dens (*Unequal* 187). Nayder points out that the Englishwoman Rosa Bud is "threatened . . . at the hands of oriental men," as her "vulnerability and innocence" contrasts with the Landless siblings (*Unequal* 188).[1] Indeed, Dickens makes use of racial prejudice and imperial anxieties throughout the narrative, casting Neville as a likely suspect in the interim before the murderer's exposure. Neville becomes a composite of supposed sympathies towards the oppressed, while also reflecting white male desire and anxieties. Neville desires Rosa, expresses gratitude to Mr Crisparkle, and yet harbors passionate instincts as an oppressed outsider. His actions are shrouded in superstitions of the white man's own invention, as indicated when John Jasper anticipates "some horrible consequences" occurring to Edwin Drood as a result of Neville's "demoniacal passion" and "savage rage" (Dickens, *Mystery* 85). Even though the prime suspect shifts to Mr Jasper in the course of the novel, the novel becomes complicit in diverting suspicion towards Neville, who is presented as constitutionally violent.

While writing *The Mystery of Edwin Drood*, Dickens also penned an article in *All the Year Round* entitled "The Ruffian" (10 August 1868). In this article, he criticized the pervasive presence of ruffians and thieves on the London streets, praising the police as "an excellent force" but arguing that the policing system was inadequate (Dickens, "Ruffian" 423). Instead of casting individual detectives as heroes, Dickens proposed the idea that "on all great occasions, when they come together in numbers, the mass of the English people are their own trustworthy Police" ("Ruffian" 423). One sees a progression in Dickens's thought here that the common people could act as detectives, without the need for professional spies. Prior to writing *The Mystery of Edwin Drood*, Dickens explored the idea of a murder mystery, in which an uncle would kill his nephew but eventually be discovered and convicted (see Slater 601). He did not indicate that a detective would heroically resolve this mystery, but it does seem likely that he was inspired (perhaps by *The Moonstone*) to heighten a sense of intrigue through the inclusion of racial others.

This study has mainly focused on the detective as an individual character while teasing out elements of detection in sensation novels. As an incomplete novel, *The Mystery of Edwin Drood* does not present a fully fleshed detective character, who in earlier novels had been incorporated to resolve lingering doubts or conveniently uncover information. The detective often appears later in a narrative and it is unclear whether Dickens might have included such a character in *The Mystery of Edwin Drood*. What the events building up to the mystery reveal, however, is that the detective might have entered the narrative where another ambivalent threat had already been identified. This sense of intrigue and mystery arises from foreign others, which Dickens seems keen to include in his novel. From the opening pages, Dickens features racial outsiders and the Orient infiltrating into the "ancient English Cathedral Town" of Cloisterham (*Mystery* 1). This inclusion of foreign outsiders, only to eradicate or dissolve their threats, would become more pronounced in later iterations of detective fiction, such as Doyle's stories. The imperial romance would feed into the development of detective stories and into the rational masculinity of the detective.

Foreign intrigue and English identity in *The Mystery of Edwin Drood*

From the first paragraph of the novel, Dickens blends the atmospheric exoticism of Turkey and Asia with the vision of an ancient English town. The exotic is imaginatively projected onto a rural (and potentially Gothic) English backdrop. The narrator gestures to the grey square tower of the Cloisterham Cathedral, remarking,

> What *is* the spike that intervenes, and who has set it up? Maybe, it is set up by the Sultan's orders for the impaling of a horde of Turkish robbers, one by one. It is so, for cymbals clash, and the Sultan goes by to his palace in long procession. Ten thousand scimitars flash in the sunlight,

and thrice ten thousand dancing-girls strew flowers. Then, follow white elephants caparisoned in countless gorgeous colours, and infinite number and attendants. Still, the Cathedral tower rises in the background, where it cannot be, and still no writhing figure is on the grim spike.

(Dickens, *Mystery* 1, italics in original)

From the evocation of the "Sultan's orders" to the "horde of Turkish robbers" to the conjured images of "ten thousand [flashing] scimitars" and "ten thousand dancing-girls," Dickens opportunistically overlays Oriental imagery against an otherwise nondescript English town. None of these conjured images are actually factual occurrences – they are merely "maybe" the imagined reason why the Cathedral tower rises in the background. Yet Dickens conjures the mystique of an imaged Orient to lend intrigue to his narrative, foreshadowing the opportunistic way in which he will later make use of Eastern characters.

Scholars have been quick to point out that, as mentioned in Chapter 2, Dickens was a fierce critic of racial others, as seen in his charged comments following the Indian Mutiny. As Timothy L. Carens points out, Dickens was hardly alone in his view of Indians as morally troubled, noting that, in the late 1860s, "it was widely believed that Indians were instinctual, impulsive, and fanatic . . . they supposedly lacked the mechanisms of self-control that guarantee sound government at the level of self and society alike" (239).[2] Dickens, like many of his contemporaries, likely saw, in the words of Audrey Fisch, "black, mixed-race, and other nonwhite characters as a potentially disruptive problem for English society" (314). But perhaps exploring whether Dickens remained a proponent or became a critic of empire here may miss the point. As a writer, Dickens opportunistically and self-servingly appropriated suggestive and evocative imagery likely to capture his readers' attention.[3] Indeed, his open willingness to scapegoat racial others as potential criminal suspects makes this unfinished novel an uncomfortable and even disturbing read for a modern audience. Dickens may expose contemporary prejudices against racial others in the process, but he does not significantly question or problematize such discriminatory perceptions. Regardless, the first monthly part of the novel sold well and the public responded enthusiastically. Sales of the first number reached 50,000 copies, 10,000 more than Dickens's previous novel, *Our Mutual Friend*, prompting him to exult to his friend James T. Fields that the novel had "very, very far outstripped every one of its predecessors" (qtd. in Slater 609).

Dickens casts suspicion on foreign others from the opening pages of the novel, where he introduces "a Chinaman, a Lascar, and a haggard woman" (*Mystery* 1). These characters do not reappear in subsequent chapters, but are associated with opium smoking dens. The descriptions of opium-smoking were based on Dickens's first-hand experiences of Shadwell in London's East End during a guided tour in autumn 1869, possibly led by Inspector Field (see Dickens, *Letters* XII, 520–51 [Dickens to Sir John Bowring, 5 May 1870]). Dickens includes racial others (such as Turkish, Chinese, and Asian characters) to combine the familiar with the exotic and unfamiliar. He sustains a sense of mystery and criminality, which he had earlier praised in *The Moonstone*, while insinuating a sense of the exotic amid the mundane. Mr Jasper is later cast as an opium-eater, while his engineer nephew Edwin plans to "[go] wake up Egypt a little" (Dickens, *Mystery* 54).[4] While the close association between the imperial romance and detective story would become more overt later in the nineteenth century, there is already opportunistic use of foreign and imperial elements here to heighten a sense of mystery in this novel. In the second monthly part, Dickens introduces Neville and Helena Landless, who walk "through the ancient streets . . . much as if they were beautiful barbaric captives brought from some wild tropical domain" (*Mystery* 43). In his working notes, Dickens wrote that the Landless siblings would have a "mixture of Oriental blood – or imperceptibly acquired nature – in them," followed by a doubly underscored "Yes" (*Mystery* 222).

Where racial others had been cast as ambivalent characters in Collins's *Armadale* (Ozias Midwinter) and *The Moonstone* (Ezra Jennings), Neville in *The Mystery of Edwin Drood* is associated with the perceived constitutional ferocity of Asia. Neville hints at his dark past, stating that he had been "brought up among abject and servile dependants [*sic*], of an inferior race" and that he may have contracted "a drop of what is tigerish in their blood" (Dickens, *Mystery* 47). Dickens willingly associates Ceylon (and more broadly, Asia) with tyranny, violence, cunning, and "tigerish" animal metaphors, underscoring an imperial view of racial hierarchy. From his first conversation with the cleric Mr Crisparkle, Neville describes himself as "secret and revengeful," "false and mean," and "suppress[ing] a deadly and bitter hatred" since his childhood (Dickens, *Mystery* 46). The image of Neville confiding in a white male cleric, instinctively trusting him, establishes a sense of patronage that only emphasizes his vulnerability in British society. Helena takes the role of confidante and protectress towards both her brother and Rosa, even as she strikes a contrast to the Englishwoman with her own "dark fiery eyes," her "lustrous gipsy-face," and "intense black hair" (Dickens, *Mystery* 52–54). Neville is characterized as harboring a "monstrous" infatuation with Rosa, who is associated with the atmosphere of springtime and virginal youthfulness (Dickens, *Mystery* 81). If Neville is a temperamentally flawed and "dangerous" character, Rosa is "an amiable, giddy, wilful [*sic*], winning little creature" with whom he is obsessed (Dickens, *Mystery* 64).

If the gentleman represents a masculine figure of ascendent respectability and social mobility, Neville is precluded from this domain of Englishness through his impulsive temperament. Mr Honeythunder states clearly that Englishness consists of Christian and gentlemanly values, such as "the justice that should belong to Christians, and the restraints that should belong to gentlemen" (Dickens, *Mystery* 153). But even Neville's complexion, as the mayor Mr Sapea points out, is "Un-English" and, as the narrator explains, "anything [declared] to be Un-English, he [Mr Sapea] consider[ed] that thing everlastingly sunk in the bottomless pit" (Dickens, *Mystery* 128). One sees here a clearer articulation of criminality as the policing of Englishness, and the association between late Victorian mystery narratives with the desired purification of English identity. Dickens may well have attempted to challenge the moral distinction between the English and un-English racial other, since he planned to locate the threat to English society within its own hypocritical confines. From this angle, Mr Jasper would be "the true monster of respectability," in Meckier's words, revealing "a hypocritical and deteriorating social system" (156, 192). Nonetheless, Dickens becomes complicit in the racial prejudice against foreign outsiders, as English virtue (represented by Rosa) is threatened and desired by a distinctly "un-English" character in the novel.

One of the more troubling scenes in which this racial complicity becomes clear is the exchange between Edwin and Neville. Edwin explicitly states to Neville that he can profess no knowledge of "white men," even though he "may know a black common fellow, or black common boaster . . . but you are no judge of white men" (Dickens, *Mystery* 61). This flippant and racist remark is doubly ironic for the novel's opportunistic inclusion of foreign others. Immediately following the scene, the narrator acknowledges the "insulting allusion to his dark skin," but Neville seems to transform into "a dangerous animal" before the reader's eyes (Dickens, *Mystery* 61). Neville confides in Mr Crisparkle that Edwin had "heated that tigerish blood," a view echoed by Mr Jasper, who says that "there is something of the tiger in his dark blood" (Dickens, *Mystery* 61). Edwin observes that Ceylon is "at a safe distance" and "a long way off," even as the novel dabbles in the air of mystery excited by the foreign siblings' arrival (Dickens, *Mystery* 60). What emerges, then, is an inclusion of Oriental imagery and Asian characters for vicarious enjoyment and commercial gain. Dickens subjects his foreign characters to suffering and scapegoating, even as he seems to extend a white flag of supposed sympathy. Neville's continued presence at Cloisterham is premised on an implied submission to this racist insult, which Edwin never genuinely apologizes for but merely agrees to forget (see Dickens, *Mystery* 86).

The character who appears as a potential detective in *The Mystery of Edwin Drood* is the lawyer Mr Grewgious. He is marked by his inscrutable expressions and reactions, especially when Mr Jasper collapses upon hearing that Edwin's engagement had already been cancelled. Mr Grewgious is partly motivated by a protective impulse towards Rosa, who considers him her guardian. In her presence, he behaves with "chivalry" and "knight-errantry," defending her against the predatory Mr Jasper (Dickens, *Mystery* 179, 183). But it is Mr Jasper who stalks the streets like a spy, not the detective character. Mr Grewgious is cast as a protector of a young woman and a persecuted foreigner, while Mr Jasper develops into a licentious, gloating, and potentially sexually violent opium-smoker. Even here, however, his criminality is expressed in subtly racial terms, as he watches Rosa with a "darkly threatening" expression" and leans over a sundial as if to set "his black mark upon the very face of day" (Dickens, *Mystery* 170). Mr Jasper's transformation into a "brigand and a wild beast" coincides with Neville's disappearance from the narrative (Dickens, *Mystery* 191). While Neville is secluded in an attic room, his physical absence allows for the displacement of criminal suspicion onto Mr Jasper. Mr Jasper stalks the streets around Neville's residence, "sneak[ing] to and fro, and dodg[ing] up and down" the neighborhood (Dickens, *Mystery* 186). The suspicious activities of the detective here are displaced onto the criminal, as Mr Grewgious acts like a policeman on the beat, aiming to elude Mr Jasper's deceptions. Mr Grewgious defends the vulnerable Rosa, while Mr Jasper appears "impassive, moody, solitary, resolute, concentrated on one idea" (Dickens, *Mystery* 204). While the novel remains unfinished, Dickens seems to resolve the contradictions and negative perceptions of the detective by distinguishing spying and surveillance as criminal activities.

Into the *fin-de-siècle*: Doyle's Sherlock Holmes

As a study focusing mainly on the period between the 1840s and the 1860s, the present reading of Doyle's detective stories merely skims the surface of a richer and broader analysis. It would be amiss, however, to omit a discussion of the most famous detective in Victorian (and British) literature. Importantly, the historical context changed in the final decades of the nineteenth century. The periodical press continued to expand in the late nineteenth century, spawning a formula for success that relied on short stories rather than serialized novels. As Winnie Chan observes, "at the end of the nineteenth century, the growth of the periodical press made short stories a necessity to any periodical with aspirations to popularity" (x). Altick notes the formula for success was threefold – "a price of 6d. or lower; plenty of light fiction and amusing non-fiction; and as many illustrations as possible" (*English* 363). The periodical press in England also became less reliant on its London audience, reaching readers across Britain and in America (see Altick, *English* 356–57). *The Strand Magazine* was one of the most successful periodicals to take advantage of these altered material

circumstances, offering stories that condensed the drama and sensationalism of earlier detective stories into readily consumable fiction. In 1896, the
circulation of *The Strand Magazine* in one month was 392,000 (including
60,000 to the USA), a number far above many other English newspapers in
the prior decade (Altick, *English* 396). *The Strand Magazine* was, as Chan
explains, a sixpence-magazine "copiously and conspicuously illustrated"
and ready "to publish sequels at the demand of its readers" (xix, 13).
Doyle was among writers enticed by the opportunity to, in Chan's words,
"convert literary wares into quick cash" offered by the booming late-cen-
tury periodical press (2).

The late nineteenth century was also distinct from the mid-century in that
it witnessed greater pessimism regarding Britain's economic and imperial
hegemony (see Ledger). Historians like Susie L. Steinbach point out that the
period between 1873 and 1896 was marked by economic decline and stagnation (92–93). Others argue that, while such estimations overstate the extent
of Britain's economic slowdown, it had clearly "slipped from its glorious
mid-century pre-eminence" of robust growth (E. Griffin, "Patterns" 92).
As a period marked also by domestic social instability, the tenor of late-
century detective stories tends less towards patriarchal triumphalism and
gestures more towards a complex socio-political landscape. In addition,
the popular perception of detectives steadily declined from around 1870
(see Saunders 168). Public mistrust in the detective force reached their peak
in 1877, when internal corruption in the Detective Branch was exposed
and extensively covered in the press. The concomitant scandal revealed, in
Shpayer-Makov's words, that "corrupt practices, including the collusion of
the police with criminals . . . were endemic in the very group considered the
elite of all detectives in the land" (31).

Prior to Sherlock Holmes's appearance in *The Strand Magazine* from
1891, Doyle published his first book featuring the famous detective. The
opening pages of *A Study in Scarlet* introduce a fatigued and war-weary
Dr Watson as a retired surgeon who served in Afghanistan. Dr Watson
was injured during his service and professes to have experienced "nothing but misfortune and disaster" as a result of his deployment in the war
(Doyle, *Study* 5). He recalls that he had seen his "own comrades hacked to
pieces at Maiwand" in Afghanistan and had been "struck down by enteric
fever, that curse of our Indian possessions" (Doyle, *Study* 5, 42). When he
returns to London, Dr Watson initially wanders about with neither "kith
nor kin" until he meets Holmes (Doyle, *Study* 5–6). The sense of imperial
fatigue and disenchantment distinguishes the late Victorian detective from
his mid-nineteenth-century predecessors. Holmes is similarly a reaction to
this imperial disenchantment, with his materialist and empiricist method of
deduction underscoring the knowability of the visible world.[5] While Doyle
himself was both a scientist and later a spiritualist, Holmes appears to

reject superstition and instinct as offering intuitive access to knowledge (see Lycett, *The Man Who Created*). The world is readable through its material traces, much as an archaeologist can piece together information about the past through its remains.

In this context, foreign others and colonial natives do not merely evoke an exotic or alluring mystique. They also feature as criminal nuisances to be apprehended by a disinterested and unaffected masculine type. Throughout his stories, Doyle introduces Holmes as a nonchalant, disaffected, and somewhat vain English bachelor. In contrast to the physically demanding and laborious work of detection in earlier novels, Holmes employs "street Arabs" or young boys to spy on suspects and gather information for him. As a "consulting detective," Holmes often refines and reinterprets information that has already been acquired (Doyle, *Study* 19–20). In *The Sign of the Four*, published three years later by the American *Lippincott's Monthly Magazine*, Holmes proudly declares that he is "the only unofficial consulting detective" in the world, transforming his profession to an exclusive vocation (Doyle, *Sign* 2). The transformation of the detective into a disaffected masculine type reflects the general fatigue of imperial administration. In the *fin-de-siècle*, the detective is "an incurably lazy devil" who does not always venture outside his room (Doyle, *Study* 25). In his own words, Holmes's work consists in "listen[ing] to their story, they listen to my comments, and then I pocket my fee" (Doyle, *Study* 20). Surveillance and spying are the exception, rather than the norm in his work. Detective work becomes a dignified intellectual activity in Doyle's stories, akin to rarefied armchair philosophizing, separate from the more vulgar and morally ambiguous work of collecting incriminating evidence.

Even as Doyle's stories focus on Holmes as a character with unique perceptive qualities, the detective always remains at a distance from the reader. As seen earlier in *The Moonstone*, the detective's mind becomes the object of scrutiny, since he provides narrative certainty and resolution. Perhaps for this reason, Jon Thompson suggests that "Holmes is the first truly complex, fully rounded, psychologically interesting detective hero" (61). Doyle presents a web of narrative possibilities, often through other detective characters, but Holmes intuits and withholds crucial information that delays narrative closure. Detective work corresponds to authoritative interpretation, as the various possibilities and scenarios are resolved through Holmes's explanation. In *The Sign of the Four*, Holmes becomes a more independent masculine figure, "a calculating machine" in Dr Watsons's words, who embodies "true cold reason" (Doyle, *Sign* 117). The investigative cases become reducible to stimulating mental exercises, as Holmes "crave[s] for mental exaltation" (Doyle, *Sign* 6). By the late nineteenth century, detective work had become material for the mass's appetite for excitement and sensation. The familiar themes of colonial theft and scheming foreigners derive from late imperial romances, as much as sensation novels. But the sensationalism of sensation novels continued to characterize the Victorian detective's work.

Notes

1 As Lonoff observed, Dickens maintained "a fundamentally Victorian reverence towards 'angels in the house'" in his fiction, contrasting with his own domestic problems around this time (168).
2 Carens argues that Collins in *The Moonstone* "question[s] the extent to which 'the English character' differs from its ungovernable colonial counterpart," a theme that Dickens seems to have picked up in *The Mystery of Edwin Drood* (239).
3 This was seen earlier, for instance, in his depiction of the Jewish character Mr Riah in *Our Mutual Friend*.
4 In relation to this, Hyungji Park writes that the novel "[exhibits] Empire as popular theatrical entertainment domesticat[ing] representations of Egypt, away from exotic mystification to homegrown cultural products" ("Going" 530).
5 For more on imperial themes in Doyle's early novels, see (O'Dell; Dearinger; Reitz 64–78; Thompson 60–79).

Coda

The ambivalence of the detective as a literary construct in Victorian sensation fiction is ultimately a story about the changing and at times contradictory anxieties of the burgeoning middle class. The ambivalence of the detective as a literary character can be explained through his simultaneous social mobility and the conservative function, he played in consolidating class boundaries. While the detective as a character moves freely across public and private domains, penetrating secrets through his powers of acute observation and defying class distinctions, his work principally benefited the middle class. As Worthington mentions, the middle class people were the primary beneficiaries of the new police, whose work involved "the protection of property through the prevention of crime" (149; see Chapter 4). The detective as a character accentuated middle-class anxieties about the erosion of class boundaries (even as the middle class was expanding throughout the nineteenth century), while his work served to consolidate their interests. The ambivalence of his characterization in sensation fiction stems from his defiance of clear-cut categorization. The detective is neither contained within established ideas of masculinity, nor within the domestic or public spheres. Instead, the detective transgresses social boundaries and flouts codes of conduct about transparency, decency, and privacy in his unrelenting quest for secrets. As such, he embodies an ascendant ideal of the self-made professional, even as he challenges existent notions of propriety in, at times, repellant ways.

As sensation novels demonstrate, the Victorian middle class was anxious to protect their social status and domestic privacy. Trodd points out the ambivalence between the desire to maintain privacy and the necessary interactions between the middle class and members of the professional and working classes. There ensued, she argues, "a whole range of worries about the values of openness and privacy, among which many Victorian writers oscillate uneasily" (*Domestic Crime* 5). The detective, as a fluid and socially mobile character, exposes middle-class anxieties because he intrudes into the domestic sphere with a publicly sanctioned authority. In

DOI: 10.4324/9781003369622-12

addition, while the middle class was anxious to protect the sanctity of the private sphere, the functioning of the household was necessarily dependent on domestic service, usually obtained from the lower classes. Hence, while the middle class was keen to distinguish themselves from the working class, their household economy required frequent interactions with and employment from members of the wider society.

These interactions were often dramatized in fiction as morally compromising. While such imagined liaisons were exaggerated for sensational effect, they gesture to an underlying fear in the middle class that their social status was not as secure or as insulated as they might have desired. The middle class may have wished to distinguish itself from the working class and their vulgar associations with labor, but their existence was entirely dependent on broader social and economic obligations, which precluded the possibility of self-containment. The middle class was implicated in a wider economy, which, taken to imagined lengths, might link them to social networks inclusive of criminal activity or wrongdoing.

Novels that depict the wife as criminal or socially deviant further reveal the middle-class anxiety that such compromising relations might infiltrate into the heart of the family unit. A bigamous wife was seen not only as a monstrous outgrowth of modern society, flouting moral norms to take advantage of enhanced social mobility, but also as exposing the tenuous ground on which the middle-class ideal rested. The bigamous wife as a figure in sensation fiction reveals cracks in a gender ideology that placed an undue burden on the "lady of the house," to quote Trodd, as "the guardian of the inner sanctuary" (*Domestic Crime* 7). Further, the bigamous wife as a literary projection gestures to the working-class and mercantile origins from which the Victorian middle class emanated.

In some ways, there are strong parallels between the bigamous wife and the detective as self-made individuals. It is unfortunate that the detective's ambivalent heroism translates into moral monstrosity and deprivation in his female counterpart, the bigamous wife. The woman who attempted to raise herself on the social ladder, through self-invention and sexual deception, encountered moral censure, particularly when she was portrayed as young and attractive. The self-made woman was a social anomaly that could hardly be countenanced, in contrast to the detective's more ambivalent portrayal. Victorian sensation fiction shaped these two characters in response to a similar set of middle-class anxieties, but it was the male detective that would evolve into an identifiable heroic type.

Works Cited

Ackroyd, Peter. *Wilkie Collins*. Doubleday, 2012.

Adams, James Eli. *Dandies and Desert Saints: Styles of Victorian Manhood*. Cornell UP, 1995.

———. *A History of Victorian Literature*. Wiley-Blackwell, 2009.

Ainsworth, W. Harrison. *Jack Sheppard: A Romance*. A. and W. Galignani, 1840.

Allan, Janice M. "The Contemporary Response to Sensation Fiction." *The Cambridge Companion to Sensation Fiction*, edited by Andrew Mangham, Cambridge UP, 2013, pp. 85–98.

Altick, Richard D. *The English Common Reader: A Social History of the Mass Reading Public, 1800–1900*. The U of Chicago P, 1957.

———. *The Presence of the Present: Topics of the Day in the Victorian Novel*. Ohio State UP, 1991.

Arata, Stephen. *Fictions of Loss in the Victorian Fin De Siecle*. Cambridge UP, 1996.

Auerbach, Nina. *Woman and the Demon: The Life of a Victorian Myth*. Harvard UP, 1982.

Auger, Emily E. "Male Gothic Detection and the Pre-Raphaelite Woman in *Lady Audley's Secret*." *Clues*, vol. 26, no. 3, 2008, pp. 3–14.

Barikman, Richard, et al. *Corrupt Relations: Dickens, Thackeray, Trollope, Collins, and the Victorian Sexual System*. Columbia UP, 1982.

Basch, Françoise. *Relative Creatures: Victorian Women in Society and the Novel*. Schocken Books, 1974.

Beller, Anne-Marie. " 'The Fashions of the Current Season': Recent Critical Work on Victorian Sensation Fiction." *Victorian Literature and Culture*, vol. 45, no. 2, 2017, pp. 461–73.

———. "Sensation Fiction in the 1850s." *The Cambridge Companion to Sensation Fiction*, edited by Andrew Mangham, Cambridge UP, 2013, pp. 7–20.

Bennett, Mark. "Generic Gothic and Unsettling Genre: Mary Elizabeth Braddon and the Penny Blood." *Gothic Studies*, vol. 13, no. 1, 2011, pp. 38–54.

Berridge, Virginia, and Griffith Edwards. *Opium and the People: Opiate Use in Nineteenth-Century England*. Yale UP, 1981.

Boz. "Full Report of the Second Meeting of the Mudfog Association for the Advancement of Everything." *Bentley's Miscellany*, vol. 4 (1838), p. 209. *ProQuest*, www.proquest.com/historical-periodicals/full-report-second-meeting-mudfog-association/docview/1310856081/se-2.

Braddon, Mary Elizabeth. *Aurora Floyd*. 1863. Edited by P. D. Edwards, Oxford UP, 1996.

———. *The Black Band or, the Mysteries of Midnight*. 1861. George Vickers, 1877.

———. "Devoted Disciple: The Letters of Mary Elizabeth Braddon to Sir Edward Bulwer-Lytton, 1862–1873." *Harvard Library Bulletin*, vol. 22, no. 1, 1974, pp. 5–35, nrs.harvard.edu/URN-3:HUL.INSTREPOS:37363293.

———. *Lady Audley's Secret*. 1862. Edited by Lyn Pykett, Oxford UP, 2012.

———. "My First Novel: *The Trail of the Serpent*." *The Idler Magazine*, vol. 3, Feb.-Jul. 1893, pp. 19–30.

———. *The Trail of the Serpent*. 1861. Ward, Lock, and Tyler, 1866.

Brantlinger, Patrick. *Rule of Darkness: British Literature and Imperialism, 1830–1914*. Cornell UP, 1988.

———. "What is 'Sensational' About the 'Sensation Novel'?" *Nineteenth-Century Fiction*, vol. 37, no. 1, 1982, pp. 1–28.

Briggs, Asa. *Victorian Things*. The U of Chicago P, 1988.

Brown, Lucy. *Victorian News and Newspapers*. Clarendon Press, 1985.

Browne, Hablot Knight. "Friendly Behaviour of Mr. Bucket, *Bleak House* (1852–3) plate." 1853. *Wikimedia*, commons.wikimedia.org/wiki/File:Friendly_Behaviour_of_Mr._Bucket,_Bleak_House_(1852-3)_plate.png.

———. "The Old Man of the Name of Tulkinghorn, *Bleak House* (1852–3) plate." 1853. *Wikimedia*, commons.wikimedia.org/wiki/File:The_old_man_of_the_name_of_Tulkinghorn,_Bleak_House_(1852-3)_plate.png.

Carens, Timothy L. "Outlandish English Subjects in *the Moonstone*." *Reality's Dark Light: The Sensational Wilkie Collins*, edited by Maria K. Bachman and Don Richard Cox, The U of Tennessee P, 2003, pp. 239–65.

Chamber's Edinburgh Journal, vol. 11–20 (new series), 1849–1853.

Chamber's Encyclopaedia: A Dictionary of Universal Knowledge for the People, vol. 4, W. and R. Chambers, 1862.

Chan, Winnie. *The Economy of the Short Story in British Periodicals of the 1890s*. Routledge, 2007.

Chase, Karen, and Michael Levenson. *The Spectacle of Intimacy: A Public Life for the Victorian Family*. Princeton UP, 2000.

Clarke, Bob. *From Grub Street to Fleet Street: An Illustrated History of English Newspapers to 1899*. Routledge, 2016.

Clarke, William M. *The Secret Life of Wilkie Collins*. Ivan R. Dee, 1991.

Cobbe, Frances Power. "Celibacy Vs. Marriage (*Fraser's Magazine*, Feb. 1862)." *'Criminals, Idiots, Women, and Minors': Victorian Writing by Women on Women*, edited by Susan Hamilton, 2nd ed., Broadview Press, 2004, pp. 50–59.

———. "Criminals, Idiots, Women, and Minors (*Fraser's Magazine*, Dec. 1868)." *'Criminals, Idiots, Women, and Minors': Victorian Writing by Women on Women*, edited by Susan Hamilton, 2nd ed., Broadview Press, 2004, pp. 90–110.

———. "Wife-Torture in England (*Contemporary Review*, Apr. 1878)." *'Criminals, Idiots, Women, and Minors': Victorian Writing by Women on Women*, edited by Susan Hamilton, 2nd ed., Broadview Press, 2004, pp. 111–44.

Cohen, Michael. "Godwin's *Caleb Williams*: Showing the Strains in Detective Fiction." *Eighteenth-Century Fiction*, vol. 10, no. 2, 1998, pp. 203–20.

Collins, Philip. *Dickens and Crime*, 3rd ed., St. Martin's Press, 1994.

Collins, Wilkie. *Armadale*. 1866. Edited by Catherine Peters, Oxford UP, 1989.

———. "The Diary of Anne Rodway: In Two Chapters, Chapter the First." *Household Words*, vol. 14, no. 330, 1856, pp. 1–7.

———. "The Diary of Anne Rodway: In Two Chapters, Chapter the Second." *Household Words*, vol. 14, no. 331, 1856, pp. 30–38.

———. *The Law and the Lady*. 1875. Edited by Jenny Bourne Taylor, Oxford UP, 1999.

———. *The Letters of Wilkie Collins*. Edited by William Baker and William M. Clarke, vol. 2 (1866–1889). Macmillan, 1999.

———. *The Moonstone*. 1868. Edited by John Sutherland, Oxford UP, 1999.

———. *No Name*. 1862. Edited by Virginia Blain, Oxford UP, 1999.

———. "The Unknown Public." *Household Words*, vol. 18, 1858, pp. 217–22.

———. *The Woman in White*. 1860. Edited by Matthew Sweet, Penguin Books, 1999.

———. "The Woman in White." *All the Year Round*, vol. 2, no. 31, 1859, pp. 95–104.

Costantini, Mariaconcetta. "Sensation, Class and the Rising Professionals." *The Cambridge Companion to Sensation Fiction*, edited by Andrew Mangham, Cambridge UP, 2013, pp. 99–112.

Cotsell, Michael. "Explanatory Notes." *Our Mutual Friend, by Charles Dickens*, edited by Michael Cotsell, Oxford UP, 1989, pp. 823–50.

Cox, Jessica. "Introduction – Blurring Boundaries: The Fiction of M. E. Braddon." *New Perspectives on Mary Elizabeth Braddon*, edited by Jessica Cox, Rodopi, 2012, pp. 1–15.

———. *Neo-Victorianism and Sensation Fiction*. Palgrave Macmillan, 2019.

Cruse, Amy. *The Victorians and Their Books*. George Allen & Unwin, 1935.

Cvetkovich, Ann. *Mixed Feelings: Feminism, Mass Culture, and Victorian Sensationalism*. Rutgers UP, 1992.

Daily News, 24 Aug. 1854. *The British Newspaper Archive*.

Dearinger, Lindsay. "Mormonism in *A Study in Scarlet*: Colonization on the Frontiers (of Sherlockian Logic)." *CEA Critic*, vol. 76, no. 1, 2014, pp. 52–71.

de Capel Wise, John Richard. "'Belles Lettres', *Westminster Review*, N.S. 30 (July 1866), pp. 268–80 [Extract]." *Varieties of Women's Sensation Fiction: 1855–1890*, edited by Andrew Maunder, vol. 1, Pickering & Chatto, 2004, pp. 157–59.

Dickens, Charles, editor. *All the Year Round*, vol. 2, no. 31, 1859, pp. 93–116.

———. *Bleak House*. 1853. Edited by Stephen Gill, Oxford UP, 1996.

———. "A Detective Police Party." *Household Words*, vol. 1, no. 18, 1850, pp. 409–14.

———. "A Detective Police Party." *Household Words*, vol. 1, no. 20, 1850, pp. 457–60.

———. "Full Report of the First Meeting of the Mudfog Association for the Advancement of Everything." *Bentley's Miscellany*, vol. 2, 1837, pp. 397–413.

———. "Full Report of the Second Meeting of the Mudfog Association for the Advancement of Everything." *Bentley's Miscellany*, vol. 4, 1838, pp. 209–27.

———. *The Letters of Charles Dickens (Pilgrim Edition)*. Edited by Graham Storey and Margaret Brown, vol. 11 (1865–1867), Oxford UP, 1999.

———. *The Letters of Charles Dickens (Pilgrim Edition)*. Edited by Graham Storey and Margaret Brown, vol. 12 (1868–1870), Oxford UP, 2002.

———. *The Letters of Charles Dickens: Volume 8, 1856–1858 (Pilgrim edition)*. Edited by Graham Storey and Kathleen Tillotson, vol. 8, Clarendon Press, 1995.

———. *Martin Chuzzlewit*. 1844. Edited by Margaret Cardwell, Oxford UP, 1984.

———. "The Metropolitan Protectives." *Household Words*, vol. 3, no. 57, 1851, pp. 97–105.

———. "The Modern Science of Thief-Taking." *Household Words*, vol. 1, no. 16, 1850, pp. 368–72.

———. *The Mystery of Edwin Drood*. 1870. Oxford UP, 1982.

———. "The Ruffian." *All the Year Round*, vol. 20, no. 494, 10 Aug. 1868, pp. 421–24.

Disraeli, Benjamin. "The State of India." *The Times*, July 28, 1857, pp. 5–7.

Doyle, Arthur Conan. *The Sign of Four*. 1890. Penguin Books, 2001.

———. *A Study in Scarlet*. 1887. Edited by Owen Dudley Edwards, Oxford UP, 1993.

Drew, John. "The Newspaper and Periodical Market." *Charles Dickens in Context*, edited by Sally Ledger and Holly Furneux, Cambridge UP, 2011, pp. 109–17.

Duggan, Christopher. *A Concise History of Italy*. Cambridge UP, 1994.

Dunbar, Ann-Marie. "Making the Case: Detection and Confession in *Lady Audley's Secret* and *the Woman in White*." *Victorian Review*, vol. 40, no. 1, 2014, pp. 97–116.

Durston, Gregory J. *Burglars and Bobbies: Crime and Policing in Victorian London*. Cambridge Scholars Publishing, 2012.

Eliot, George. *The George Eliot Letters*. Edited by G. Haight, vol. 4 (1862–1868), Yale UP, 1954.

Eliot, Simon. "The Business of Victorian Publishing." *The Cambridge Companion to the Victorian Novel*, edited by Deirdre David, Cambridge UP, 2001, pp. 37–60.

Eliot, T. S. "Wilkie Collins and Dickens (1927)." *Selected Essays: 1917–1932*, Harcourt, Brace and Company, 1932, pp. 373–82.

Emrys, A. B. *Wilkie Collins, Vera Caspary and the Evolution of the Casebook Novel*. McFarland, 2011.

Emsley, Clive. *The English Police: A Political and Social History*, 2nd ed., Pearson Education, 1996.

Encyclopaedia Britannica, 3rd ed., vol. 7, A. Bell and C. Macfarquhar, 1797.

Encyclopaedia Britannica, 8th ed., vol. 10, Adam and Charles Black, 1856.

Encyclopaedia Britannica: A Dictionary of Arts, Sciences, Literature and General Information, 11th ed., vol. 11, Cambridge UP, 1910.

" 'The Enigma Novel', *Spectator* (28 December 1861), p. 1428." *Varieties of Women's Sensation Fiction: 1855–1890*, edited by Andrew Maunder, vol. 1, Pickering & Chatto, 2004, pp. 3–7.

"Evans v. Robinson." *Globe*, 22 Aug. 1854. *The British Newspaper Archive*.

Ferguson, Christine. "Sensational Dependence: Prosthesis and Affect in Dickens and Braddon." *Literature Interpretation Theory*, vol. 19, no. 1, 2008, pp. 1–25.

Finn, Margot, et al. "Introduction." *Legitimacy and Illegitimacy in Nineteenth-Century Law, Literature and History*, edited by Margot Finn et al., Palgrave Macmillan, 2010, pp. 1–24.

Fisch, Audrey. "Collins, Race, and Slavery." *Reality's Dark Light: The Sensational Wilkie Collins*, edited by Maria K. Bachman and Don Richard Cox, The U of Tennessee P, 2003, pp. 313–28.

Flint, Kate. *The Victorians and the Visual Imagination.* Cambridge UP, 2000.

Forrester, Andrew. *The Female Detective.* 1864. The British Library, 2012.

Foyster, Elizabeth. *Marital Violence: An English Family History, 1660–1857.* Cambridge UP, 2005.

Free, Melissa. " 'Dirty Linen': Legacies of Empire in Wilkie Collins's *The Moonstone.*" *Texas Studies in Literature and Language,* vol. 48, no. 4, 2006, pp. 340–71.

Frost, Ginger S. *Living in Sin: Cohabiting as Husband and Wife in Nineteenth-Century England.* Manchester UP, 2008.

Garrison, Laurie. *Science, Sexuality and Sensation Novels: Pleasures of the Senses.* Palgrave Macmillan, 2011.

Gaskell, Elizabeth. *North and South.* 1855, edited by Angus Easson, Oxford UP, 1998.

Gaukroger, Stephen. *The Collapse of Mechanism and the Rise of Sensibility: Science and the Shaping of Modernity, 1680–1760.* Oxford UP, 2010.

Gilbert, Pamela K. *Disease, Desire, and the Body in Victorian Women's Popular Novels.* Cambridge UP, 1997.

Gilmour, Robin. *The Idea of the Gentleman in the Victorian Novel.* George Allen & Unwin, 1981.

Griffin, Ben. *The Politics of Gender in Victorian Britain: Masculinity, Political Culture and the Struggle for Women's Rights.* Cambridge UP, 2012.

Griffin, Emma. *Bread Winner: An Intimate History of the Victorian Economy.* Yale UP, 2020.

———. "Patterns of Industrialisation." *The Victorian World,* edited by Martin Hewitt, Routledge, 2012, pp. 90–107.

Gruner, Elisabeth Rose. "Family Secrets and the Mysteries of *The Moonstone.*" *New Casebooks: Wilkie Collins,* edited by Lyn Pykett, Macmillan, 1998, pp. 221–43.

Haining, Peter, editor. *Hunted Down: The Detective Stories of Charles Dickens.* Peter Owen, 1996.

Hammerton, A. James. *Cruelty and Companionship: Conflict in Nineteenth-Century Married Life.* Routledge, 1992.

Harrison, Kimberly, and Richard Fantina. "Introduction." *Victorian Sensations: Essays on a Scandalous Genre,* edited by Kimberly Harrison and Richard Fantina. The Ohio State UP, 2006, pp. ix–xxiii.

Hartman, Mary S. *Victorian Murderesses: A True History of Thirteen Respectable French and English Women Accused of Unspeakable Crimes.* Schocken, 1976.

Hayter, Alethea. *Opium and the Romantic Imagination.* U of California P, 1968.

Hayward, William Stephens. *Revelations of a Lady Detective.* George Vickers, 1864.

Hearder, Harry. *Italy: A Short History.* Cambridge UP, 1990.

Heller, Tamar. "Blank Spaces: Ideological Tensions and the Detective Work of *The Moonstone.*" *New Casebooks: Wilkie Collins,* edited by Lyn Pykett, Macmillan, 1998, pp. 244–70.

Herbert, Christopher. *War of No Pity: The Indian Mutiny and Victorian Trauma.* Princeton UP, 2008.

Hewitt, Martin. *The Dawn of the Cheap Press in Victorian Britain: The End of the 'Taxes on Knowledge', 1849–1869*. Bloomsbury, 2014.

Hughes, Tom. "The Public Undoing of Mrs Mary Evans." *Marylebone Lives: Rogues, Romantics and Rebels; Character Studies of Locals since the 18th Century*, edited by Mark Riddaway and Carl Upsall, Spiramus Press, 2015, pp. 102–5.

Hughes, Winifred. *The Maniac in the Cellar: Sensation Novels of the 1860s*. Princeton UP, 1980.

Humphreys, Anne. "Breaking Apart: The Early Victorian Divorce Novel." *Victorian Women Writers and the Woman Question*, edited by Nicola Diane Thompson, Cambridge UP, 1999, pp. 42–59.

Hutter, A. D. "Dreams, Transformations and Literature: The Implications of Detective Fiction." *New Casebooks: Wilkie Collins*, edited by Lyn Pykett, Macmillan, 1998, pp. 175–96.

"Italian Distrust." *All the Year Round*, vol. 2, no. 18, 1859, pp. 105–6.

Jameson, Fredric. *Raymond Chandler: The Detections of Totality*. Verso, 2016.

Jay, Elizabeth. "Introduction." *East Lynne*, by Ellen Wood, edited by Elizabeth Jay, Oxford UP, 2005, pp. vii–xxxix.

———. "Note on the Text." *East Lynne*, by Ellen Wood, edited by Elizabeth Jay, Oxford UP, 2005, pp. xl–xliii.

Johnson, Edgar. *Charles Dickens: His Tragedy and Triumph*, vol. 2, Simon and Schuster, 1952.

Kaplan, E. Ann. *Motherhood and Representation: The Mother in Popular Culture and Melodrama*. Routledge, 1992.

Karpenko, Lara. "'A Nasty Thumping at the Top of Your Head': Muscularity, Masculinity, and Physical Reading in 'The Moonstone'." *Victorian Review*, vol. 38, no. 1, 2012, pp. 132–54.

Kestner, Joseph A. *Sherlock's Sisters: The British Female Detective, 1864–1913*. Routledge, 2003.

Knight, Stephen. *Form and Ideology in Crime Fiction*. Macmillan, 1980.

Knowles, Nancy, and Katherine Hall. "Imperial Attitudes in *Lady Audley's Secret*." *New Perspectives on Mary Elizabeth Braddon*, edited by Jessica Cox, Rodopi, 2012, pp. 37–58.

Kucich, John. *The Power of Lies: Transgression in Victorian Fiction*. Cornell UP, 1994.

Ledger, Sally. "In Darkest England: The Terror of Degeneration in *Fin-de-Siècle* Britain." *Literature & History*, vol. 4, no. 2, 1995, pp. 71–86.

Leighton, Mary Elizabeth, and Lisa Surridge. *The Plot Thickens: Illustrated Victorian Serial Fiction from Dickens to Du Maurier*. Ohio UP, 2018.

Liggins, Emma, and Andrew Maunder. "Introduction: Ellen Wood, Writer." *Women's Writing*, vol. 15, no. 2, 2008, pp. 149–56.

Linton, Eliza Lynn. "The Wild Women: As Politicans (*Nineteenth Century*, July 1891)." *'Criminals, Idiots, Women, and Minors': Victorian Writing by Women on Women*, edited by Susan Hamilton, 2nd ed., Broadview Press, 2004, pp. 161–69.

Lloyd, Amy J. "Emigration, Immigration and Migration in Nineteenth-Century Britain." *British Library Newspapers*. Gale, 2007. www.gale.com/binaries/content/

assets/gale-us-en/primary-sources/intl-gps/intl-gps-essays/full-ghn-contextual-essays/ghn_essay_bln_lloyd1_website.pdf.

Lonoff, Sue. "Charles Dickens and Wilkie Collins." *Nineteenth-Century Fiction*, vol. 35, no. 2, 1980, pp. 150–70.

Louttit, Chris. "M. E. Braddon, Bohemian Networks and the Shaping of a Sensational Author." *Women's Writing*, vol. 29, no. 1, 2022, pp. 28–44.

Lycett, Andrew. *The Man Who Created Sherlock Holmes: The Life and Times of Sir Arthur Conan Doyle.* Free Press, 2007.

———. *Wilkie Collins: A Life of Sensation.* Hutchinson, 2013.

Macdonald, Tara. "Sensation Fiction, Gender and Identity." *The Cambridge Companion to Sensation Fiction*, edited by Andrew Mangham, Cambridge UP, 2013, pp. 127–40.

Mallett, Phillip. "Preface." *The Victorian Novel and Masculinity*, edited by Phillip Mallett, Palgrave Macmillan, 2015, pp. vi–xiii.

Manavalli, Krishna. "Collins, Colonial Crime, and the Brahmin Sublime: The Orientalist Vision of a Hindu-Brahmin India in the Moonstone." *Comparative Critical Studies*, vol. 4, no. 1, 2007, pp. 67–86.

Mangham, Andrew. " 'Drink It Up Dear; It Will Do You Good': Crime, Toxicology, and *The Trail of the Serpent.*" *New Perspectives on Mary Elizabeth Braddon*, edited by Jessica Cox, Rodopi, 2012, pp. 95–112.

———. " 'Murdered at the Breast': Maternal Violence and the Self-Made Man in Popular Victorian Culture." *Critical Survey*, vol. 16, no. 1, 2004, pp. 20–34.

———. *Violent Women and Sensation Fiction: Crime, Medicine and Victorian Popular Culture.* Palgrave Macmillan, 2007.

———. " 'What Could I Do?': Nineteenth-Century Psychology and the Horrors of Masculinity in *The Woman in White.*" *Victorian Sensations: Essays on a Scandalous Genre*, edited by Kimberly Harrison and Richard Fantina. The Ohio State UP, 2006, pp. 115–25.

Mansel, H. L. "Sensation Novels." *The Quarterly Review*, vol. 113, 1863, pp. 482–514.

Maunder, Andrew. "General Introduction." *Varieties of Women's Sensation Fiction: 1855–1890*, edited by Andrew Maunder, vol. 1, Pickering & Chatto, 2004, pp. vii–xxxi.

———. " 'I Will Not Live in Poverty and Neglect': *East Lynne* on the East End Stage." *Victorian Sensations: Essays on a Scandalous Genre*, edited by Kimberly Harrison and Richard Fantina. The Ohio State UP, 2006, pp. 173–87.

———. " 'Stepchildren of Nature': *East Lynne* and the Spectre of Female Degeneracy, 1860–1861." *Victorian Crime, Madness and Sensation*, edited by Andrew Maunder and Grace Moore, Ashgate, 2004, pp. 59–71.

Maunder, Andrew, and Grace Moore. "Introduction." *Victorian Crime, Madness and Sensation*, edited by Andrew Maunder and Grace Moore, Ashgate, 2004, pp. 1–14.

Maxwell, Catherine. *Second Sight: The Visionary Imagination in Late Victorian Literature.* Manchester UP, 2008.

McCuskey, Brian W. "The Kitchen Police: Servant Surveillance and Middle-Class Transgression." *Victorian Literature and Culture*, vol. 28, no. 2, 2000, pp. 359–75.

Meckier, Jerome. *Hidden Rivalries in Victorian Fiction: Dickens, Realism, and Revaluation.* The UP of Kentucky, 1987.

Mill, John Stuart. *Autobiography*. 1873. Edited by Mark Philip, Oxford UP, 2018.

———. "Civilization." *The London and Westminster Review*, vol. 25, April 1836, pp. 1–16.

Miller, D. A. *The Novel and the Police*. U of California P, 1988.

Moore, Grace. "Turkish Robbers, Lumps of Delight, and the Detritus of Empire: The East Revisited in Dickens's Late Novels." *Critical Survey*, vol. 21, no. 1, 2009, pp. 74–87.

Moretti, Franco. *Signs Taken for Wonders: Essays in the Sociology of Literary Forms*, translated by Susan Fischer et al., Verso, 1988.

Mossman, Mark. "Representations of the Abnormal Body in *The Moonstone*." *Victorian Literature and Culture*, vol. 37, no. 2, 2009, pp. 483–500.

" 'Mrs Wood and Miss Braddon', *Littell's Living Age* (18 April 1863), pp. 99–103." *Varieties of Women's Sensation Fiction: 1855–1890*, edited by Andrew Maunder, vol. 1, Pickering & Chatto, 2004, pp. 57–64.

Mukherjee, Upamanyu Pablo. *Crime and Empire: The Colony in Nineteenth-Century Fictions of Crime*. Oxford UP, 2003.

Nayder, Lillian. "The Empire and Sensation." *A Companion to Sensation Fiction*, edited by Pamela K. Gilbert, Wiley-Blackwell, 2011, pp. 442–54.

———. "Rebellious Sepoys and Bigamous Wives: The Indian Mutiny and Marriage Law Reform." *Beyond Sensation: Mary Elizabeth Braddon in Context*, edited by Marlene Tromp et al., State U of New York P, 2000, pp. 31–42.

———. "Science and Sensation." *The Cambridge Companion to Sensation Fiction*, edited by Andrew Mangham, Cambridge UP, 2013, pp. 154–67.

———. *Unequal Partners: Charles Dickens, Wilkie Collins, and Victorian Authorship*. Cornell UP, 2002.

Nemesvari, Richard. "Manful Sensations: Affect, Domesticity and Class Status Anxiety in *East Lynne* and *Aurora Floyd*." *The Victorian Novel and Masculinity*, edited by Phillip Mallett, Palgrave Macmillan, 2015, pp. 88–115.

———. "Robert Audley's Secret: Male Homosocial Desire in *Lady Audley's Secret*." *Studies in the Novel*, vol. 27, no. 4, 1995, pp. 515–28.

" 'Novels Past and Present', *Saturday Review* (14 April 1866), pp. 438–39." *Varieties of Women's Sensation Fiction: 1855–1890*, edited by Andrew Maunder, vol. 1, Pickering & Chatto, 2004, pp. 151–56.

O'Dell, Benjamin D. "Performing the Imperial Abject: The Ethics of Cocaine in Arthur Conan Doyle's *The Sign of Four*." *The Journal of Popular Culture*, vol. 45, no. 5, 2012, pp. 979–99.

Oliphant, Margaret. "Novels." *Blackwood's Edinburgh Magazine*, vol. 102, 1867, pp. 257–80.

———. "Sensation Novels." *Blackwood's Edinburgh Magazine*, vol. 91, 1862, pp. 564–84.

Ousby, Ian. *Bloodhounds of Heaven: The Detective in English Fiction from Godwin to Doyle*. Harvard UP, 1976.

Page, Norman, editor. *Wilkie Collins: The Critical Heritage*. Routledge, 1976.

Paget, Frederick. " 'Afterwood' to *Lucretia. The Heroine of the Nineteenth Century. A Correspondence Sensational and Sentimental* (London, Masters, 1868) [Extract]." *Varieties of Women's Sensation Fiction: 1855–1890*, edited by Andrew Maunder, vol. 1, Pickering & Chatto, 2004, pp. 210–18.

Pallo, Vicki A. "From Do-Nothing to Detective: The Transformation of Robert Audley in *Lady Audley's Secret.*" *The Journal of Popular Culture*, vol. 39, no. 3, 2006, pp. 466–78.

Park, Hyungji. "Empire, Women, and Epistemology in the Victorian Detective Plot." *British and American Fiction*, vol. 15, no. 1, 2008, pp. 133–56.

———. " 'Going to Wake Up Egypt': Exhibiting Empire in 'Edwin Drood.' " *Victorian Literature and Culture*, vol. 30, no. 2, 2002, pp. 529–50.

Pedlar, Valerie. "Behind the Scenes, Before the Gaze: Mary Braddon's Theatrical World." *Popular Victorian Women Writers*, edited by Kay Boardman and Shirley Jones, Manchester UP, 2004, pp. 186–207.

" 'The Philosophy of 'Sensation", *St James's Magazine*, 5 (October 1862), pp. 340–46." *Varieties of Women's Sensation Fiction: 1855–1890*, edited by Andrew Maunder, vol. 1, Pickering & Chatto, 2004, pp. 16–26.

"The Police and the Thieves." *Quarterly Review*, vol. 99, June 1856, pp. 160–201.

Pool, Daniel. *What Jane Austen Ate and Charles Dickens Knew*. Touchstone, 1994.

Pykett, Lyn. "Collins and the Sensation Novel." *The Cambridge Companion to Wilkie Collins*, edited by Jenny Bourne Taylor, Cambridge UP, 2006, pp. 50–64.

———. "Mary Elizabeth Braddon." *A Companion to Sensation Fiction*, edited by Pamela K. Gilbert, Wiley-Blackwell, 2011, pp. 123–33.

Rae, W. Fraser. "Sensation Novelists: Miss Braddon." *The North British Review*, vol. 43, 1865, pp. 180–204.

Reitz, Caroline. *Detecting the Nation: Fictions of Detection and the Imperial Venture*. The Ohio State UP, 2004.

"Revelations of a Lady Detective." *George Vickers*, 1864. *British Library*, www.bl.uk/collection-items/revelations-of-a-lady-detective.

Richards, Evelleen. "Huxley and Woman's Place in Science: The 'Woman Question' and the Control of Victorian Anthropology." *History, Humanity and Evolution: Essays for John C. Greene*, edited by James R. Moore, Cambridge UP, 1989, pp. 253–84.

Riley, Marie. "Writing for the Million: The Enterprising Fiction of Ellen Wood." *Popular Victorian Women Writers*, edited by Kay Boardman and Shirley Jones, Manchester UP, 2004, pp. 165–85.

Roberts, Lewis. "The 'Shivering Sands' of Reality: Narration and Knowledge in Wilkie Collins' *The Moonstone.*" *Victorian Review*, vol. 23, no. 2, 1997, pp. 168–83.

Robinson, Kenneth. *Wilkie Collins: A Biography*. Macmillan, 1952.

Ruskin, John. "Fiction – Fair and Foul." *The Ethics of the Dust; Fiction, Fair and Foul; The Elements of Drawing*, Dana Estes, 1900, pp. 153–219.

Russell, William. *Recollections of a Detective Police-Officer*. J. & C. Brown, 1856.

Russett, Cynthia Eagle. *Sexual Science: The Victorian Construction of Womanhood*. Harvard UP, 1989.

Sanders, Andrew. "High Victorian Literature, 1830–1880." *The Oxford Illustrated History of English Literature*, edited by Pat Rogers, Oxford UP, 1987, pp. 327–78.

Saunders, Samuel. *The Nineteenth Century Periodical Press and the Development of Detective Fiction*. Routledge, 2021.

Schroeder, Natalie, and Ronald A. Schroeder. *From Sensation to Society: Representations of Marriage in the Fiction of Mary Elizabeth Braddon, 1862–1866*. U of Delaware P, 2006.

Secord, James A. *Victorian Sensation: The Extraordinary Publication, Reception, and Secret Authorship of Vestiges of the Natural History of Creation*. The U of Chicago P, 2000.

"The Sensation Times, and a Chronicle of Excitement." *Punch*, vol. 44, 1863, p. 193.

Shanley, Mary Lyndon. "'One Must Ride Behind': Married Women's Rights and the Divorce Act of 1857." *Victorian Studies*, vol. 25, no. 3, 1982, pp. 355–76.

Shpayer-Makov, Haia. *The Ascent of the Detective: Police Sleuths in Victorian and Edwardian England*. Oxford UP, 2011.

Shuttleworth, Sally. *Charlotte Brontë and Victorian Psychology*. Cambridge UP, 1996.

Slater, Michael. *Charles Dickens*. Yale UP, 2009.

Smajić, Srdjan. *Ghost-Seers, Detectives, and Spiritualists: Theories of Vision in Victorian Literature and Science*. Cambridge UP, 2010.

Smiles, Samuel. *Self-Help; with Illustrations of Character and Conduct*. Harper & Brothers, 1860.

Smillie, Rachel. "Now You See Her – Now You Don't: Household Spies in *Aurora Floyd* and *Lady Audley's Secret*." *Clues: A Journal of Detection*, vol. 33, no. 1, 2015, pp. 8–17.

Smith, Denis Mack. *Modern Italy: A Political History*. The U of Michigan P, 1997.

Smith, Jonathan. *Charles Darwin and Victorian Visual Culture*. Cambridge UP, 2006.

Steinbach, Susie L. *Understanding the Victorians: Politics, Culture, and Society in Nineteenth-Century Britain*. Routledge, 2012.

Stephen, James Fitzjames. "Detectives in Fiction and in Real Life." *The Saturday Review*, vol. 17, no. 450, 1864, pp. 712–13.

Stevenson, Robert Louis. *The Letters of Robert Louis Stevenson*. Edited by Bradford A. Booth and Ernest Mehew, vol. 1 (1854-April 1874), Yale UP, 1994.

Surridge, Lisa. *Bleak Houses: Marital Violence in Victorian Fiction*. Ohio UP, 2005.

Sussex, Lucy. *Women Writers and Detectives in Nineteenth-Century Crime Fiction: The Mothers of the Mystery Genre*. Palgrave Macmillan, 2010.

Sussman, Herbert. *Victorian Masculinities*. Cambridge UP, 1995.

Sutherland, John. "Explanatory Notes." *The Moonstone*, by Wilkie Collins, edited by John Sutherland, Oxford UP, 2008, pp. 467–502.

———. *The Stanford Companion to Victorian Fiction*. Stanford UP, 1989.

Symons, Julian. *Mortal Consequences: A History – from the Detective Story to the Crime Novel*. Harper and Row, 1972.

Talairach-Vielmas, Laurence. *Moulding the Female Body in Victorian Fairy Tales and Sensation Novels*. Routledge, 2007.

Tambling, Jeremy. "Opium, Wholesale, Resale, and for Export: On Dickens and China (Part Two)." *Dickens Quarterly*, vol. 21, no. 2, 2004, pp. 104–13.

Tange, Andrea Kaston. *Architectural Identities: Domesticity, Literature, and the Victorian Middle Classes*. U of Toronto P, 2010.

———. "Picturing the Villain: Image-Making and the Indian Uprising." *Victorian Studies*, vol. 63, no. 2, 2021, pp. 193–223.

Taylor, Jenny Bourne. *In the Secret Theatre of Home: Wilkie Collins, Sensation Narrative, and Nineteenth-Century Psychology*. Routledge, 1988.

———. "Introduction." *Willkie Collins the Law and the Lady*, edited by Jenny Bourne Taylor, Oxford UP, 1992.

Taylor, Jenny Bourne, and Russell Crofts. "Introduction." *Lady Audley's Secret*, by Mary Elizabeth Braddon, edited by Jenny Bourne Taylor, Penguin Classics, 1998, pp. vii–xli.

Thackeray, William Makepeace. *Vanity Fair*. 1847. Edited by Helen Small, Oxford UP, 2015.

"'Thackeray and Modern Fiction', *London Quarterly Review*, 22 (July 1863), pp. 375–408 [Extract]." *Varieties of Women's Sensation Fiction: 1855–1890*, edited by Andrew Maunder, vol. 1, Pickering & Chatto, 2004, pp. 76–81.

Thomas, Keith. "The Double Standard." *Journal of the History of Ideas*, vol. 20, no. 2, 1959, pp. 195–216.

Thomas, Ronald R. "Detection in the Victorian Novel." *The Cambridge Companion to the Victorian Novel*, edited by Deirdre David, Cambridge UP, 2001, pp. 169–91.

———. *Detective Fiction and the Rise of Forensic Science*. Cambridge UP, 2003.

———. "The Moonstone, Detective Fiction and Forensic Science." *The Cambridge Companion to Wilkie Collins*, edited by Jenny Bourne Taylor, Cambridge UP, 2006, pp. 65–78.

Thompson, Jon. *Fiction, Crime, and Empire: Clues to Modernity and Postmodernism*. U of Illinois P, 1993.

Tomaiuolo, Saverio. *In Lady Audley's Shadow: Mary Elizabeth Braddon and Victorian Literary Genres*. Edinburgh UP, 2010.

———. "Sensation Fiction, Empire and the Indian Mutiny." *The Cambridge Companion to Sensation Fiction*, edited by Andrew Mangham, Cambridge UP, 2013, pp. 113–26.

Tosh, John. *A Man's Place: Masculinity and the Middle-Class Home in Victorian England*. Yale UP, 1999.

Trichet, Yohan, and Agnès Lacroix. "Esquirol's Change of View Towards Pinel's Mania without Delusion." *History of Psychiatry*, vol. 27, no. 4, 2016, pp. 443–57.

Trodd, Anthea. *Domestic Crime in the Victorian Novel*. Macmillan, 1989.

———. "The Policeman and the Lady: Significant Encounters in Mid-Victorian Fiction." *Victorian Studies*, vol. 27, no. 4, 1984, pp. 435–60.

Tromp, Marlene. "The Dangerous Woman: M. E. Braddon's Sensational (En)gendering of Domestic Law." *Beyond Sensation: Mary Elizabeth Braddon in Context*, edited by Marlene Tromp et al., State U of New York P, 2000, pp. 93–108.

———. "Mrs. Henry Wood, *East Lynne*." *A Companion to Sensation Fiction*, edited by Pamela K. Gilbert, Wiley-Blackwell, 2011, pp. 257–68.

———. *The Private Rod: Marital Violence, Sensation, and the Law in Victorian Britain*. The UP of Virginia, 2000.

Varese, Jon Michael. "The Woman in White's 150 Years of Sensation." *The Guardian*, 26 Nov. 2009, www.theguardian.com/books/booksblog/2009/nov/26/woman-in-white-150-years-sensation.

Walkowitz, Judith R. *City of Dreadful Delight: Narratives of Sexual Danger in Late-Victorian London.* U of Chicago P, 1992.

Waters, Karen Volland. *The Perfect Gentleman: Masculine Control in Victorian Men's Fiction, 1870–1901*, 2nd ed., Peter Lang, 1999.

"What is a Gentleman?" *Chamber's Journal*, vol. 5, no. 129, 21 June 1856, pp. 399–400.

White, Jerry. *London in the Nineteenth Century: A Human Awful Wonder of God.* Vintage, 2008.

Wilkes, John. *The London Police in the Nineteenth Century.* Cambridge UP, 1977.

Willey, Vicki Corkran. "Wilkie Collins's 'Secret Dictate': *The Moonstone* as a Response to Imperialist Panic." *Victorian Sensations: Essays on a Scandalous Genre*, edited by Kimberly Harrison and Richard Fantina. The Ohio State UP, 2006, pp. 225–33.

Wolfram, Sybil. "Divorce in England 1700–1857." *Oxford Journal of Legal Studies*, vol. 5, no. 2, 1985, pp. 155–86.

"'Women's Novels', *The Broadway*, N.S. 1 (1868), pp. 504–9." *Varieties of Women's Sensation Fiction: 1855–1890*, edited by Andrew Maunder, vol. 1, Pickering & Chatto, 2004, pp. 219–25.

Wood, Ellen. *East Lynne.* 1861. Edited by Elisabeth Jay, Oxford UP, 2005.

Worthington, Heather. *The Rise of the Detective in Early Nineteenth Century Popular Fiction.* Palgrave Macmillan, 2005.

Yoon, Sarah. "Revisiting New York as an Existential Metaphor in Paul Auster's *The New York Trilogy*." *The Explicator*, vol. 76, no. 1, 2018, pp. 40–43.

Index

For Product Safety Concerns and Information please contact our EU
representative GPSR@taylorandfrancis.com
Taylor & Francis Verlag GmbH, Kaufingerstraße 24, 80331 München, Germany